PLACE OF TEMPTATION

THE DARK HEART OF YORKSHIRE

DI HASKELL & QUINN SERIES
BOOK 6

BILINDA P. SHEEHAN

D1739212

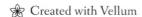

ALSO BY BILINDA P. SHEEHAN

Watch out for the next book coming soon from Bilinda P. Sheehan by joining her mailing list.

A Wicked Mercy - DI Haskell & Quinn Crime Thriller

Death in Pieces - DI Haskell & Quinn Crime Thriller Book 2

Splinter the Bone - DI Haskell & Quinn Crime Thriller Book 3

Hunting the Silence - DI Haskell & Quinn Crime Thriller Book 4

Hidden in Blood - DI Haskell & Quinn Crime Thriller Book 5

Place of Temptation - DI Haskell & Quinn Crime Thriller Book 6

Lake of Tears - DI Haskell & Quinn Crime Thriller Book 7

No Safe Place - DI Haskell & Quinn Crime Thriller Book 8

All the Lost Girls-A Gripping Psychological Thriller

Wednesday's Child - A Gripping Psychological Thriller

PLACE OF TEMPTATION

CHAPTER ONE

"The mind is its own place, and in itself can make a heaven of hell, a hell of heaven.."

—JOHN MILTON, PARADISE LOST

xoGeeSoupxo: Last I heard, Olive Scott has completely lost her marbles.

MardArse5108: Where'd you hear this?

xoGeeSoupxo: I've got my sources ;) And they say Olive is toast. She's going to miss her deadline. She'll be lucky if the publishers don't demand that she give the advance back.

Georgiex094: You mean she's gone mad?

xoGeeSoupxo: Yup. Full on cuckoo for cocopops. Thinks God is talking to her, telling her to save the world. LOL

CremeEggFanatic: Holy shit! For realz?

SinEater81: Who told you that GS?

xoGeeSoupxo: Like I said I've got my sources.

SinEater81: You sure they're telling you the truth? Maybe there's more to the story than meets the eye?

xoGeeSoupxo: Hahaha anyone would think you liked Olive. You've never had a nice word to say about that stuck up cow. Why change now?

CremeEggFanatic: Maybe SinEater is Olive...

MardArse5108: Not likely she hates her as much as we do.

SinEater81: Olive is a poisonous b*tch. The sooner she falls off the map the better.

xoGeeSoupxo: There's the SinEater we know and love.

SinEater81: Lolz, I never went anywhere. I'm just saying be careful who you get your information from.

xoGeeSoupxo: No worries doll. I've seen it myself. Olive is a crazy cow choking the life out of everyone who gets too close.

SinEater81: Good to know ;)

CHAPTER TWO

WHEN TOBY WAS FINALLY SETTLED in bed, Libby stacked the dishwasher, with 90s pop music from her Alexa turned down low so as not to wake her son. She flicked on the kettle. This was her favourite part of the evening. Even thinking it caused a pang of guilt, but she ignored it as she scraped away the remnants of spaghetti hoops and garden peas from Toby's dish into the bin. It wasn't a crime to think like that. And it didn't make her a bad mum to enjoy the peace and quiet.

With the kettle boiled, she grabbed her grey mug. Pausing in front of the cupboard, she considered her options. Weigh-in day was coming up at Slimming World. Last week had been a disaster, two whole pounds on. When Brenda had read it out in front of the group, Libby had felt like a criminal.

To make matters worse, Brenda had pulled her

aside after the meeting to talk to her. "Are you sure you're serious about this, love? You're not making the progress you should be. You did so well in the beginning. Is there an issue with the recipes?"

Libby had lied, telling Brenda she'd added her calories up incorrectly. The look on Brenda's face had said she didn't believe a word of it.

"Fuck you, Brenda," Libby whispered as she pulled open the cupboard and grabbed a Kit-Kat. The memory of Brenda's sour expression filled her mind and Libby grabbed a second chocolate bar. She'd skip the meeting this week, and work extra hard next week instead.

Content with her choice, she put the dishwasher on and made her way to the living room. Setting her steaming cup of Yorkshire tea on the side-table along with the Kit-Kats, she dropped down onto the grey, crushed velvet couch. Picking up her phone, she scrolled through her Instagram page, double-tapping a couple of images of home interiors. The circles at the top of the screen told her that some of the influencers she followed had created some 'stories'. Tearing open the first Kit-Kat, she sank back against the cushions as she clicked on the first video.

The on-screen woman's energy as she danced around her living room with a hoover left Libby feeling inadequate. Why couldn't she look like that when she did the cleaning? The videos continued to play. Another influencer taught her how best to apply contour. Not that Libby would ever find the time to indulge herself like that. She was lucky if she found the time to throw her hair up into a top-knot, and brush her teeth before the nursery run and her part-time job in Asda.

Feeling thoroughly unsatisfied with her lot, Libby left Instagram and the flawless lives of the influencers behind. Popping open her browser, she typed in the address of her favourite website. The people there understood her, they knew how hard it was to constantly have your inadequacies highlighted by those who had it all.

Rattle's website loaded quickly, the plain interface making it all the easier to navigate. Libby clicked through to the threads regarding her favourite Instagrammers. Scanning the page, she sipped at her tea as she opened up a bookmarked thread about Holly Thomas and read the back and forth commentary.

> Georgiex094: Can't believe she's flogging the same old tat again!

> Mard-Arse5108: She'd sell her own mother, if she thought she might get a quid for her. Silly cow is everything that's wrong in this world. I wouldn't piss on her if she were on fire...

The last comment was followed by a row of laughing emoji faces.

Bringing up the comment box, Libby let her

fingers do the talking. They flew across the screen, as she allowed her pent up vitriol drip out through the words.

"You're so right Mard-Arse5108. Every second story is an ad for some kind of crap. She claims to care about the climate, but she's always flogging some useless bit of plastic. It'll all wind up in landfill anyway. Can't believe I used to fall for this shit. Thank god for Rattle and all you lot opening my eyes to the lies that go on. Did you see how last night she was on crying to the camera again about all the trolls out to get her? No one in their right mind would touch her with a fifty-foot stick!" For good measure, Libby added three vomit face emojis.

It took only a moment for Mard-Arse5108 to respond with a rolling-eye emoji.

Mard-Arse5108: I was the same. I woke up one day and thought, why am I buying all this useless crap? As for her crying over trolls, I say, if you're going to insist on living your life as an insta-hun, then you better be prepared for people to call you out on your bullshit. Why she thinks she can pull the wool over so many people's eyes, I don't know. I swear, these people need to grow a thicker skin.

"They're just sad because they know they've been rumbled. All we're doing is showing the world how false they are. Why should I be kind, when you're busy fleecing all those poor sheep?" Libby responded with glee.

Giggling to herself, Libby continued to comment on the thread. Every so often she left the Rattle website and returned to Instagram in search of the latest influencer on the chopping block. However, she never stayed away too long, always choosing to return to the place where she felt most comfortable.

> Mard-Arse5108: Someone needs to take this silly cow down a peg or two. Where's SinEater when you need her.

Libby grinned and quickly typed out a reply. "I'd love to see the smile wiped off her face. It'd serve her right if someone reported her for failing to disclose an ad on all of her sponsored content."

> SinEater81: @Mard-Arse5108 you rang? :D

> SinEater81: She needs worse than that. Prison is too good for her. Someone really needs to make her suffer for everything she's done...

Reading over the message, Libby's curiosity was piqued. "What else has she done, SinEater81?"

A moment later, SinEater81 posted again. It was a screen shot of a private message exchange wherein

Holly Thomas made threats against a girl named Rita. The final message from Holly caused Libby's breath to catch in the back of her throat.

"You know, the world would be a better place if you just went and killed yourself! Nobody would miss you..."

> Mard-Arse5108: Someone needs to share that with the tabloids. They'd lap it up. Expose Holly to the world for the real scum-bag she is.

Libby started to respond, but was cut off as SinEater81 posted again.

> SinEater81: Feel free... It's not the first time she's done this.

The message was followed by a link.

Unable to help herself, Libby clicked on the link and was redirected to another site. The screen brightened and a message thread appeared. It took Libby a moment to realise each message was a screen shot from a different conversation. Attached to each message was Holly's unmistakable grinning face.

"Did you see that fat cow on the dance floor last night? Don't know why Daniel bothers with her. He's lucky she doesn't suffocate him when she rolls over in the bed... All the self-induced vomiting in the world won't help you shift those double chins, Chelsea."

"If I get one more message asking for help with

some bleeding heart charity I'll go insane. No, Karen, I don't want to donate to your pathetic spawn's surgery fund. Pay for it yourself like the rest of us hard workers."

The messages went on, and on. And as Libby read on, she quickly realised each comment became progressively worse. Her phone buzzed next to her, making her jump. Glancing away from the screen, she picked it up and was relieved to see *his* name attached to the message.

Her fingers flew over the screen as she typed out a reply. A heartbeat later the phone began to ring and when Libby answered the call, his soothing voice washed over.

"I've missed you." His husky voice caused goose flesh to pebble her skin.

"I miss you too. When can I see you again?" Libby chewed at her bottom lip, half expecting him to fob her off.

"How about now?"

Her heart skipped in her chest. "Toby's asleep..."

"Then we'll just have to find something to keep you quiet." His words sent a shiver of desire racing over her skin. The phone went dead and Libby scrambled to her feet to check her appearance in the mirror.

A private message dinged on her tablet. Pausing her primping and preening, Libby snatched up the device.

SinEater81: If there's one thing I
hate, it's hypocrites and liars.

Libby smiled to herself. "You and me both..." She started to type something else, but a gentle knock on the front door sent her heart rate soaring. Flipping the cover on the tablet shut, Libby dropped the device back on to the couch. all thoughts of Holly Thomas and her behaviour forgotten.

She raced to the door.

CHAPTER THREE

SITTING behind the wheel of her Toyota Yaris, Olivia took a deep calming breath. It felt like a lifetime since she had set foot inside the team's headquarters. Twelve weeks of recovery and rehabilitation could do that to you. Nervous butterflies erupted in her empty tummy. Against her mother's wishes, Olivia hadn't been able to stomach the idea of a cup of tea, never mind actual, solid food. Now she was beginning to think that had been a mistake.

It was ridiculous really. What did she have to be nervous about? It wasn't as though she hadn't seen the team in those twelve weeks.

In some ways, she'd seen more of them in the past three months, than she might have done had she never been injured. Just thinking about it, brought her out in a cold sweat. She still had nightmares. Dr

Quinn told her it was a form of PTSD but as far as Olivia was concerned it was much more than that. She was a trained officer, she should have stopped Alfie Douglas. If she hadn't rushed headlong into things, she could have been prepared. Of course, when she mentioned this to Dr Quinn, Harriet had tried to redirect her thinking. She'd told her that dwelling on what might have been was a waste of her time.

Olivia didn't agree. For her, dwelling on it meant she would do better in the future.

A knock on the glass made her jump. Turning towards the passenger window, she was pleased to see DC Timothy Green grinning at her. He spoke to her, but his words were muffled by the glass between them. Rather than open the window, she popped the door. He stepped back, giving her a moment to grab her meagre belongs and climb out.

Her hand went self-consciously to the collar of her shirt. She raised it and smoothed it into place, ensuring it covered the scar.

Tim glanced away, giving her a moment to carry out this small ritual. Olivia's stomach flipped. He understood. Just knowing that he got it, made it easier.

"You all set?" he asked, peeking back at her.

She returned his smile. "As ready as I'm ever going to be."

"I did this last week, it was easy. You'll walk it."

"I hope so," Olivia said. The butterflies were back, only now they didn't feel so much like butterflies but elephants crashing around in her stomach. "They're not going to make a fuss, are they?"

Tim shrugged. He was clearly aiming for nonchalance, but instead overshot the mood by a mile. The ghost of a smile he was trying to keep buried peeped through, leaving Olivia in no doubt as to what awaited her.

"They're going to make a fuss, aren't they?"

He laughed, and threw an arm over her shoulders. "They missed you, that's all."

"You said they didn't make a big deal of you returning."

"That was deliberate," he said. His easy smile put her at ease. "If I told you, you'd just have weaselled your way out of it."

Olivia groaned. "It's that bad, is it?"

He laughed as he dragged her towards the automatic doors. "Just you wait and see."

"Great," Olivia grumbled, but deep down there was a part of her that flipped with joy. She'd never been so close to any other team she'd worked with in the past. The idea of having colleagues who treated her more like family filled her with happiness. "Fine, let's just get it over with."

. . .

MOMENTS LATER, Tim urged her ahead as they approached the main doors into the office. Through the glass, Olivia could see that everyone appeared to be going about their business as usual. The sight caused some of her nervous energy to dissipate. She shoved open the main door and stepped into the shared office space.

"For she's a jolly good fellow!" The song rang out, taking Olivia by surprise. Other voices joined in, and Olivia spotted DI Haskell and Appleton as they clapped along with the beat.

PC Indira Shah came from the direction of the small staff kitchen. In her hands she carried a large cake covered with a blue, and yellow icing that reminded Olivia of the high-visibility Battenberg pattern on the marked cars. Across the top of the cake, written in a script font was, 'Welcome Back DC Olivia Crandell'.

She glanced up at the room and the group of people surrounding her blurred as her eyes filled with tears. Her nervousness had been unwarranted because, as she brushed the tears away, Olivia couldn't shake the feeling that returning to the team felt like coming home.

CHAPTER FOUR

JOAN SAT ON THE COUCH, iPad forgotten in her lap, and a half empty teacup on the side table at her elbow. Her gaze was only half fixed on the television screen. She'd lost track of the time she'd spent sitting but her legs had started to feel a little numb, so it seemed safe to assume it was quite a while.

What was it she had intended to do?

The house was silent. Nigel had mentioned something about an appointment he had to keep. Closing her eyes she tried to recreate the conversation but her thoughts felt ephemeral, unsubstantial. Every time she tried to latch on to one, to catch it in her mind's eye, it broke apart like seaweed sucked away on an outgoing tide. Her thoughts drifted further from the shores of her mind.

Life seemed to be something lived by other people, not by her. At least Nigel was happy.

Resentment stirred in her gut. No sooner had the emotion started to form, it dissipated.

Joan wanted to cry. Raising her hand to her cheek, she was unsurprised to find her face dry and her eyes gritty. Dr Oswalt had told her dry eyes were a side-effect of the medication. He'd also reminded her that her inability to cry was a symptom of her underlying condition.

Joan deliberately pushed the intrusive thought aside. Nigel would pick up some drops for her when he had a chance. She would remind him. Or had she already asked him? She wasn't sure.

Scrambling her hand over the couch cushions, she searched for her phone. It wasn't there. A hazy memory of her plugging it in returned to her.

She glanced down at the forgotten iPad in her lap. Next to her, the laptop had been discarded among the cushions. Had she written anything today? She couldn't remember. And the act of trying to recall the hazy events of the day made her head ache.

Joan continued to stare at the iPad screen, her face dimly reflected in its surface. Eyes flat, hair limp, bloated pale face. A vision struggled to swim to the surface of her memory.

Her stomach rumbled, breaking the moment, and she turned from the screen. It was always the same. She was either hungry, or nauseous. Sometimes, both at once. Drawing a breath, she heaved herself out from between the cushions. Pain tweaked her in the space between her ribs and stomach. Breath caught in the back of her throat and she winced, waiting for the pain to pass.

Her legs were not her own. They wobbled as though undecided about their role. She briefly wondered if they would support her at all. The feeling passed and Joan took a tentative step towards the door. She stumbled as her slipper—which was only partially on her foot—caught in the bunched up rug next to the couch. Joan caught herself, barely managing to stay on her feet. Was this how newborn animals felt?

Stuffing her foot all the way into her wool-lined slipper, she flexed her toes. Headlights flashed by on the road outside, momentarily flooding the living room with unnatural light. Joan caught a glimpse of her own jaundiced reflection in the mirror over the mantelpiece as the headlights swept over her. The sight conjured a memory she'd carefully buried.

"So much for the camera on this phone." Irritation coated Nigel's voice. "I still can't take a bloody clear picture of the moon." Glancing over his shoulder, he eyed Joan speculatively. The glint in his eye caused her to shrink against the shadows of the house. She knew that look. The night air nipped at the exposed flesh of her arms, causing it to pebble.

"Don't..." The word hovered, half formed on her

tongue. Nigel snapped the picture before she could turn away.

"Perfect. Who needs the moon when I've got you?" His hoarse laughter brought heat flooding into her face. Holding the phone up, Nigel presented her with the photograph he'd taken. "My very own moon face."

The memory faded, but the humiliation remained. As Nigel always reminded her, he wasn't saying these things to be mean. It was simply the truth. And sometimes the truth hurt.

For one split second, her misery overwhelmed the haze caused by her combined medications. The emotion flooded through her system, filling her up to the point of overflow. She was disgusting. Nigel would leave her. There was no doubt in her mind.

As quickly as it had come, the feeling faded into apathy. Pulling her gaze away from the mirror, she sloped out to the kitchen. Her feet barely lifted from the carpet because lifting them was too much effort. Her slippers *shushed* across the floor.

Maybe if she spoke to Dr Oswalt, on her own this time, he would agree to her cutting down the dosages on some of her medications. It seemed unlikely. Dr Oswalt and Nigel were convinced she required everything she had been prescribed.

Pausing at the fridge, Joan pulled it open and stared in at the paltry contents. Nigel would not be happy that she'd forgotten to do a food shop. Closing the door, she crossed to the cupboards and opened them one at a time.

A half-empty multi-pack of crisps called to her and she snatched it down. She spotted an extra large chocolate bar shoved down the back of the cupboard and pulled it free. She tore through the wrapper exposing the chocolate beneath. White mould bloomed across the brown squares. Snapping off a chunk, Joan shoved it into her mouth anyway.

She remembered buying it in the time before. That was how she saw her life now. Cut into pieces like the chocolate bar. There was the time before her hospitalisations, the spaces between, and then there was now.

The chocolate bar had come during one of those between times. Probably a celebratory treat for a some milestone or other in her recovery.

The chocolate turned to ash on her tongue.

Nigel would be so disappointed with her.

Turning to the bin, she thought about throwing the chocolate out. She clutched the bar. So wasteful.

Abandoning the cupboard, she shuffled over to the place where her phone was plugged in and charging. She picked it up, but was surprised to find the screen dead and the phone unresponsive.

Uncomprehending, she twisted the phone in her hand, but tit remained dead. Her eyes travelled up along the charger wire to the power point. The plug was on the counter and not in the socket where it was supposed to be. Had she forgotten to plug it in? It wouldn't be the first time.

She shook her head as though the action could clear some of the cobwebs from her brain. She was sure she'd plugged it in. Ever since Nigel had cancelled the landline—according to him it was a drain on their finances—it became imperative to Joan that she keep her phone charged. It was her only life-line to the outside world.

With her eyes closed tight, she leaned heavily on the kitchen worktop. She'd caught Nigel unplugging her charger once before. Or she'd thought she had. He'd dismissed the accusation as nonsense. *"Joan, why would you say that? Why would I disconnect it? Without it, I can't contact you when I'm staying out late for work. And what if something happened to you? What if there was an emergency, Joany-Pop? Or you became sick again?"*

He was right. Of course, he was right. Nigel worried about her. He would never do something like that. It was all her. She was so forgetful.

Sighing, she plugged the charger in and waited for the phone to return to life. The screen flashed and a memory stirred deep in her mind. *She was standing at the counter, the tremor in her hand wors-ening as she'd reached for the charging cable and plugged it into the base of the phone.* It stuck out in her memory because the white apple logo that appeared on the screen had shocked her sensitive

21

eyes. That had been before Nigel had sat her down and made them both a cuppa to drink. And...

Joan cringed, fighting with the fog in her brain. What happened next? She screwed her eyes shut, willing her mind to cooperate for once.

It returned to her in pieces. She'd dozed off on the sofa. Somewhere in the recess of her mind she recalled Nigel standing over her, complaining about the lack of lunch and her laziness. Or had that been yesterday?

Shaking her head, she set the phone back down. Maybe she really was losing her mind. After all, those memories felt very real, and yet there was no escaping the fact that phone had never been plugged in.

Glancing down at her watch, she was dismayed to discover the time. Half past six. Nigel should be home soon. And when he did, he would want his evening glass of wine.

She crossed to the fridge and was relieved to find the bottle of Pinot Grigio chilling on the shelf. His wine. She preferred red, but Nigel would never let her have any because of the possible interaction with her medication.

With a sigh, she grabbed the crisps and chocolate and carried them back to the living room, where she settled on the couch. With greasy fingers, she picked up the laptop and switched it back on. The screen flared to life, the flickering cursor on the empty white screen mocking her. She hadn't written a single word today.

For a moment, fear tightened her chest. Her last deadline had passed in a haze. Everyone said they understood, but Joan wasn't convinced. If she didn't turn something in soon...

Nigel would be so angry if she screwed up and they had to return the advance payment to the publishers.

Joan pushed the uncomfortable thoughts aside. She needed to think. The news was always good for ideas. It was always full of stories about people committing crimes.

She flicked through the channels, searching for some kind of news report that might spark something in her dulled mind. Headlights spun over the ceiling and Joan sat up a little straighter, half expecting it to be Nigel. But the car passed by and she sank back among the cushions, the chocolate and crisps her only companions.

CHAPTER FIVE

THE EVENING WAS DRAWING in when Harriet left her office. The pink and yellow sunlight faded, sinking below the level of the tallest buildings. This slow demise allowed shadows to creep from their hiding places like small night creatures scurrying from their dens. Twisting and stretching, they crept outwards, growing bolder, like fingers reaching, searching for a weakness.

The *hum* and *click* of the lights as they flickered to life overhead were comforting, familiar. These splashes of bright yellow luminance provided pools of protection for those who remained on campus, each illuminated patch of ground driving back the shadows, forcing them to crowd around the edges of each mini sun.

As Harriet crossed the tree lined walkway that took her to the carpark, she spotted a familiar face.

Misha McDermid stood huddled by the library. She brushed at her pale face. Even from this distance, Harriet could tell that not everything was as it should be. Pace faltering, she considered her options. Would it be inappropriate to approach her student?

Get a grip, Harriet. Not everything needs to be examined so closely. She hated that the anonymous complaint lodged against her had infected her ability to be a good teacher. Every action she made now was scrutinised over and over. It was exhausting. But, until Dr Baig declared her to be in the clear, it felt necessary.

Harriet chewed her lip. Misha swiped at her cheeks again and closed her eyes. She looked wretched. With her mind made up, Harriet changed direction and hurried towards the student.

It was stupid to feel so connected to Misha; almost responsible. She wasn't Louise, and no matter what Harriet did now, nothing would change the past.

Pausing, she coughed gently and waited for the student to notice her. When Misha glanced up, her eyes were bloodshot and red rimmed, causing the blue of her iris to stand out in sharp contrast.

"Dr Quinn, sorry," Misha said, clearing her throat awkwardly. She averted her gaze and straightened her shoulders. "I didn't see you coming. I was just taking a quick study break."

"You don't need to explain yourself to me," Harriet said. "Is everything all right?"

Misha nodded, her bright smile forced. She momentarily met Harriet's gaze before letting her eyes flick away. "Yeah, of course. Why would you ask?"

Well, the fact that you're standing out here, and have clearly been crying tells me something is wrong. Harriet resisted the urge to state the obvious. "Is it the research topic? It's certainly a broad area to dive into." She skirted around the truth of the matter. When she'd heard Misha's plans to write a paper on the connection between childhood trauma and violent crimes, Harriet's trepidation had been only too obvious. It was a heavy topic for anyone to tackle, but especially so for someone with Misha's background.

Misha shook her head, but Harriet knew there was something she wasn't saying. Had diving into the existing papers, and statistics brought unpleasant memories to the surface?

"You don't think I can handle it." It wasn't a question and that made Harriet uncomfortable. It wasn't her job to assuage the ego of her students. Instead, she was there to help guide them on their chosen paths. If they bit off more than they could chew, and they all inevitably did, then it was down to her to be honest with them. After all, she wanted them to succeed in their chosen areas. But she knew better than anyone how long it took to build coping mechanisms to deal with the more graphic aspects of their work.

"I didn't say that." Harriet tried for diplomacy but she could tell from the look on Misha's face that she'd fallen woefully short of the mark. "It was just a question. I wouldn't be doing my job as your lecturer if I didn't ask."

"You missed our meeting last week," Misha said, glancing off to the side. "I thought maybe you were bored with my research."

It seemed like an odd observation, but it wasn't the first time Misha had said something which jarred. Harriet shook her head. "That's not it," she said. "I had a meeting with the police. My work with them often means I have to juggle my priorities a little."

"Martha said you would reschedule, but..."

"Oh, right. God, I'm sorry," she said. "With everything—" Harriet cut herself off. Misha didn't need to hear her excuses. She needed action. Rummaging around in her bag, she pulled out the burgundy planner Drew had bought her for Christmas. Or at least he'd *said* it was a Christmas present. The fact that he'd given it to her almost a month after the holiday suggested otherwise. She flipped it open and caught Misha eyeing it.

"That's really pretty," Misha said.

"Thank you," Harriet said. "A gift from a friend."

Misha nodded. "Lucky you."

Was it her imagination, or had there been there an edge to Misha's voice when she'd said that? Harriet quickly dismissed the idea. She was reading too much into those around her, as usual. Drew had said it was a problem she needed to curb, and Harriet found herself agreeing with him.

"I'm free next Tuesday, if you'd like to meet then?"

Misha pulled a face and chewed the nail on her index finger. "Yeah, I guess so."

"Is there a problem?"

Misha shrugged. "I suppose it doesn't matter."

"No, talk to me."

"I'm struggling with some of the papers I've found," Misha said. As she spoke, her eyes brimmed with tears. "It's brought up some painful memories."

Harriet nodded sympathetically. Just as she'd suspected. "Of course. Well, it's not too late to swap your paper if that—"

Misha shook her head. "That's not what I meant, Dr Quinn," she snapped. "My mother never turned away from a fight, and neither will I." She swallowed hard, and her gaze softened again. "I'm sorry. It's just a sore point. I've spent my life feeling as though I would never live up to the ghost of my mother's memory." She sighed. "And now I've got this wonderful opportunity to prove myself worthy, and I'm screwing it all up."

"I'm sure that's not true."

"It is," she said. There was an edge of panic in her voice. "She would be so disappointed in me. That's why I was really counting on our meeting. I knew if I could just talk it through with you, it would be all right."

"Tuesday is not that far away," Harriet said gently.

"My mother always said talking things through with you helped her to grasp situations more clearly." Misha spoke as though she hadn't heard Harriet.

Harriet furrowed her brow. "Weren't you a baby when..."

Misha nodded and colour crept into her cheeks. "She didn't tell me this personally. Well, maybe she did, but I don't remember it." She shrugged. "I wanted to feel closer to her, so I went looking through her things." Misha leaned closer, her voice dropping to a conspiratorial whisper. "I found some of her journals. My mother was always an enigma to me, but with the journals, it was like finding a window into who she was. She wrote quite a bit about you in them."

Guilt gnawed at Harriet. She glanced down at her schedule.

"I really don't have anything else free. Tuesday at 1pm..."

"You probably think me reading her journals is an invasion of her privacy."

Harriet shook her head. "She was your mother, Misha. I can understand you wanting to bridge that gap between you." And Harriet did understand. She'd spent years trying to do the same thing with her own mother.

Misha's expression brightened. "I knew you'd get it, Dr Quinn." She glanced down at her watch. "You know, I'm free right now. We could discuss the research I've dug up. Oh, wait, I don't have it with me." Misha frowned. "You could pop over to mine. I could get my flatmates to clear out—"

Harriet shook her head. "Not this evening, Misha. I've already got plans."

"Maybe tomorrow night?"

Harriet smiled kindly. "You know I don't meet students outside of hours."

"But you meet your PhD students after hours."

"That's different—"

"Please, Dr Quinn. I could really use your help on this. I'll even cook dinner, and I could show you the journals."

The pleading note in Misha's voice tore at Harriet's heart. But Dr Baig's voice rang in her head.

"I really can't, Misha. Next Tuesday is the best I can do."

"I suppose you're too busy with your police meetings." There was an edge to Misha's voice that reminded Harriet of Louise.

"The work I—"

Misha shook her head, cutting Harriet off. "You don't owe me anything, Dr Quinn. Next Tuesday will have to do."

Before Harriet could say another word, Misha turned away. "I need to get back to my study."

Stunned, Harriet watched the young woman stalk away.

Before Misha reached the double doors, she paused. "You know, you're nothing like the person my mother wrote about. She talks about you like you're this saint. But you're just like everyone else. Self-interested. Your problems are the only ones that matter." She swiped at the tears that tracked down her cheeks. "I suppose I should have known better than to trust you."

With that, she was gone, leaving Harriet to stare after her in shocked silence.

CHAPTER SIX

DREW HUNG BACK and watched the rest of the team crowd around DC Crandell. It was good to have everyone back where they were supposed to be, and not just because of the guilt he carried over everything that had gone down with Alfred Douglas. Part of him knew it was silly to feel so responsible for the others, but he couldn't help it.

"Looks like things can get back to normal around here now," Melissa whispered as she leaned towards him.

"I'm not sure normal is a word I'd describe for this lot," Drew said with a smile.

"You still on for tomorrow night?"

"Of course," Drew said. His words belied the nervousness he felt. Their newly budding relationship—not that he was positive he could call it that, yet—still left him feeling discomfited. He wasn't sure if it was the fact that it was a work relationship that bothered him, or if there was something else at play.

Melissa shot him a hundred-watt smile, tilting her head coyly to the side as she looked him up and down. "You know, if you wanted, we could meet for a drink after work."

Drew shook his head. "Not tonight," he said. "Paperwork." He shrugged, not daring to offer a further explanation. And it wasn't a lie, he did have a pile of paperwork to get through. But guilt stuck him in the gut all the same because doing paperwork wasn't the only plan he had.

However, the last time he'd told Melissa he was meeting Harriet, a weird atmosphere had grown between them.

"Yeah, sure, of course," Melissa said, taking a small step back from him. "You're right. We said we were going to take this slow." She smiled at him, and from where Drew stood he could have sworn it was a smile tinged with sadness. "I suppose I'm just a little more sure of everything."

He didn't argue with her, there was little point in it. The conversation would only wind up going around in circles, and Drew was definitely not in the mood for that. It was easier to pretend he couldn't see her emotions as they played out across her face.

"Great."

Melissa stared at him for a beat longer, and Drew wondered if she was going to call his bluff. When she didn't, he sighed inwardly. "I've got to run," she said. "Gregson wants me to finish up the reports I'm working on."

"Which reports?" he asked.

"The drugs seizure in Leeds. It's not looking like we'll net anything bigger than David Grantly."

"He's plenty big."

She shook her head. "He's destroying those kids' lives with his county lines bullshit, but I know he's not the top of the food chain."

"Did you mention this to the monk?"

Melissa shot him a withering look. "What do you think, Sherlock?"

"I'm just asking," he said. "No need to be defensive."

She sighed, and looked away. "I've got to go. Save me a piece of cake, will you?"

Drew nodded as she hurried back to her office. Turning his attention back to the gathering, he studied the others as they interacted with Olivia. She caught his eye, and broke away from the group of people surrounding her. Making her way through the desks, she paused next to him.

"Brought you this, guv," she said, offering him a slice of cake.

"Cheers." He took the offered paper plate happily. The sharp scent of lemon caught his nose, and he dipped his head to the cake, inhaling the scent appreciatively. "Lemon curd? PC Shah really went all out."

"She did," Olivia said, glancing back over her shoulder at the PC who stood chatting with colleagues.

"You're lucky they didn't ask *me* to pick one out," he said.

"I don't think they make cakes out of Pot Noodles," Olivia said, proving she was a little too familiar with his dietary habits.

"Ouch," he said. "I'm not that bad."

Olivia raised an eyebrow at him. The humorous glint in her eyes gratified him. When he'd watched her get stretchered out of The Grand, he'd been certain she was a goner. Luckily, she was a fighter.

As though she could sense the direction of his thoughts, Olivia shifted uncomfortably, her hand automatically moving to her throat. She smoothed her shirt collar into place.

"How are you feeling?"

Her eyes widened imperceptibly before she glanced down at her shoes. "I'm fine," she said offhandedly. "All healed up."

"That's not what I meant," he said. "But I'm glad to hear you're physically fitter."

"Oh, I am." Olivia raised her chin defiantly. "The moment they gave me the all-clear to get back to training, I went."

"I heard," Drew said. "But I never expected anything less from you. Have you spoken to anyone?"

Olivia's expression twisted into a grimace, there and gone in an instant. "Guv, I'm fine. Really."

"You know that's not what I'm asking, DC Crandell."

She flinched, her shoulders rounding.

Drew sighed. What had started as a friendly chat, now seemed to be veering down a more professional path, and that was not what he wanted. "I'm not very good at this," he said kindly. "But I've had a little experience with these things and I know the toll it can take if you don't let someone in to help." He tried to school his features into something warmer and more approachable.

Olivia glanced towards the small groups in the office. He could see the conflict as it warred on her features. "I'll take that under advisement, guv," she said.

"Talk to Dr Quinn if that'll make you feel better. She's not a stranger."

Maz caught Olivia's eye and waved her over. "I'm going to..." she trailed off.

"Of course, go."

She walked away, leaving Drew alone with the piece of cake on the paper plate. He glanced down at it but his mouth was dry. The thought of stuffing cake down his throat didn't exactly fill him with joy. Instead, he set it to one side for Melissa.

DC Green grinned at him from the other side of the space, and Drew's stomach dropped. He still had nightmares about Tim's injuries. And while the young officer seemed to be doing much better, Drew was acutely aware that he was tied to a desk for the forceable future.

With a sigh, he reached down to the drawer in his desk and grabbed the packet of cigarettes he'd stashed there for just such a moment. Without a backwards glance, he escaped from the office, and made a beeline for the back stairs.

CHAPTER SEVEN

DRAWING her coat tighter around her body, Harriet rapped on the wooden door and then stood back. Turning her face up towards the sky, she was surprised to discover there wasn't even a cloud in sight. The inky darkness spread out in front of her, studded with the twinkling light from distant stars. Breathing out, she watched as a cloud of white drifted away over her head and into the chilly night air. The distant sound of the waves lapping against the shoreline brought her the type of calm she didn't normally experience.

Drew pulled open the door to his cottage. Warmth rushed out, swirling around Harriet's legs as it pushed back the worst of the nippy spring air.

"You're late," Drew said, the ghost of a smile hovering on his lips. "We'll have to reheat the food."

"Sorry," Harriet said, as she followed him inside.

From inside her bag, she produced a bottle of red wine. "I had to stop to pick this up."

Taking it from her, he gestured for her to follow him into the living room. There remained a couple of cardboard boxes against the back wall, but considering how few opportunities Drew actually had to unpack, Harriet thought he was doing remarkably well. "It's looking wonderful," she said, noting the new forest green throw on the couch. Several scatter cushions lay haphazardly across the chairs, the tags still hanging from the corners. "You've really upped your game since I was last here."

Drew grinned. "Melissa thought I needed some new stuff. She reckons it'll help me feel at home here faster."

Harriet kept her smile fixed in place. His relationship with Melissa was a relatively new one. It was something they didn't discuss. A mercy Harriet was only too happy to cling to. Despite being glad to see him moving on, her usual curiosity did not extend to asking questions about it. "Did she help you pick the new things out?"

"She showed me how to order them online," he said. "The thought of going to a shop…" He shuddered, drawing a smile from Harriet.

"You're right. I don't exactly see you fluffing cushions in Dunelm, or Next."

"Not a chance. You want to eat in here, or the kitchen?"

Harriet shook her head. "What and risk destroying your new stuff so soon? The kitchen will do just fine."

Drew rolled his eyes, but led the way into the room next door. A brand new table stood in front of the double doors that led out into the small back garden. Judging by the discarded cardboard box next to it, he'd only just put it together.

"Another new purchase, I see."

Drew shook his head sheepishly. "Actually I bought that before I moved into this place. Haven't managed to assemble it until now."

"Work has been that busy?"

He shook his head. "No, I just didn't have a Phillips screwdriver."

Harriet started to laugh, drawing a sideways glance from Drew as he pulled open the the plastic bag on the counter and set out the containers of food. "Are you going to stand there and laugh at my ineptitude, or will you help me serve this?"

Stifling her laughter, Harriet headed for the cutlery drawer. Grabbing the utensils they needed, she laid them out on the table as Drew placed the food on plates. "Olivia came back to work today," he said, breaking the companionable silence between them.

"That's great," Harriet said. "She needs it. Last time I spoke to her, I thought she was developing a little bit of cabin-fever."

Drew nodded. "I get that. She prefers to be in the thick of it."

Harriet paused. "What is it?"

"What do you mean?" He returned to the cupboards and grabbed the glasses and the bottle of wine.

"There's something you're not saying."

Sighing, he unscrewed the lid before he poured a generous measure in each glass. "I think she could do with talking to someone."

"Did she say something to you?" Harriet took her seat at the table and grabbed a spoon. Drew had already begun helping himself, and she followed suit, heaping rice and madras onto her plate. The scent hit her nose, and her stomach grumbled appreciatively. This had been yet another day where she'd become so caught up in her work that she hadn't taken the time to grab lunch. And then her meeting with Misha had thrown her off course entirely. If it wasn't for the protein bars Martha left in her office drawers, Harriet wouldn't have eaten at all.

Drew shook his head as he took a large helping of saag-aloo and added it to his already full dish. "I brought it up with her," he said. "I suggested she should maybe speak with you."

"Me?" Harriet jerked her head up in surprise. "Why me?"

"Because you're you," Drew offered weakly. "Why, do you not want to speak with her?"

Harriet shook her head, and shifted some rice around the plate with her fork. "That's not what I meant."

"Then what is it?"

"Well, counselling requires a specialised practitioner. That's not really my area of expertise."

"You get inside the heads of murderers and lunatics every day of the week," Drew said around a mouthful of dinner.

Harriet shot him a dirty look. "We don't use language like that."

He nodded. "Sorry." He swallowed and levelled his gaze on her. "But Crandell should be a cake walk by comparison."

"Olivia is no doubt suffering from PTSD," Harriet said. "That's not something I can treat. I could definitely direct her to someone who could walk her through the treatment." She sighed. "Anyway, I'm not sure how comfortable Olivia would be, speaking to me."

"What do you mean?"

"It might require her to discuss some more personal matters. Because I'm a colleague, she might not feel comfortable with me knowing that much detail about her. And then there's the conflict of interest matter."

"What conflict of interest?" Drew had set his fork aside and was studying her intently.

"What if my assessment of her differed from the

one given when she was signed back to work? I would be obligated to inform both you and Gregson. It would just complicate things for her needlessly."

Leaning back in his chair, Drew sipped at the glass of wine. He grimaced. "This is basically battery acid."

Harriet grinned. "Sorry."

He straightened in the chair and picked his fork up again. "So I shouldn't have said anything to her?"

Shaking her head, Harriet glanced down at her plate. "Quite the contrary. It shows you care, Drew, and that alone is worth something. If Olivia comes to me, I'm not going to turn her away."

"But?"

"But, if she's amenable to it, then I will direct her to someone much more qualified."

Drew scooped a heap of rice into his mouth and chewed thoughtfully. When he finished, he nodded. "That's all I'm asking."

They returned to their companionable silence as they ate.

"How are things up in the university?" Drew asked.

His question caused Harriet's breath to catch in the back of her throat. After her run in with Misha earlier that day, she had found it difficult to focus on anything. And she hadn't yet mentioned anything to him about Dr Baig's initial conversation with her at Christmas regarding inappropriate behaviour. Truth be told, so much had happened since then that Harriet had pushed it entirely out of her mind, or at least she had tried to.

"Fine," she said. "I had a little bit of an issue with one of my students today. They weren't keen on the idea of having to wait for a one-on-one meeting."

"Don't they understand you're an in-demand, busy woman?"

Harriet smiled and glanced down at her plate. "Not exactly. They wanted to meet after hours."

Drew glanced up at her. "A meeting at night?"

"Well, I wouldn't exactly call 6pm night," Harriet said hurriedly.

"Why would they think you'd meet them after six?"

"I've had some evening meetings with my PhD students after I fell behind."

"But surely you're all caught up now?"

She sighed and picked up her wine. "I may have put off some meetings with my students."

"That's not like you," Drew said astutely. He was right. It wasn't like her.

"With my work for the police..."

"We haven't been loaded down with cases recently," he said, eyeing her thoughtfully.

He was right again. There hadn't been the usual caseload to contend with. She spent her time blaming her work with the police for putting off the meetings with her students, but if she were honest with herself, that wasn't strictly true.

"You remember around Christmas I seemed a little off after a meeting with Dr Baig?"

Drew screwed his face up in consternation. "I think so."

"You said when I was ready to tell you, I could."

"Aye, sounds like something I'd say."

"There was a complaint made at the university against me."

Drew laughed, his eyes crinkling up at the corners as he leaned back in his chair. A moment passed and he looked back at her, the mirth fading from his face. "Wait, you're serious?"

Harriet nodded, and chewed her bottom lip unable to meet his eye.

"Why would anyone lodge a complaint against you?"

"Allegedly, my behaviour has bordered on inappropriate."

Drew's derisive snort caused Harriet to look at him. "Bloody heck. That's the most ridiculous thing I've ever heard. You inappropriate? Christ, Harriet, why didn't you say anything before?"

She shrugged. She knew the truth, but the idea of spilling it out to Drew filled her with dread.

"Don't lie to me." He softened his voice. "Why didn't you say anything?"

Harriet pushed away from the table and crossed

to the sink. Grabbing a glass, she filled it with water and sipped at the contents as she stared out into the darkness beyond the window.

"Harriet?"

"I was ashamed," she said, heat burning in her face. "I pride myself on keeping a professional distance." Her shoulders dropped and she set the glass back down on the counter. "Being a woman in academia... most people think it must be so easy." Her laughter was bitter and hurt her ears. "Don't misunderstand me, it's much better than it was. And Dennis is trying very hard to ensure a level playing field for all. But it's still predominantly a boys' club. I've always accepted that. It drives me to work harder, I suppose." She glanced at him. Drew was sitting at the table, his body-language open and relaxed as he listened to her. It gave Harriet the courage she needed to continue.

"It was just easier to keep it to myself."

"So why are you telling me now?"

"I don't really know," she said with a smile. "Maybe it's the wine."

"Did Dr Beige tell you who made the complaint against you?"

She didn't bother to correct the nickname he'd given to the head of her department. Harriet shook her head. "He said it wouldn't be appropriate."

"Horse shit," Drew said vehemently. "The coward just wanted to save face." Climbing to his feet, he crossed the kitchen. He paused in front of Harriet and placed his hands on her shoulders. "I know you. You would never do something like this. You're simply not capable of it."

Harriet pulled away from him, and paced the floor. "I just don't know who would say it. I've been searching my mind for any incidents that might have occurred."

"Harriet, you've done nothing wrong."

She shook her head. "We can't say that. This person, whoever they are, clearly feels as though I've crossed a boundary."

"Bloody snowflake," Drew said.

"That's not really fair," she said. "If this was anyone else besides me telling you this, would you be so understanding?"

Drew shrugged. "But it's not anybody else."

"No, and I think that's clouding your judgement," she said. "I appreciate the vote of confidence though." She grinned at him.

"And all of this is the reason you've been putting off meetings with your students?"

She nodded. "There's a part of me that worries I'll cross some line, and I won't even know it." Pinching the bridge of her nose, she closed her eyes. "I've never felt like this before. I've always considered myself to be a reserved person, and now with this..." She let her hands drop back to her side. "I feel like I have to walk on eggshells with everyone who walks through the door of my office. It's messing with my head."

Drew grew quiet. Harriet moved back to the table, giving him the time to cement the thoughts in his head.

"Has it occurred to you that this might have something to do with Dr Connors?" he said.

Harriet tried to hide her surprise and failed. "Why would this have anything to do with him?"

Drew shrugged. "I don't know, but we both know he's a bitter bastard. I wouldn't put anything past him. Could he have slipped one of your students a few extra quid to lodge the complaint against you?"

Harriet immediately shook her head. "No, he wouldn't."

"Wouldn't he? Have there been any other complaints?"

She folded her arms across her chest defensively, hugging her body. "Well, no. Not that I know about."

"And would Dr Baig keep something like that from you?"

She shook her head. "No, he would tell me. He's obliged to inform me."

"Well then," Drew seemed relieved. "It looks cut and dried to me. Dr Connors is trying to put the frighteners on you. He probably hopes to intimidate you into dropping your case against him. Didn't he come and see you over the Christmas holidays?"

Harriet had never even considered the possibility

that Dr Connors could be involved in something so despicable. But the more she thought about it, and the more Drew sketched it all out for her, the more plausible it became. "I suppose."

"Come on, Harriet. You know what he's like."

She did. "I guess I never looked at it like that. I think I was always so close to the situation that I couldn't see the wood from the trees."

"And if you'd said it to me earlier, I could have put your mind at ease sooner." He grabbed the wine bottle. "You should probably go back to holding your student meetings without the worry of crossing some non-existent line."

She glanced down at the table. "Well I've still got some catching up to do. Once I'm done with these last few, I'll try to stay on top of it a little better." As she spoke, she thought about Misha. She'd been unfair. The young woman had asked for help, and Harriet had cut her off. As soon as she had the opportunity, she would change that.

Drew topped up her glass.

"I've got to drive home," she said.

He shook his head. "Don't be daft. Look at all the times you let me stay over." A grin spread over his face. "It's your turn to take the couch."

Laughing, Harriet shook her head. "I can't. I really do need to get back to mine. I've got an early morning appointment at the university. And you said it yourself, I need to get back on track."

Drew slid into the seat opposite her. "Well, we can at least finish our food." She couldn't argue with him there. Settling across from him, she allowed her worries to wash away as Drew filled her in on the office politics.

CHAPTER EIGHT

LIBBY CLICKED ON TO *RATTLE*.

In the time she had been away, the forum had exploded with activity. Comments zipped by so fast, Libby could barely keep up with the barrage. The entire situation was like a car-crash happening in slow motion, and Libby was unable to look away.

> Georgiex094: OMG! It hit the Sun.

> Mard-Arse5108: Where did you get these messages from, SinEater81?

The message was quickly lost as others piled on.

> Georgiex094: Remind me to never get on SinEater's bad side!

The message struck a chord with Libby and she found herself agreeing. For a moment she felt guilty for joining in with the others. She considered logging out, but was unable to look away from the vitriol that spread through the forum for a woman they'd never even met.

> SinEater81: She checked into a garden centre near Harrogate earlier today.

> MardArse5108: Anyone nearby fancy dropping in to get some information on her? Maybe she lives in the area.

Several Rattle members agreed to check up on it. Feeling sick, Libby scrolled back up the thread in an attempt to get some clarity. It took her a moment to read through the most recent messages. Holly Thomas had dropped off the map since the messages had been made public. And while she'd issued a public apology it seemed the Rattle forum were not in a very forgiving mood.

> CremeEggFanatic: Bitch deserves to get what's coming to her...

> TheGreedyTruthx0x0: If I knew where she was I'd out her in a heartbeat. No way I'd protect someone like that.

> MardArse5108: How do we take her down?

> SinEater81: The same way you'd eat an elephant MardArse... One bite at a time. :D:D:D:D

"Hey, maybe we should take a minute. We don't know how true any of this is..." Libby's hands trembled as she hit *send* on the message.

> SinEater81: Oh, hey, Holly! Nice you could join us. Pushed any teenagers to suicide lately?

Libby's palms grew sweaty as she read the message.

"I'm not Holly," she responded. They wouldn't listen, they never did. She'd seen this happen too many times in the past with others in the group. The moment a member presented a dissenting opinion they were instantly ostracised, and ridiculed mercilessly. Nothing she could say to them would make them change their minds.

> Mard-Arse5108: Just like Holly to weasel her way out of the truth...

Libby's mouth went dry. What had been a bit of fun and a way to blow off steam was slowly morphing into something else. Something she wasn't entirely comfortable with.

> Mard-Arse5108: I've got her!

The message was followed by a link to a pin on a map.

Libby didn't bother to click on it, and instead, signed out of the forum before anyone else could pile on.

CHAPTER NINE

MALCOLM SET the handbrake and turned off the ignition. Only a handful of cars were scattered around the small car park, giving him a choice of spaces. He leaned back into the seat and stared out at the expanse of landscape that stretched in front of him. From this vantage point he could make out the sweeping grandeur of the moorland. The rich hues beckoned to him. Spring had not yet fully sprung, but even now, he could see the lush green starting to spread across the ground.

Reaching over into the footwell of the passenger seat, he grabbed his backpack. Hoisting it over the centre console, he rummaged through the contents. The familiar brush of his map and his notebook filled with his observations on the bird populations in the area met his fingertips. Tugging the thermos free, he deftly unscrewed the lid and quickly poured out half a cup of the strong Yorkshire tea he'd brewed before leaving home.

A quick cup before he set off.

Swallowing down a mouthful of the strong brew, he was surprised to find it still hot enough to scald his tongue. A low hiss of discomfort escaped him as he rolled his lips back over his teeth in a grimace.

Slipping his hand into the side pocket of his blue pack, he closed his fingers around the small velvet box. Removing it from the relative safety of his bag, he felt a tight knot form in the centre of his chest. All his carefully laid plans lay in tatters. And for what?

Tearing his gaze away from the view, he cast a sideways look at his phone. Still no word from her. It smarted to think of how they'd left things. If she could just admit he was right, everything could go back to normal. But Rosie's stubborn refusal to admit she'd been wrong about him left Malcolm hanging in limbo. And now, sitting here at the place where they'd first met, Malcolm was alone.

The idea that he had an anger problem was almost too ridiculous to credit. But Rosie had levelled the accusation at him just the same.

A blue SUV pulled off the road and stalled at the entrance to the car park. The driver quickly restarted the engine and the car lunged forward. Rolling his eyes, Malcolm took another swig of his tea. When the

SUV came to a stop next to his car, Malcolm's mood slid further into irritation. He jammed the ring box into his backpack. Incredulously, he took in the half empty car park before glancing back at the blue SUV which had stopped next to him.

What was wrong with people? Of all the places she could have parked—and it *was* a she, he noted with a sneer—she had to park right next to him? The driver pushed open her door, narrowly avoiding hitting Malcolm's car.

He tutted under his breath. The blonde woman smiled brightly at him, raising her hand in friendly salute. Malcolm kept his gaze fixed on the view that spread out before him.

The woman's phone rang, the strident sound breaking through Malcolm's contemplation, and a moment later the blonde woman's high voice cut through the silence as she answered it.

"Hiya!" The way she drew on the 'a' sound, elongating it so that it was almost comedic, drew a shudder from Malcolm. Turning his head to the left, he caught sight of a curly haired black dog watching him from the back seat. As soon as he made eye contact with the animal it began to bark and whine as it scratched at the window.

"Bess, no! Hold on, I have to let Bess out of the car," the woman blathered into the phone that was now pressed to her ear.

Tension sang through Malcolm's shoulders as he observed the woman wrangle the dog from the back of the car. At least she kept the creature on a lead. Some dog owners wouldn't have bothered. It was no wonder the bird populations was in decline.

A moment later and the woman and dog departed from the side of the car. She resumed her conversation, her voice shredding the peace as she waited to cross the A169.

Malcolm downed the last of his tea and screwed the cap back onto the thermos. He'd give it a couple of minutes and with any luck, the woman would be out of sight when he started down the path to the Hole of Horcum.

By the time he stepped out of his car and locked the doors, he felt his earlier mood dissipating. This was exactly what he needed. A chance to take his mind off the situation with Rosie. Perhaps his plans for their future together had been hasty. Considering her behaviour, how could he look at her as his future wife? Especially when all she wanted to do was criticise him at every turn.

Malcolm crossed the road quickly and started down the rough trail. Five minutes passed as he made steady progress along the path. Pausing to gaze across the underbrush, he searched for the faintest signs of movement among the flora. Peace washed over him and he closed his eyes.

The yapping of a dog broke through the blissful

silence. Malcolm's eyes snapped open in time to see the same black dog from the SUV launch itself from the undergrowth and cross the path twenty feet in front of him.

The dog dived into the overgrown scrub on the opposite side and a moment later the sound of panicked flapping heralded a small brown bird that scrambled into the air.

Shock rendered Malcolm momentarily dumbstruck. He watched as the dog bounced through the tangled bushes and bracken. The same bushes and bracken that created the perfect nesting ground for the birds Malcolm had come to seek out.

Tinkling laughter brought Malcolm back to himself and he felt his rage rise until it was a lump of barbed wire that dug into the back of his throat.

"Oi!" His voice, a half strangled shout, tore from his dry mouth. The dog continued to yip excitedly as Malcolm quickened his pace over the muddy ground. It was going to ruin everything. If the birds had already begun to nest—and Malcolm was positive they had—then the untold damage this stupid bloody dog could do didn't bear thinking about.

The dog bounded through the scrub and a flurry of birds scattered into the air on Malcolm's left.

Malcolm spotted the woman. "Excuse me!" He was hoarse. His heartbeat hammered a tattoo against his ribcage. "Your dog should be on a lead. That animal needs to be controlled! Excuse me!"

The woman, who was now only a few feet away turned in his direction, the asinine smile on her face fading as she spotted Malcolm barrelling towards her.

Grunting with the exertion, Malcolm fought to keep his footing on the uneven pathway. He'd lost sight of the dog, but he could still hear it.

"Your dog." Malcolm panted heavily. "You need to keep it on its lead."

The woman shook her head and spoke into the phone. "Give me a minute, I've got some madman ranting at me." The dismissive tone in her voice only served to send Malcolm's blood pressure spiralling.

The rage built in the centre of his chest, exacerbated by the rolling of the woman's eyes.

"What's your problem?" She tossed her head, the helmet of blonde hair on her head barely moving despite her actions.

Malcolm paused a few steps in front of her. "The dog," he said, hating the way his laboured breathing made him appear weak. "From the first of March all dogs must be kept on leads."

"What?"

"Are you deaf, or just stupid?" Malcom snapped.

"You can't talk to me like that." She raised the phone back to her ear.

"Listen to me," Malcolm said, anger colouring his voice. "The dog needs a lead. You can't just let it run free and disturb the nesting birds."

"This bloke is hassling me," she said into the phone.

Malcom shook his head before he took a step towards her. "You're not listening—"

"Help!" Her voice rose in panic.

The sound of something crashing towards them through the undergrowth made Malcolm turn. He spotted the dog as it emerged through a gap in the bracken.

"Bess, come here! Bess!" The woman's voice was pitched high and tinged with fear.

What she had to be afraid of, Malcolm wasn't sure.

His thoughts trailed away as the dog trotted past him. With its tail wagging back and forth, the dog proudly kept its head aloft as though to show them both what a good job it had done.

"Bess, drop it," the woman said. There was no mistaking the note of disgust in her voice.

Sweat trickled down Malcolm's spine as he watched the dog drop to its belly, the bone still clasped between its jaws. The dog seemed utterly unimportant now. He took a step towards the animal. It rolled its chocolate drop eyes in his direction, a low growl escaping from its mouth. The sound emanated from a place behind the large bone in its mouth.

"We need to call the police," Malcolm said. Sweat, cold and clammy, slicked his palms. His tongue was suddenly too large for his dry mouth. He ran his tongue over his bottom lip but it felt like sandpaper.

"The police?" The woman was incredulous. "First you follow me, ranting and raving, and now you want to call the police? If anyone is entitled to—"

"Shut up." What little patience Malcolm had left had fled. He turned his attention to the woman in front of him. "Your dog," he said, fighting to keep his composure. "Your dog has dug up a crime scene."

He was by no means an expert. Accountancy didn't exactly lend itself to the identification of human remains. However, an unusual upbringing assured Malcolm that the dog, crouched between them, had a femur in its maw.

She continued to stare at him. "Don't be ridiculous. It's just a bone from an animal, or..."

As she spoke, Malcolm tracked backwards, following the same path the dog had taken. A couple of steps into the underbrush and his worst fears were confirmed. There would be no birds nesting here for quite some time.

"You need to call the police," he told the woman again, unable to tear his gaze from the disturbed shallow grave that was visible beneath the vegetation.

"You're overreacting," the woman said. The stumbling of her footsteps signalled she was closing the distance between them.

Malcolm bit his tongue, his eyes fixed on the

ripped and dirt-covered denim jean leg that was poking out above ground.

Despite expecting it, Malcolm started when the woman's scream ripped the air. Only then did he pull his eyes from the macabre scene in front of him.

"Please..." His breathing laboured as he pulled a clean breath through his nose. "Just call the police."

CHAPTER TEN

"SIR." Olivia's voice cut through Drew's solitary contemplation.

He glanced at her. "What is it?" He scratched at the spot on his arm beneath his sleeve where he knew the useless nicotine patch lay. May as well have been a piece of sellotape for all the good it did him.

He'd slipped the day before, stress causing him to give into his addiction. But that was then. Today, he was determined to do better.

Why he was even bothering to try and give up was beyond him. There was always something just waiting around the corner to knock him off course. His mother had said he'd learn to regret sneaking behind the bike shed for a quick smoke between classes when he was in school. It seemed she'd been right.

"They've got a body over at the Hole of Horcum."

"Are they looking for an SIO?"

Olivia nodded. "Forensics are already on site, but they need—"

"I'll go," Drew said. "It'll get me away from that mounting pile of paperwork I've yet to clear."

Olivia smiled tightly. "I could…"

Drew started to shake his head before she even managed to finish the sentence. "You're on desk duty for the foreseeable. You know the score."

"But, guv, I've been cleared to return to duty."

"*Desk* duty," Drew clarified. "You know how these things work. We all have to play ball. You were lucky—," he cut himself off before he could finish the sentence. But it wasn't soon enough. He watched the colour drain from Olivia's face, her shoulder's stiffening in response to his careless mistake.

"I'm sorry," he said.

"No, sir, it's fine. You're right. I'm lucky to be alive. I suppose desk duty is my punishment for being so careless."

Before Drew could refute her statement, Olivia disappeared back into the building, leaving him to stare after her.

"Well, shit." He huffed out a breath. Would he always stick his foot in it? With a shake of his head, he followed Olivia back in through the doors.

. . .

"I DON'T THINK DC Crandell is too happy about missing out on this one," Maz said from his place in the passenger seat. "In fact, she looked proper pissed off when she came back to the desk."

Drew followed the road that led through the moors. In the distance, he could make out the emergency vehicles that had beat them to the scene.

"Nobody likes to be on desk duty," he said diplomatically.

"Nothing worse," Maz replied. "I wound up on desk duty when I was still a uniform."

Drew glanced over at the ambitious DS next to him. "I didn't know that."

Maz shrugged. "Stupid really. Got called to a domestic, or that's what we thought. Turned out it was a house party gone sideways. It had spilled out onto the street. When we arrived and tried to disperse the crowd, I got jumped."

From the corner of his eye, Drew watched as Maz twisted his fingers over and back in his lap. His short bitter laugh did nothing to cover his discomfort at reliving such memories.

"It was my own fault." Maz sighed.

"I hope they picked up the one who assaulted you," Drew said.

"Slap on the wrist," Maz said with a shake of his head. "Got off with a suspended sentence."

Drew kept his gaze on the road ahead. Flexing

his clenched fingers on the steering wheel, he tried to keep his anger in check. They all had a similar story. But that was the risk with taking a job that put you at the sharp end of the public's worst moments. Not that it was an excuse. He'd long thought there should be harsher sentencing for those who chose to attack front line workers.

Not that anyone was going to listen to *him* any time soon.

"I'm sorry to hear it," Drew said.

Maz straightened in his seat. "No need. I bet you've had your own fair share of close shaves."

Drew pulled into the car park that was very nearly fully occupied. Maz had caused a dark memory to tug at the back of his mind. With a tight smile, he agreed with the DS.

A sharp rap on the window on Drew's side jerked his attention back to the situation at hand.

A uniformed officer stood outside the car with a wet clipboard clutched in his dripping hands. His watery blue eyes kept a sharp eye on Drew, despite the misty rain that clung to his eyelashes. He kept his chin tucked down into the top of his high-vis coat. He looked perfectly miserable.

Rather than roll down the window, Drew pushed open the car door, forcing the officer to take a step back or risk having the door slam into him. The wind took Drew by surprise and he was compelled to cling onto the door more firmly than he'd initially expected.

"Sorry, this is a closed area. You'll have to—," The officer's voice was hoarse, with a nasally quality.

Drew cut him off before he could finish his practiced speech. "DI Haskell," He flashed his identification. "And this is DS Arya. We got a call about a body."

The officer sniffed loudly, confirming Drew's suspicions that he was probably coming down with a cold. Standing out in the rain wouldn't do him any favours.

"Sorry about that," The officer shivered as a particularly large drop of water disappeared inside the collar of his coat. "Didn't recognise you." He jotted something down on the clipboard, which he tilted in Drew's direction. "Just making a note of everyone coming and going, sir."

Drew smiled sympathetically. "How far to the scene?"

The officer inclined his head in the direction of a path on the other side of the road. "Over the road, sir. A short walk down the path to the scene itself. They've got a tent set up already to preserve the site. And over there, they've set up an exhibits tent."

Turning his face up into the rain, Drew relished the feel of the cool mist that fell over his cheeks and mouth.

From his place at the boot of the car, Arya called

to the uniformed officer. "What's it like to get in and out of the scene?"

From the corner of his eye, Drew became aware of Arya stripping out of his normal sensible shoes. He tugged a pair of hiking boots on.

"It's a little muddy in places," the officer said. "But nothing too serious."

Maz shot him an appreciative smile as he slammed the boot shut. "Great."

Another car pulled into the carpark and the officer shuffled off in that direction, leaving Drew and Maz.

"You don't want to change your shoes?" Maz asked as he came level with Drew.

"These will do," Drew said indicating his heavy black boots. "Anyway, he said it's not too bad down there."

Maz looked unconvinced. "With all the people moving in and out, if it's not already soup, then it will be shortly."

"Go hiking often?" Drew asked as they waited to cross the road.

Maz nodded sheepishly. "Mum thought it would be a good hobby for us all."

Drew glanced at him in surprise. "I've met your mum, she doesn't strike me as the hiking type."

Maz sighed. "It was after dad had his first heart attack. She needed to get him active so we all chipped in."

"You ganged up on him, you mean." Drew's smile took the sting out of his words.

"It's the only exercise he's willing to do." Maz's face broke out in a grin. "You should hear the way he moans about it, though. Anyone would think we were trying to finish him off instead of getting him healthy."

"I'm sure he appreciates it, really."

"Oh, he loves it. He just won't admit it."

As they spoke they crossed the road and started down the path. Ahead, Drew could see the small white tent erected by forensics. Off to their right lay the Hole of Horcum, or the devil's punchbowl as he'd often heard it referred to. How it had earned that name eluded him.

The view, as Drew paused to look across at it, left him breathless.

Resuming their trek, they reached the second cordon faster than Drew expected. There, they were greeted by another uniformed officer. Drew towered over her, feeling like a giant in comparison to her petite frame. She was buffeted by the wind sweeping over the moors. Drew fought to keep his expression neutral as she struggled to stay on her feet and maintain her composure.

He was so concerned with his thoughts that he forgot to watch his step. As his left foot came down in the mud, he lost his balance.

He went down, hard. Catching himself on a large

tuft of bracken, he narrowly avoided winding up on his arse. But the cold muddy water soaking through the side of his trouser leg told him he hadn't entirely avoided the ground. Swearing proficiently enough to make any sailor proud, Drew fought to right himself.

The officer opposite hid her grin in the collar of her coat.

"You all right, sir?" Maz reached out, offering Drew a steadying hand.

"Thanks," Drew said, awkwardly accepting the offered help.

Once upright again, he caught the sheepish eye of the uniformed officer who had only just managed to keep her laughter at bay. Freya wouldn't have hesitated to tell him his fall was *instant karma*. She had believed in things like that, along with horoscopes and having her tarot cards read. He often wondered if her fascination with all things pertaining to the occult, and a life after, had come about because of her attempts to take her own life. Maybe believing there was something else made her feel less alone, soothing the pain in ways he would never make sense of.

As though she could sense the sudden shift in his mood, the officer opposite straightened up. Her expression was guarded, as though she expected Drew to chastise her for laughing. He softened his expression, smiling at her in an attempt to lighten the tension that had sprung up.

"Always knew I'd make a tit of myself," he said.

"It's very muddy, sir." Her brown eyes danced with humour as she gave a pointed look at the side of his dirty trousers.

"Where is the CSM?" Drew decided changing the subject was the best course.

"He's in the tent, sir... but, I'll need to take your names."

After sharing the information, Drew and Maz ducked beneath the cordon and followed the track down to the tent.

A man wearing a white Tyvek suit emerged and strode toward them. As he reached them, he lifted his gaze from the ground and his eyes widened in surprise. The CSM pulled his mask down, uncovering the lower portion of his face. He quickly stripped off the outer forensic gloves he wore and dropped them into an evidence bag.

"DI Haskell, I didn't expect to see you here." His surprise was genuine as he eyed Drew speculatively.

"David Farley, isn't it? We worked together on the mispers in Darkby."

The ghost of a smile pulled at the corner of Farley's mouth. "If I remember correctly, you and a Dr Quinn attended the Oliver Poole scene." His expression darkened. "A terrible tragedy. Such a waste of a young life."

Drew remained silent. They all felt it and saying anything more, to Drew's mind, felt trite. He met

Farley's gaze head on. He could see the toll the case had taken on the CSM reflected in his blue eyes.

"Well, it's good to see you again." Drew made a point of looking past him to the tent. "What have we got here?"

Farley's gaze tracked back up the path. "Shouldn't we wait for Dr Quinn?"

There was something in the familiar way Farley mentioned Harriet that irked Drew.

"No, Harr—, I mean Dr Quinn had other matters to attend to."

The light in Farley's eyes faded and his smile dimmed. "That's a real shame. Would have been nice to get someone with Dr Quinn's expertise to share her take on the scene." Farley glanced up at Drew. "Not that I don't appreciate your insights, Detective Inspector."

Tension pricked along the back of Drew's neck before it spread upwards and tightened his scalp. "Well, you'll just have to make do with us."

The ghost of a smile appeared on Farley's face. "Not a problem. Shall we get on with it?" Without waiting for a reply, he turned in the direction of the tent, his expression contemplative as he watched a SOCO emerge from the depths of the tent with a camera slung around his neck. "After an initial examination we believe the body is that of a female. This doesn't appear to be the primary crime scene. More likely a deposition site."

"Who found the body?" Maz asked.

Farley's smile returned. "Well, that's a little bit complicated. We've got a dog walker and it was her dog who made the discovery."

"That doesn't sound so complicated," Drew said.

"She also claims that the second witness was following her along the trail. She says he started to harass her when the dog retrieved the femur of our victim."

"And where are these witnesses now?" Drew couldn't keep the eagerness from his voice. It was foolish to get too excited about a lead so early in the case. But Drew wasn't a fan of coincidences and this felt like a big one.

"Back up at the road," Farley said. "Uniforms have taken their details." He grimaced as he glanced over at the tent. "The dog did a number on the remains; scattered them throughout the bracken. And we've got natural predation to contend with, as well."

"What does that mean for the investigation?" Maz asked.

"Well, it's not great." Farley edged closer to the crime scene. "To be honest, we were lucky that whoever buried the body here used a carpet to do it."

"So not an accident then?" Drew asked drily.

Farley glanced at him, surprise drawing his eyebrows upwards towards the white hood of his coverall. "Certainly not, DI Haskell."

Silence stretched between them. Farley was good at his job. Drew knew that if he gave the man a few minutes to gather his thoughts, he would give him something to work with.

"Based on the disposal method, murder is my working theory," Farley said. "But as far as cause of death, I'll leave that to the forensic pathologist and anthropologist to make a determination."

"Fair enough," Drew said.

One of the crime scene officers gestured for Farley to rejoin them. "I need to supervise," Farley said. "But you're welcome to suit up and I'll walk you through the scene."

"I'll do that," Drew said. "Thanks."

Farley hurried away and Drew paused next to Maz. "I want you to go back to the tent and get some details from the two witnesses. We need to know what really happened out here."

Maz nodded and jogged slowly back up the path, leaving Drew to follow Farley's tracks. He dressed quickly in a Tyvek suit, donning the face mask and double gloves on autopilot. He stepped into the tent, grateful for the treadplates that provided a pathway through the worst of the mud covered scene.

Farley stood to one side of the tent, his attention fixed on another person, who was working in the bracken.

"What's going on?" Drew asked, keeping his

voice low. There was a sombre atmosphere inside the tent and it seemed only fitting that he respect it.

"They've found something else," Farley said. There was an odd note in the other man's voice. Drew didn't know him particularly well, but something about the way he stood fixated on the scene caused the sweat gathering at the small of Drew's back to turn icy.

Drew caught a glimpse of something wrapped in plastic. The sight of the item tugged at a memory in the recess of his mind.

The woman on the ground straightened up and Drew caught a glimpse of her. "We have the remains of a second body." The voice was familiar to him as belonging to that of the forensic anthropologist who had worked alongside them on the Darkby case.

Drew tried to see past her but he couldn't make out the complicated scattering of remains in the ground, never mind determine if there was a second body present. While he couldn't remember the anthropologist's name off the top of his head, he knew she was good at her job. Liked and well respected. If she said they had a second body, then it was true.

The cloth she carefully unfolded bothered Drew. It was small, painfully small. His stomach twisted around on itself. The colour drained from his face.

He caught a flash of what looked to his untrained eye like an animal motif printed on fabric. The plastic wrapped blanket was muddy and water logged from being in the ground, but that didn't account for all of the staining that covered it. The dark patches on the blanket—and Drew was now certain it was a blanket—could be chalked up to bodily fluids due to decomposition. Apart from a few patches that had been protected by the plastic it had been wrapped in, the colour of the blanket was faded. A sick feeling formed in the pit of Drew's stomach as he watched them carefully expose the contents.

Silence fell over those gathered inside the tent. Drew balled his hands into fists by his sides as he watched the anthropologist scrutinise the contents closely.

"These appear to be the remains of an infant. Approximate age below two years."

Drew's breath caught in the back of his throat. The mask he wore suddenly suffocated him as the urge to flee the scene became overwhelming.

"I'll need to take everything back to the lab for closer examination before I can share any other pertinent details," the woman said.

"Would a body look like this if it had been here for the last few years, say 2017?" Drew was relieved to discover his voice was steady and betrayed none of the emotions coursing through him.

She straightened up and faced him. "It's certainly a possibility, but I'm not willing to say anything concrete until I can have more time with the remains."

"I think anything you find out will just confirm what we already know," Drew said. His gaze travelled back to the small wrapped bundle on the ground. It was so tiny... Then again, five years in the cold, wet ground, abandoned to the mercy of the wild and windswept moors was a long time for any remains.

"Gwen Campbell and her infant daughter went missing November 2017. The husband insisted she'd left of her own volition. If memory serves, he said she was going to Middlesborough to visit her mother, but she never arrived. The investigation at the time turned up nothing. They recovered her car several miles outside of Middlesborough abandoned and burnt out in a field."

"You can't make assumptions like that," the anthropologist said. "We need more information."

Drew's lips compressed into a grim line. "And you'll hear no argument from me. But that blanket..." He pointing to what remained of the child's blanket. "That was listed during the investigation as having gone missing. Her husband made a case at the time that perhaps Gwen had run away with the child. And talking to others who knew the couple raised some questions about the state of their marriage."

Turning away from the sad bundle, he closed his eyes.

"No wonder they call this place the Devil's punchbowl," Farley said.

"I suppose the killer thought the bodies would never surface. He'd have been right too, if the dog hadn't discovered the carpet."

"If they find the skull, we might be able to identify the victim based on dental records."

"They haven't found the head yet?" Drew asked, his eyes snapping open.

Farley shook his head. "If we're lucky, it simply rolled out while the dog was tearing it all apart. But we're not done combing the area."

"And if we're unlucky?"

Farley's expression was grim. "You can see the size of this place, not to mention how wide open it is. If we're unlucky enough, we might never find it at all."

Drew swore beneath his breath.

"We'll keep looking," Farley said, his smile grim. "We won't give up until we're forced to."

"Thanks," Drew said. "I appreciate that." With one last lingering look at the tiny bundle of remains on the ground, he turned and made his way out of the tent. He spotted Maz in conversation with a PC at the edge of the cordon. Drew stood to one side and waited for the DS to finish up.

"You all done, sir?" Maz asked.

Drew nodded. His lips compressed into a grim line as he stripped out of his coveralls. "When we get back to the office I want you to dig out everything you can on the Gwen Campbell case."

"The mother and baby that went missing?" Maz asked. He cast a look over his shoulder as he hurried to keep pace with Drew. "You think that's them?"

"They've found two bodies," Drew said, his long strides carried him away from the scene. "One of them is an infant."

"Shit..." Maz drew out the syllables. "When the press get a hold of this."

"The proverbial shit will hit the fan," Drew finished for him. "That's why we need to stay ahead of this at all costs. If that is Mrs Campbell and her child, then they've been sitting under our noses the entire time and we never knew it."

"With all due respect sir, we couldn't have known."

"It's our job," Drew said quietly. "And when the public hear about it, they won't look upon any of this favourably. We need to make sure we've done everything we could have. I want every 't' crossed, and every 'i' dotted. Leave no stone unturned on this."

"Yes, guv," Maz said.

The sickly feeling stayed with Drew all the way back to the car. He'd dealt in cases like this before, but this one was different. Personal, even. He hadn't been a DI when Gwen Campbell had gone missing. He'd worked the case as a DS. Everything pointed towards Declan Campbell being responsible, but they hadn't been able to prove it. And then the situation with Freya had taken a turn and...

He closed his eyes. He couldn't let old memories cloud what he knew to be true. Declan Campbell had murdered his wife and child.

And as soon as they had enough evidence, Drew would be paying Declan a visit.

CHAPTER ELEVEN

FLOPPING into the chair at her desk, Harriet allowed herself a moment's indulgence and closed her eyes. The morning had been far busier than she'd initially thought. Each appointment with her students had overrun, pushing her further and further behind schedule. It wasn't only mid-morning and she already knew her day was so badly off track that there weren't enough hours left in the day to make it right.

Despite all of that, she hadn't been able to get her conversation with Drew out of her mind. He was right. Keeping everyone at arm's length served no purpose. Not to mention the theory he had floated about Dr Connors being the one responsible for the complaint.

The more Harriet contemplated it, the more she was inclined to believe that Drew was on to something. Jonathan was a vindictive man. And he had warned her that he would make her pay for everything she had done to him.

No, not what she had done to him. There was no point in blaming herself. Jonathan had brought it all down onto his own head. She had simply been the one to blow the whistle on his misconduct. He had nobody but himself to blame for the predicament he now found himself in.

The memory of Misha's tear-stained face popped unbidden into Harriet's mind. The young woman was clearly struggling and Harriet had turned her away instead of helping.

Feeling guilt for her hasty actions, Harriet tapped out a quick email inviting Misha to attend a meeting to discuss her work that afternoon. Several minutes passed and Harriet did what she could to focus on the work in front of her. When her email dinged, she pulled it open on the computer and scanned the screen.

Even through the written word, Harriet was under no illusions as to Misha's mood. Her curt response, that she would be unable to attend any such meeting due to work commitments, told Harriet in no uncertain terms that the young student was still upset.

Sitting back in her chair, Harriet contemplated her next move. Not that she needed to. She already knew how to sort the problem out, but it required a face-to-face conversation that Misha clearly wasn't in the mood to have. With no other alternative, Harriet replied.

"I understand that you're still upset. If you would like to discuss the matter further, my office door remains open."

Tapping her fingers against the desk's surface she contemplated saying more, but changed her mind. With the message winging its way to Misha, Harriet decided to throw herself head first back into her work. Opening a new paper she'd begun to research, she immersed herself in the topic of *Paraphilic Tendencies in Young Men Exhibiting Incel Behaviour.*

"Dr Quinn?" Martha's voice pulled Harriet from her deep contemplation.

Jerking in the chair, she glanced over at the woman framed in the doorway. The light from the outer office bathed Martha in strange shadows that left Harriet feeling somewhat disquieted. Clearly, she'd spent too long researching her topic and it was now colouring her perceptions of reality.

With a small laugh, she shook off the uneasiness that had settled over her. "Can I help you, Martha?"

"I was just wondering if you wanted me to get you something to eat."

A beat passed between them. Harriet stared at the woman. It seemed something had happened to cause a slow, but progressive thaw, in Martha's interactions with her. Just what had precipitated such an event? It had been happening slowly, over time.

"I'll go out and grab something for lunch," Harriet said quickly.

"Lunch has been and gone," Martha said. "You've been locked up in here all morning."

"What?"

Surprised, she glanced down at her watch. Ten past two. Shock settled over her. Hours had passed since she had started to write. As though to emphasise Martha's question, Harriet's stomach chose that moment to grumble loudly.

"I didn't realise," she said. "Please tell me you went to lunch, Martha."

"Of course I did." Martha sniffed loudly. "You know, you shouldn't let this place take too much from you."

"I just lost track of time," Harriet said.

Martha's eyebrows climbed upwards to her hairline. "You do that a lot when you're stressed about something. You're not letting Dr Baig get to you, are you?"

Surprised, Harriet shook her head. "Well, no..." She broke off as a thought occurred to her. There wasn't much happened on campus that Martha didn't know about. And to Harriet's mind it wasn't inconceivable that Martha might have some idea as to who had made the complaint about her in the first place.

"Martha, what do you know of the situation Dr Baig spoke to me about?"

Martha's lips compressed into a thin line of disapproval. "If you're insinuating that I'm a gossip—"

Harriet shook her head, cutting the other woman off. "No, nothing like that. I just, well..." Harriet spread her hands in front of herself.

Martha pursed her lips and sighed. "I know you give your all to everything you do." She paused, as though needing a moment to compose her thoughts. When she resumed speaking, she levelled Harriet with a stern expression. "But I also know there are those who would seek to take advantage of such nature. And Dr Baig, while he's a good man, leans towards being risk averse. I'm not saying that's entirely a bad thing," she added hurriedly. "But it also makes him far too cautious and prone to jumping the gun."

"So you know a complaint was made against me?" The idea that everybody knew of the situation left Harriet feeling numb. It was a serious breach.

Martha nodded. "I had heard."

Harriet let her chin drop towards her chest, shame burning in her cheeks.

"I also know it's horse shit," Martha said.

For a moment, Harriet wasn't sure she'd heard correctly. "I'm sorry, Martha, I thought for a moment you—"

"You heard right," she said. "Don't let them get to you. The work you do," Martha paused as though she were struggling to get her thoughts in order. "Well, it's important. You help people. You're not here, like the rest of 'em, hiding behind their computer screens and their dusty old books. You're out there." She waved towards the windows. "Helping to set the world to rights. That should count for something."

Harriet smiled. "You would think so."

Martha opened her mouth to continue and then at the last second seemed to change her mind. "Well, enough of me rambling on. I suppose you know all of this, anyway."

"It was kind of you to say," Harriet said.

Martha's expression soured. "I didn't say it to be kind. I was stating facts. Nothing kind about that."

"I just meant—"

Martha cut her off before she could say another word. "I know what you meant, Dr Quinn. I'm not some bleeding heart liberal who takes a wishy-washy stance on things. I speak my mind and I stand up for what I believe in. I thought you would understand that." She strode to the door. "I've got some typing to do before I finish for the day."

Martha stalked out of the room before Harriet could add anything further. So much for thinking Martha was thawing towards her. Two steps forward and fifty back.

Clicking through to her email, Harriet was

surprised to see that Misha had responded to her last message.

"I'll be at the campus coffee shop at half two if you still want to talk."

Taking a quick peek at her watch, Harriet was glad to discover it had only just gone half two. Perhaps if she hurried, she could catch Misha before she left campus for the day.

She signed out of the system and switched off her computer. Standing, she waited for the feeling to return to her legs. How long had she been sitting here, exactly?

Her stomach rumbled as though to answer her question. Gathering up her belongings, she turned off the lights and beat a hasty retreat from the room.

When she reached the outer office, she found Martha with her head buried in a mountain of what looked to Harriet like admin work. The older woman barely glanced in Harriet's direction as she made a beeline for the door. Martha's irritation permeated the air like a cloud of cheap perfume. Turning a page, Martha sniffed loudly, letting Harriet know her temper had not yet abated.

"Good night, Martha," Harriet said, pausing at the door.

Martha kept her eyes glued to the work in front of her. "Close the door on the way out," she grumbled. "No point in letting all the warm air escape."

Smothering a smile, Harriet did as she was told.

CHAPTER TWELVE

PADDING ACROSS THE WARM, white marble tiled floor of her walk-in-closet, Holly settled in front of her cameras. Tilting her head, this way and that, she studied herself on the camera screen, searching for any traces of imperfection, anything that might impact her ability to hold her audience's attention. For most people, flaws were merely an everyday occurrence. A little concealer here, and a dab of foundation there would hide them. Then again, most people did not have a sizeable audience with a voracious appetite studying their every detail like their lives depended on it.

No, even the smallest defect could be fixed upon by those who relied on her to fulfil their fantasies. A flaw like that would cost her money. And, for someone like Holly, that was simply unacceptable.

Sliding her mint, oversized cardigan off one

shoulder, she scrutinised the golden glow on her skin. She had spent the better part of the morning buffing and slathering herself in creams and lotions. Flipping her long, rose-pink locks back over her shoulder, she blew out a deep breath in an attempt to relax her features. Her shell-pink gel-nails clicked across the computer keyboard as she leaned over and filled in her password.

The screen flashed to life, her own reflection staring back at her. Closing her eyes, she imagined how good it would feel when the video was complete. A long hot shower awaited her. She'd promised herself the night off after this, something she desperately needed.

A chance to recharge her batteries.

Fixing a smile on her features, she practiced different poses, and expressions, while watching herself on the computer screen. Reaching over, she turned up the ring-light, illuminating more of the room behind her. The floor to ceiling shelves filled with designer handbags and expensive shoes glittered subtly in the background.

Grabbing her phone from the place she'd discarded it on the floor, Holly scrolled through her emails. Most of the people who subscribed to her channel were nothing more than perverts as far as she was concerned. Some of the things they asked her to do left her feeling dirty. Nobody was forcing her to make the private videos, but they brought in the most money. And if there was one thing Holly excelled at, it was maximising her potential earnings. After all, if she wanted to be a millionaire by the age of twenty-five she needed to hustle now.

Pulling up the email she wanted, she scanned the list of requests and settled on one. With a heavy sigh, she got to her feet and made her way to the kitchen. An online shop had seen to it that everything she could possibly need to create the video was available to her. Tugging open the fridge, she quickly looked over the items she had. Pulling out the squirty cream, she set it aside on the counter. She grabbed the strawberries, a couple of extra large, cooked, cumberland sausages, and a bowl of prepared lime jelly. She pushed all thoughts of being disgusted to the back of her mind. It wasn't her place to think about stuff like that. Dwelling on how disgusting it all was would only make it harder for her to do her job.

Carrying the items carefully through to her dressing room, she set them on the rubber mat she'd laid out. Not a chance was she willing to risk getting stuff like this all over her engineered flooring. Returning to the kitchen, she grabbed the cold tea she had brewed earlier. Taking it, and a cup, back through to her dressing room, she set it next to the food.

Slipping out of her robe, she set her phone up inside the ring light. Turning to her closet, Holly grabbed the pink bow-tie, bunny ears, and obligatory white, fluffy bunny tail. After all, a Mad-Hatter's Tea Party required a white bunny rabbit. Getting dressed up was her favourite part of making the videos. With everything in place, she studied herself in the mirror behind the camera. After a quick adjustment to the bunny ears, she smiled.

An hour later, Holly stopped filming. She was sticky with residue. The cream and jelly had combined to form a kind of glue, which had taken her by surprise. Her stomach was uncomfortably full. When she glanced down, where her tummy had been flat before, it was now rounded.

"Great..." She muttered beneath her breath. Discomfort churned her guts. Something thick plopped down the side of her face as she moved her head and she shuddered. The cold jelly slithered down her cheek and she swiped it away. Crawling towards the ring light, she disconnected her phone.

A noise in the room next door drew her attention.

"Hello?"

Silence greeted her. Pushing onto her feet, Holly ignored the jelly and crushed fruit that fell onto the rubber mat around her feet. Grabbing her robe, she pulled it on as she hurried to the closet door.

"Hello?" Again, nothing. "John, is that you?"

Of course, Holly knew, if it was John he would have answered her by now. Sure he liked to mess around sometimes but he wasn't interested in scaring her.

The creak of a floorboard somewhere in the apartment set her pulse racing. Her stomach cramped uncomfortably. Normally, by now she would have purged herself of the excess food she'd consumed.

"This isn't funny, John," she said, the tremor in her voice giving away her fear.

A shadow moved in the hall and fear skittered down Holly's spine. "Who is it? Who's there?" As she spoke, she moved back into the room, her eyes pinned on the place where she had seen the shadow. She stepped onto a a piece of jelly on the floor and her foot slid out from under her.

Even as her arms windmilled, she knew the precarious predicament she found herself in. She hit the floor with a dull thud, her wrist taking the brunt of her fall. With the wind momentarily knocked out of her, Holly lay there stunned. Opening her eyes, she was disgusted to discover her false eyelashes on her right eye had become stuck together. Groaning, she rolled onto her side. The pain in her wrist increased as she tried to put her weight on it. Whimpering, she cradled her arm against her body.

She drew in a shaky breath as she tried to get to her feet, but the slippery surface on the floor made it virtually impossible.

"Poor Holly..." The voice from the bedroom

caused Holly to panic. She crawled towards her phone as bile crept up her throat.

A heavy boot thrust into the place between her shoulders stopped her. Holly's chest hit the floor and she whimpered. "Please..."

"Please, what? You want to be famous, don't you, Holly?"

The frightened woman tried to roll away, but her attacker straddled her body, pinning her in place. She stretched her hand out, fingers straining towards the phone that had skittered across the floor when she'd dropped it. As though able to anticipate her movements, Holly's assailant yanked her arm back, almost wrenching it out of the socket, and bent it up behind her back. She cried out, the bone yielding with an audible snap as Holly's face was pressed into the messy, rubber mat. Vomit coated her tongue; the combination of fear and pain forcing the excess food out of her stomach and back onto the mat.

A dark chuckle reached her ears. "I'm going make you so famous, Holly. Everybody will know your name, you gluttonous whore..."

"No..." she moaned, straining to escape the person holding her and the acrid vomit that puddled in front of her.

Fingers laced through her hair, lifting her head away from the floor. For a moment, Holly thought her attacker was helping her to get up. She struggled to right herself. But it soon became clear that the person holding her had no intention of letting her get up.

With her arms pinned behind her, and nothing to protect her face when her attacker slammed her head down onto the floor, her head bounced against the rubber mat. The young woman moaned, tasting blood mixed with the earlier vomit as her vision blurred. The action was repeated until, mercifully, Holly gave up and slipped into the oblivion offered by unconsciousness.

CHAPTER THIRTEEN

PULLING her coat tightly around her body, Harriet stepped into the campus coffee shop. The space was cramped with people milling around ordering drinks and generally socialising. The drone of voices mingling together created a constant buzz of noise that made it difficult to concentrate.

Such close quarters left Harriet feeling somewhat claustrophobic. She avoided spaces like it for this very reason. It wasn't that she believed the cause of her discomfort was rooted in any real phobia, it was just that she had always been far more comfortable in smaller groups. It was easier to concentrate on the people around her when there was less distraction. And in her line of work, being able to focus was invaluable.

Scanning the crowd, her hope of catching her student before she left slowly evaporated. Misha was nowhere to be found among the groupings of customers. Clearly, Harriet had missed her opportunity to set things straight with the intense young woman.

Disheartened, she turned back to the door. As she placed her hand on the handle and pushed against the weight of the door, Misha appeared on the other side. Even with her head down, rain drops glistening in her hair, she was instantly recognisable.

It was more than that if Harriet was honest with herself. There was an uncanny resemblance to Louise and every time Harriet was confronted with it, she felt blindsided all over again.

Misha adjusted her bag strap, settling it higher on her shoulder as she looked up. Her mouth dropped open into a round oval, surprise settling in her gaze.

"Dr Quinn." Misha was breathless, but she recovered herself swiftly. "You came."

"I wasn't happy about how we left things yesterday," Harriet said. "You were clearly upset and I was rigid and uncaring." She sighed. "I know I shouldn't let it happen, but I've had a lot on my mind recently. And try as I might, against my better judgement, I've obviously allowed it to bleed into my interactions with my students... with you."

Misha ducked her head and gave a small shrug. "I shouldn't have pushed. I know you're a busy woman. You don't have time to deal with all the petty problems of the students you teach."

Was it Harriet's imagination, or was there an edge to Misha's words? Technically she wasn't wrong. It wasn't Harriet's place to intervene in the problems of her students. The idea was to allow them the space to come up with their own conclusions; not to hold their hand throughout. But that wasn't how Harriet liked to treat her undergrads. In the past she had told them she was there for them, no matter what.

And where has that got you?

When the young student looked up again, Harriet quickly disabused herself of that notion. The look of uncertainty on Misha's face; the sheer vulnerability in her expression spoke volumes to Harriet. She was failing at her job, and it was high time she put a stop to it before something that couldn't be so easily rectified, slipped through the cracks.

"If you've got a problem with the curriculum, then it's my place to help clear it up." Harriet smiled widely in an attempt to put the young woman at ease.

Misha dropped her gaze to the ground. "I really don't know where to begin."

"Well, how about we sit down and have a quick look at what you've got, for a start. We can go from there."

"I've got to meet someone right now." Misha glanced at her watch. "And I'm already running late."

"Tomorrow then—"

"I could do later this evening." There was a hopeful sparkle in the young woman's eyes that hadn't been there before.

Hesitating, Harriet noted the cautious voice in the back of her mind, warning her not to get too involved. It was Drew's voice that cut through the negativity. *"You should probably go back to holding your student meetings without worrying about crossing some non-existent line."*

Drew was right. Fear could not come between her and the job. While fear could sometimes be a useful emotion — adding a little more zip to your step when running from a bear, or more likely for her, a criminal — in this instance, it served no purpose beyond making her, and the students she interacted with, miserable.

"Later sounds fine. Is there somewhere particular?"

Misha's smile lit up her face. "We could meet in the campus bar. Maybe half seven. I'll be finished my meeting then."

"Won't that be a little noisy?"

Misha shrugged. "I don't think so. It's always quiet early in the evening. Things don't get busy around here until nine, or ten."

"Half seven is fine."

"Thanks, Dr Quinn. I really appreciate this."

"You don't need to thank me, Misha. It's my job."

The woman's smile wilted at the edges. "Yeah, of course. Well, I'll see you tonight."

Misha left. As she moved further into the crowded coffee shop, her shoulders rounded and she kept her head down. Harriet studied her progress for a couple of beats; her mind a mix of thoughts. She wanted to help Misha, but, despite Drew's intervention, there was still a nagging voice in the back of her mind that told her she was missing something important.

Of course, there was only one way she was going to get to the bottom of it. And Harriet would get to the crux of the matter. Perhaps in a less formal setting, Misha would be more inclined to open up to her. With a sigh, Harriet pushed out through the coffee shop doors. Tonight, she would have some kind of answer.

CHAPTER FOURTEEN

HARRIET CLIMBED the stairs to the team's office. Pushing open the door, she was unsurprised to find the place a hive of activity. She scanned the office and caught sight of Olivia hunched over her desk. The detective constable stared off into space, her gaze somewhat vacant. Crossing the floor, Harriet paused next to the DC's cluttered desk. She was so used to seeing the space immaculately tidy that to see it in such disarray took her by surprise.

"DC Crandell?" Harriet spoke gently, conscious that she didn't wish to startle the other woman.

Olivia didn't move. Either she hadn't heard her name, or she was ignoring Harriet.

Harriet felt it safe to assume it was the former. The DC had never struck her as someone who would be deliberately rude.

"Olivia." Harriet reached out and touched the

other woman's shoulder. Olivia jerked, her eyes swivelling to Harriet's. There was a moment of blind panic that flitted through her gaze, but it was gone in an instant.

"Sorry," Olivia said, with a small shrug of her shoulders as though that alone was enough to get rid of whatever thoughts plagued her. "I was miles away."

"How are you getting on?"

"I'm fine," the DC said hastily. "I was just thinking some things through. Nothing to worry about," she added, glancing sideways at Harriet.

With a small smile, Harriet indicated the vacant chair. "Can I sit?"

"Yeah, go ahead." There was a defensiveness to Olivia's voice that hadn't been there a moment before. The officer was clearly on her guard, and Harriet wondered just what had been said to her regarding her return to work and the state of her mental wellbeing.

"How does it feel to be back?" Harriet kept her voice light and neutral.

"You don't have to worry about me, doc," Olivia said quickly. "I've been given a clean bill of health. I'm not going to crack up anytime soon."

"Even if you were, it wouldn't be anything to feel ashamed about," Harriet said. "Being a little unsure after the kind of trauma you experienced, it's understandable."

"Well, I feel fine," Olivia said with more conviction than was necessary. Hearing it made Harriet wonder just who she was trying to convince; Harriet, or herself. "I'm not shaky. Just glad to be back." She began to shuffle some of the disordered papers on her desk. "Just counting down the minutes until they give me the all clear to come off desk duty."

Harriet smiled. "That must difficult. I know you prefer to be out there."

Olivia flopped back in her chair and glanced over at Harriet. "Has DI Haskell asked you to come and talk to me?"

"Would it bother you if he had?"

"That's a yes," Olivia said. Picking up a biro from the table, she twirled it around in her fingers. "He asked me to speak to you."

"And, what did you say?"

"I don't need to speak to anyone," Olivia said tightly. "I'm fine. Really. What happened, well it could have been any one of us. I was just in the wrong place at the right time." Her shoulders were rigid and her grip on the pen changed, growing firmer until her fingers whitened beneath the pressure. "It's what I signed up for. I knew when I came into this job that getting hurt was only a matter of time."

"There's a big difference between thinking it might happen, and the reality of it actually happening," Harriet said. "As much as we might try to prepare ourselves for something like that, we are, at the end of the day, only human."

Olivia kept her attention fixed on the desk. "Yeah, well, doing this job means you don't have the luxury of thinking like that."

"I can see how you might believe that," Harriet said.

"Look." Olivia sighed. "I appreciate the pep-talk, but I'm fine. I made a stupid mistake and I paid the price. Do I wish it hadn't happened? Of course I do. But I can't change the past. I can only look forward."

Harriet knew when it was time to back off. "I'm glad you're back," she said. "If you ever want to talk about it, you know where I am."

Olivia glanced at her, surprise etched into her features. "You mean, you're not going to pressure me into speaking with you?"

Harriet shook her head. "What purpose would it serve? I'm not here because Drew— DI Haskell asked me to speak with you. I would have sought you out no matter what. I'd like to think we're friends."

Olivia stared at her for a moment, and then swallowed hard as she returned her attention to the desk. "Thanks, Dr Quinn."

"But the offer stands. If you find yourself needing to talk, as a friend or something more, you know where to find me."

Olivia nodded. "Thanks..."

"Look after yourself, DC Crandell. This team needs you."

The DC gave her a small, shy smile. "I'd like to think so."

"It's the truth."

Harriet stood, leaving Olivia to return to her paperwork. As she made her way through the tables, she spotted Drew in DI Appleton's office. From a distance, they seemed to be engaged in some kind of heated argument. When Melissa reached out to touch Drew's face, Harriet looked away. Taking a seat at Drew's desk, she turned her back to the office, choosing instead, to fix her attention on the report Drew had been working on.

A crime scene photograph caught her eye and she worked it free of the pile. She studied the image. A plastic wrapped bundle in a shallow hole. Harriet wasn't particularly familiar with the area. She wasn't exactly the outdoorsy type. Trekking through mud had never been her cup of tea. She was much more comfortable at home with her books.

As she pored over the image, Harriet sensed a terrible loneliness about the scene. She found the next image and her suspicions were confirmed. The sad remnants of what had once been a living, breathing, dreaming human were scattered across the muddy surface of, what to her looked like a faded carpet. Despite everything, Harriet was still often confounded by the sheer lack of humanity in those who committed such crimes.

"We're waiting on forensics." Drew's voice took her by surprise. Harriet was pulled from her own spiralling thoughts with a jolt. "Sorry, I didn't mean to startle you," he said, as he moved around the table and took his seat.

She watched as he buried his face in his hands and blew out a long breath. "I shouldn't have been poking around."

"You're not." Drew let his hands drop back onto the table with a dull thud. "I was going to ask your opinion on this anyway. The remains were discovered this morning up near the Hole of Horcum."

"Any idea who it is?"

"They," Drew corrected her. "They found a second, smaller body wrapped up with the first."

Harriet glanced back down at the image. There was nothing in the picture to indicate the discovery of a second body, but she knew from everything Drew had said the body could only be that of a child.

"I asked Maz to dig out everything he could find about Gwen Campbell."

A distant memory tugged at Harriet. "I think I remember there was something on the news about her. She went missing with her child... An eight month old baby?"

"Ten months," Drew corrected her. "They made an appeal for any information at the time. Her husband *appeared* to be pretty cut up about the entire thing."

Serial killers and mass murderers were, for Harriet, easy to comprehend. The compulsions that drove them to commit some truly heinous atrocities could be examined and picked apart. But it was the other types of crime that baffled her. The killers who murdered those closest to them, for seemingly no reason beyond their own desire to inflict their will upon the world, were an unknowable quantity. That even the most ordinary of humans could be driven to such measures, made her question everything she knew.

"There's something you're not telling me," she said, studying the photographs Drew pushed over to her.

"How do you do that?" Drew asked, his hand rested on the edge of the nearest picture. "How do you know when there's something I haven't mentioned?"

"Instinct," Harriet said quietly. "And I suppose I'm growing to know all of your little foibles."

"I have foibles?" There was a hint of humour in Drew's voice.

"We all do," Harriet said. "But you're..." She struggled for the correct description. "You wear your emotions on your sleeve."

"I'm that transparent?"

Harriet grinned at him. "Why, would you prefer if I found it difficult to read you?"

He snorted a half-hearted laugh. "It'd make life easier. But for what it's worth, yeah, there's something I haven't mentioned. Declan Campbell, the husband, he was broken up about it all, but it turned out he was having an affair."

"So you think it was an act?" Harriet raised an eyebrow at Drew.

"Maybe, I don't know. It's not like I can go accusing him of spinning us all a line. I remember watching a statement he gave, and it didn't sit right with me."

"And did the rest of the team feel the same way?"

Drew shook his head. "They had their suspicions. Spent months looking into him from every possible angle, but they couldn't find anything. And he wasn't giving anything away. Cool as a cucumber during the interviews they conducted with him." Closing his eyes, Drew balled his hands into fists. "But if this is his wife and baby, then I want to be the one who breaks the news to him."

"So you can study his reaction."

Drew nodded. "Exactly. I'd like you to be there too."

"Of course. How soon do you expect to know—"

Drew cut her off by climbing to his feet. "No time like the present."

Harriet glanced back down at the pictures. "What year did Gwen go missing again?"

"November 2016." There was a tightness to Drew's voice that ripped Harriet from her contemplation of the images.

"2016. Didn't Freya..."

"February 2017," Drew said quickly. He snatched the car keys from the desk and tugged his coat on with more force than was necessary. "I already know what you're thinking," Drew said quietly.

"I doubt that very much," Harriet said softly. She returned her attention to the pictures. Forcing Drew to dredge up old memories wouldn't do either of them any good. The best thing he could do right now was to focus on the case in front of him. If he wanted to talk to her, then he could.

Clearing her throat, Harriet grabbed her bag from the floor. "I thought you said you needed to know if the remains belong to his wife and child."

"We need to inform him of the discovery. It's standard procedure and it prevents family members finding out through the press coverage. The press will have a field day with this one." Drew sighed. "Normally, I'd send a FLO over, but this is different."

"Lead the way," Harriet said as she gathered up the photographs and preliminary report Drew had drawn up. The journey would give her the opportunity to review the evidence that had been recovered.

. . .

DREW PARKED at the bottom of the Campbells' driveway. The house itself was large and well appointed, positioned in the middle of a large parcel of land, with nothing but green fields on either side, and the view from the front of the house looking out onto grazing land. It surprised Harriet. Everything she had read in the files and records provided to her by Drew suggested the Campbells, while comfortable, had not been wealthy.

"Looks like Declan landed on his feet after his wife's disappearance," Drew said. There was an edge to his voice. When Harriet shot him a sideways look, she noted the way his hands tightened on the steering wheel.

"That doesn't make him guilty," Harriet said.

"You're right," Drew said. "But I can still remember the look on the smug bastard's face when he was pleading with the public for information on his wife's whereabouts."

"You can't let any preconceived ideas colour your perspective now," Harriet said. "When you go in there, you need to approach him with a fresh mindset."

He grinned. "I know. Doesn't mean it's easy to do."

Harriet opened her door and stepped out onto the gravel driveway. "If he's guilty." She shot Drew a meaningful look. "I know you won't rest until you have him."

"You've got a lot of confidence in me," Drew said.

"Why wouldn't I? You've proved yourself more than capable of getting the right result."

Drew smiled and opened his mouth to respond, but he was interrupted by a man in his early forties stepping out through the front door. A young, sullen, teenage boy, dressed in a football kit followed hot on his heels.

"There's no point in arguing, Simon," the older man said. His attention was fixed on the keys in his hand. "You're coming to Tuscany with us if I have to drag you there--"

"Dad..." The uncertainty in Simon's voice was enough to pull Declan Campbell's attention away from his keys. He looked up, surprise flitting over his handsome features as he took in Drew and Harriet. The surprise was momentarily doused, only to be replaced with panic.

"Is there something I can help you with?" Declan asked, his voice strained. "You know, if you're with the newspaper, I already gave your boss my answer."

"We're not with the papers," Drew said smoothly.

Declan's lips pulled together into a pained expression. "Then what?"

Drew pulled out his warrant card and flashed it in front of Declan's face. "DI Haskell, and this is my colleague, Dr Quinn. Could we have a moment of your time?"

Declan's expression changed instantly.

"This is about mum, right?" Simon, who had until that moment hung back, took a step forwards. There was an eagerness to his face that pulled at Harriet. "You know where she is, yeah?"

"I think this might be best discussed in private," Drew said gently.

"Don't forget you've got a lunch appointment—" A woman appeared in the doorway of the house. "Oh, I didn't realise we had visitors."

Harriet hung back and studied the group dynamic. Instantly, the tension in the air ratcheted up.

"Simon, head back inside, there's a good lad," Declan Campbell said. His gaze never left Drew's face. "You too, Beth."

Simon tucked his chin down towards his chest, his shoulders tightening as he glanced back at the woman behind him. "Dad, I'm old enough to stay. I want to know about mum."

"Wait, they've found, Gwen?" Beth took a tentative step out into the porch. "Declan?"

"I'm DI Haskell," Drew said, taking a small step forwards. "And this is my colleague, Dr Harriet Quinn. And you are?"

"Beth Smith..." She glanced in Declan's direction. "Declan and I—"

"Not now," Declan snapped. He sucked in a breath, and Harriet could tell it was genuinely an effort for him to control his feelings. When he opened his eyes again, the tumultuous emotions were gone. He moved back to his son and clapped a hand on his shoulder. "Please, Si, go back inside."

"Dad, I can handle it."

"I know you can," Declan said smoothly. "But Beth, and the baby... Well, she needs you to be strong now, ok?"

Simon cast the woman who had moved up beside him a wary glance. " I suppose..."

"Good lad." Declan pulled his son towards him in what could only be described as part headlock, part embrace. He released the teenager, and ruffled his hair swiftly as he pushed him back towards the house.

"Declan?" Beth shot him a quizzical look. As much as she tried to keep her expression neutral, Harriet could see the look of hurt that passed through her pale blue eyes.

"Go inside, Beth. I'll deal with this."

"Maybe we should all go inside," Drew said quickly.

Declan shook his head. "No, thank you." Declan's tone was clipped. "Out here is fine."

Drew closed the gap between them. "Mr Campbell, I'm here today to inform you that a discovery was made this morning."

Declan waited until the woman and the boy had disappeared into the house. The door closed softly behind them. It was only then that Declan turned to face Drew.

"You've got some nerve. My son and I have moved on with our lives. We don't need you coming here, disturbing our peace."

"Excuse me?" Drew failed to keep the surprise out of his voice. Not that Harriet could blame him. Declan Campbell had certainly managed to turn the tables in the blink of an eye.

He rounded on Drew. "Go on then, what is it this time? You said you got a call. Somebody called in a report about some woman fitting the description of my missing wife, right? Well, I hate to break it to you, but it won't be her."

Before Drew could respond, Harriet saw an opening. "What makes you say that, Mr Campbell?"

"And who are you again?" Declan snapped at her, his hostility growing with every passing moment.

"Dr Quinn." She took a step up towards him, holding her hand out in front of her. "I assist the police with their enquiries."

Declan's expression shifted, growing more wary. His mercurial mood intrigued Harriet.

"Why would the police require the help of a doctor?"

"I'm not a medical doctor," Harriet explained, letting her hand drop back to her side. "I'm a forensic psychologist. I'm here to help them sift through the information and pluck out the important facts."

Declan Campbell shook his head, dropping his chin towards his chest in a move reminiscent of his son's just moments before. He jammed his hands into his pockets, his shoulders tightening as he stared at the ground. "I don't know why you're here. She left me years ago. Abandoned us both, and took our baby--" His voice cracked over the words. It took him a moment to regain his composure. "She took Evie with her."

He shot a quick glance back at the house. "Do you know how damaging that is to a young child's mind? To have his mother abandon him like that. Forget about what it has done to me. Her running off like that has destroyed our son's ability to trust." He lifted his chin and met Harriet's gaze head on. "Even if you find her, I want nothing to do with her."

"And what about your daughter?" Harriet asked gently.

"Excuse me?" Confusion clouded Declan's eyes.

"I assume your hatred towards your wife doesn't extend to your daughter as well."

Declan pulled his hands from his pockets. It seemed clear to Harriet that he was done with the conversation. "I've made my position clear," he said. "Now, I really must insist. You've wasted enough of our time already. My wife..." He met Harriet's eyes fleetingly. "And my daughter are gone. I made my peace long ago that I would never see them again. Gwen was a selfish bitch who only ever thought of herself and the things that would benefit her. I'm not going to bring someone that destructive back into my son't life. At least not if I can help it."

A moment passed and Declan looked between Harriet and Drew. "We're done here," he said finally.

"Mr Campbell, we have reason to believe we have found your wife," Drew interjected. "That's why we're here. We wanted to tell you before the story breaks on the news."

"I told you already. My wife is gone."

"A discovery of a body, near the Hole of Horcum was made," Drew said. "A team was put together and during a search of the area the remains of two bodies were unearthed."

The colour drained from Declan Campbell's face. "That's impossible."

"You found her!" Simon Campbell exploded out through the front door. "You found mum, didn't you?"

"We really should discuss this elsewhere," Drew said.

"No..." Declan Campbell said, taking a small step backwards. "She made her choice. She left us." There was a conviction to his voice that rang hollow to Harriet.

"Can I see her?" Simon Campbell asked. "I want to see mum!"

"We should discuss this inside, Mr Campbell," Drew said quietly.

Declan met Drew's eyes. He nodded and his voice shook as he spoke. "Fine. In my office. We can talk in my office."

"Dad?" Simon asked uncertainty coating his words. "Can I see mum?"

"It's not her, Si," Declan said, glancing over at his son. "Go to your room. When I get this sorted, everything will go back to normal."

Pain and fear spread across Simon's face, and Harriet had to fight the urge to reach out to him as he took a step back from his father. "You're a liar. Nothing is normal. You did this... It's your fault she's gone."

Before Declan could say anything to his distraught son, Simon took off at a run. He raced down the side of the house and disappeared from sight.

"I have to go after him," Declan said, taking a step in the direction his son had taken.

"I'll have a uniform go after him," Drew said quickly. "He'll be fine."

"I can go," Harriet said. She met Drew's eye and he gave a small nod in response. "You," Drew called back over his shoulder to the marked car that had pulled into the drive behind them. The officers were already on the drive and walking towards them. "Go with her." Harriet started down the path next to the house.

"Not her," Declan shouted. He reached for Harriet, but she side-stepped him and quickly picked up her pace. He came after her, his hand tangling in the collar of her coat. He jerked hard, causing her to stumble backwards into the gable end of the house. The stone bit into Harriet's hands as she put them out to brace herself as Declan Campbell fought to stop her. Before he could land a blow, Drew was there.

"Mr Campbell," Drew caught the other man's arms, forcing him back into the wall. Drew glanced in Harriet's direction ."Are you all right."

"I'm fine. I'll go and find Simon."

"Not her," Declan screamed, fighting against Drew's hold. "He's just a child. He doesn't know what he's talking about!"

Harriet didn't wait to hear the rest of Declan's *spiel*. Instead, she followed the path that stretched down the side of the house, a young, female officer at her back.

"Let me go," Declan shouted. "Simon! Simon!"

Blocking out the man's cries, Harriet raced away.

REACHING THE BACK GARDEN, Harriet spotted Simon's legs as they disappeared into a tree-house. Crossing the grass, Harriet paused near the base of an old, rickety ladder that had clearly seen better days. The idea of scaling the rotten rungs caused cold sweat to break out down her spine.

"Simon, my name is Dr Quinn," she said, placing a hand on the rung at eye-level.

"Dr Quinn." The female uniformed officer who had followed her into the garden, shook her head. "I don't think going up there is such a good idea."

"Normally, I'd agree," Harriet said, swallowing past the lump in her throat. "Simon, you can call me Harriet. Would you mind if I come up?"

"Fuck off!" Simon's angry voice carried down from the top of the tree. "Just leave me alone."

"You asked about your mum," Harriet said, testing the weight-bearing capabilities of the treehouse ladder. "You clearly want to talk about her to someone. Why not me?"

"You didn't know my mum," he said, but he was quieter, the anger more subdued than it had been a moment ago. "Why would I want to talk to you about her?"

"Because I'm a good listener," Harriet said. She swung herself onto the ladder. It creaked beneath her, and she closed her eyes half expecting the first rung to give way beneath her. When it didn't, Harriet dragged herself up onto the next step. It held. "You miss her."

Silence closed around her as she continued to climb. The entrance to the tree house came into view, and Harriet heaved herself over the edge, resting her elbows on the wooden planks that made up the small platform. Scanning her surroundings, Harriet spotted Simon sitting in the bough of the tree a few feet away. His long legs swung back and forth, his spine pressed to the dark bark of the tree.

"Simon, tell me about her."

He turned his head to the side and met her gaze. "I don't care what he says, she was an amazing mum." Tears brimmed on his lashes, and he dashed them away roughly with the back of his hand. "I could tell her anything."

"And is there something you wish you could tell her now?"

He squeezed his eyes shut, his head lolling back against the tree. "He's a liar."

"What makes you say that?" Harriet tried to keep her voice neutral, but the effort of keeping herself propped in the entrance to the tree house was beginning to take its toll on her. Her arms and shoulders burned with exertion. Heat built in her muscles. She couldn't remember the last time she'd been so active. Probably the one and only time she'd allowed Bianca to drag her to a yoga class in the local studio. Her friend had sworn it was a class for beginners, but Harriet's limp noodles for limbs begged to differ. She'd sworn from that moment on she would never again attend something so hellish.

"He lied about everything. He said she left. That

she abandoned us. But I knew she wouldn't do that. She would never have left me behind. It's all his fault."

"Why would you think that, Simon?"

Simon swallowed hard. Even with the distance between them, Harriet could see his Adam's apple as it bobbed in his throat. "I don't want to talk about it anymore."

"Why don't you come down," Harriet said, studying the unstable structure that surrounded them. "It's not safe in here."

"She used to come up here with me... to get away from him." There was a hoarseness to Simon's voice. He glanced over at Harriet. "The day he said she left. When he told me she'd abandoned me, he didn't know I'd stayed home."

"You don't have to carry this anymore, Simon."

"He'll kill me if I say it." The admission was given in a whisper.

"My friend DI Haskell won't let him. I promise you that."

Simon glanced down at the ground. "They had a fight. I stayed out here, because I didn't want mum to know I'd skipped school. But I heard her scream."

"And are you sure it was your mother you heard scream?"

He nodded mutely. He slid out of the tree and dropped to the wooden platform. The moment his weight hit the boards, the entire structure shook.

Dust, and dirt rained down on Harriet, but Simon seemed unperturbed by the state of the tree-house.

"We should go down, Simon. This isn't safe."

"I need to show you something."

"Simon, you can show me on the ground."

"No. It's just..." He cut off with a yelp as he stepped onto a rotted board and his foot disappeared through the floor. He dropped like a ton of bricks and the tree house shook in its moorings. Without thinking, Harriet lunged forwards and caught his hand. His frightened eyes met hers head on.

"You're going to be all right, Simon," she said, keeping her voice even. From her vantage point, Harriet could see that it was only his foot which had broken through the boards. "Can you pull your leg free?"

"I think so," he said. He tugged and twisted. His face screwed up in pain, but he finally managed to pull himself free.

"Now, slowly," she warned. "Crawl towards me." She started to move back, her hand on his arm. But Simon wriggled free of her grasp. A board above her dropped and Harriet ducked her head, but not before the edge of the board clipped the side of her head. Gritting her teeth, she ignored the pain.

"I need to get it."

"Simon, it doesn't matter," Harriet said sharply.

"It'll just take a minute..." The tree groaned and the structure shook around them as Simon scampered towards the back of the tree house. Fear gnawed at Harriet. While it wasn't far to the ground, such a fall would leave him injured, not to mention what the structure of the tree house might do if it dropped on top of him.

"Simon, please. We need to go. Whatever it is, it can wait."

"Dr Quinn, please. You need to come down. It's not safe," the uniformed officer's voice called up from the ground.

Simon chewed his lower lip nervously as he edged close to the back of the structure. Dropping to his hands and knees, he crawled the last few feet to the back wall. Harriet's heart edged into her mouth as she pulled herself up through the opening in the plat-form. If she really stretched out, she could probably reach him...

"Dr Quinn?" The officer on the ground called up to her. But Harriet was forced to ignore her. She needed to keep her wits about her. She couldn't afford to be distracted by anyone else. Something warm trickled down over her eyebrow. Raising her hand, she swiped at the spot and her fingers came away wet with blood. Harriet focused her attention on the young man ahead of her. Another rotten board broke apart near Simon and Harriet watched as a handful of wood-lice dropped out onto the floor of the tree house. She couldn't reach him, not from here.

Simon pulled a board off the back of the tree house. Harriet placed her hand tentatively on a board in front of her, only for it to crumble and break up beneath her weight. How had he managed to scramble up here in the first place without the whole lot collapsing around his ears?

"Nearly there," he said as he pulled a plastic lunch box from the hole he'd revealed. He shifted and the tree holding them aloft creaked ominously.

Pulling herself up through the hatch, Harriet braced herself against the rotting boards. Leaving the relative safety of the ladder behind, she crept into the main structure of the treehouse. Everything shifted and groaned beneath her as she reached for Simon.

"It's not worth it," she said from between gritted teeth. "Whatever it is, it doesn't matter."

He glanced back at her. "Got it!" He held an iPhone with a cracked screen in his hand. Grinning, he started to crawl back in Harriet's direction.

"Simon, come down from there!" Declan Campbell's frightened voice echoed in the garden. "It's not safe. Simon, come down!"

Ignoring everything but the boy in front of her, Harriet reached out. She grabbed his arm as soon as he was within touching distance. Her heartbeat found a steadier rhythm, one that didn't involve an attempt to beat straight out through her chest. Wrapping both arms around Simon, she guided him back towards the hatch.

"I recorded them." Excitement coloured his voice as he edged towards her. "I recorded the fight."

Harriet helped him to the hatch and directed him to the ladder.

"When I told Dad that I knew what happened he told me it was in my head. I hid the phone so he wouldn't know—"

"It's all right, Simon, we can discuss this once we're on the ground."

He twisted in her grip and faced her as he prepared to descend. "He's the reason she's gone." Simon's voice broke as a small sob tore from him. "I think he killed her. I think he killed my mum."

Harriet tried to keep her composure as she listened to his admission. "Simon—"

The top rung of the ladder gave way with a deafening crack. She reached out for the boy but it was already too late. Simon dropped through the hole like a stone.

CHAPTER FIFTEEN

JOAN SLUMPED down on the couch. The pain in her stomach was back, but she did her best to ignore it. Nigel had told her it was just in her head. What had he called it? A phantom pain. He was probably right. He usually was.

She gripped the remote control in her hand, quickly flicking through the channels.

As she passed the BBC News Channel, a familiar face triggered a cascade of memories in her mind, but her body—on autopilot—had already moved past the channel. She clicked back, and was disappointed to find the image had changed. Instead of the photograph that had been there moments before, some footage showed a crew of white coverall-wearing people scurrying back and forth on the moor. They moved in and out of camera shot like big, white ants.

Joan stirred, straightening up on the sofa as she turned up the volume. The reporter droned on about the work being done at the scene. Words like *remains*, and *murder* were thrown around. Joan's brain was sluggish, and it took her a moment to fully grasp everything the journalist was saying.

A breaking news banner scrolled across the bottom of the screen. *Remains of missing woman Gwen Campbell found at Hole of Horcum in North Yorkshire.* The name pulled at her. She'd known a Gwen, hadn't she? It had been a number of years ago, but she was certain she'd known a woman called Gwen. Of course, the chances that it was the same person...

Joan's mind trailed off as the screen displayed a picture of a smiling woman. In her arms, she held a small child.

Bile, fiery and bitter coated the back of Joan's throat. The remote control dropped from her hand unnoticed, hitting the floor with a dull thud. Joan's eyes were glued to the screen. She raised her hand to the small scar that traced over the side of her temple. As the journalists shared what little details they had, Joan ran her finger back and forth on the knot of scar tissue. Her memories were murky. Much of them had been eroded by the combination of anti-anxiety, and anti-psychotic medications she took, but what she *did* know left her with a feeling of fear.

"Gwen..." The name left her feeling shaky and

emotional. This was Gwen. This was her friend... and she was dead. Dread coursed in Joan's veins. She glanced over at the bottle of pills on the table. It would be so easy to take one. It's what Nigel would want her to do. She closed her eyes and a hazy memory of Gwen filtered through the fog in her mind. Joan sat back and drew a cushion into her lap. As the reporter prattled on, she hugged the cushion to her chest.

She knew Gwen... but there was more to it than that. Her mind, however, refused to give up its secrets and so she sat there in silence, tears gliding down her cheeks as Gwen's smiling face burned itself into her retinas.

CHAPTER SIXTEEN

THE WORLD SEEMED to slow on its axis. Pain tore through Harriet's arms and back as the weight of the teen dragged her forwards. "I've got him, Harriet. You can let go now." Drew's reassuring voice wrapped itself around her and she felt Simon's weight disappear.

Nerves gripped her as she manoeuvred to the hatch. She glanced down and felt relief when she saw that Drew's presence wasn't a hallucination. He was setting Simon on the ground. He turned to look up at her. "You'll have to trust me," he said.

The urge to disagree with him was strong, but as she took in the sight of the broken top rungs of the ladder, Harriet knew arguing was pointless. Instead, she swallowed back her discomfort and edged to the opening. Swinging her legs through the hole, she was relieved to feel Drew's strong hands catch her foot. He guided her to the remaining rungs.

"That's it," he said. The concentration was plain in his voice. As she lowered herself, Harriet's breath caught in the back of her throat as Drew wrapped his arms around her. He held her tight and helped her down the final steps. Finally, with the ground beneath her feet, Harriet's fear began to dissipate.

"What were you thinking, following him up there?" The edge in Drew's voice took Harriet by surprise. Shrugging free of his grip, she started to turn to face him. But Drew caught her shoulders before she'd even finished moving. "Bloody heck, you're bleeding. Why didn't you say you were hurt?"

"I'm fine."

"You're not fine. You've split your head." He glanced over her shoulder. "PC—"

"Would it have been better if I'd let him go up there alone and get hurt?"

Drew's brow furrowed in consternation. "Well, no, but—"

"Then I'd appreciate you not lecturing me on health and safety."

"I'm responsible for you, Harriet, when you're out here with me." His gaze softened. "You're hurt." He reached for her, but she moved away.

"I'm fine." Her hand automatically went to her head. The moment she touched the cut, she winced and her fingers came away damp. "Ouch."

Drew's expression grew concerned. "We need to get you looked at."

"I said I'm fine, Drew. I meant it."

He searched her face, a slight quirk at the corners of his lips telling her he wasn't angry any more. "Will you let me get you cleaned up?"

"Later," she said. "I'm more interested in finding out what Simon has on that phone. And why it was so important that he'd risk his neck to get it."

Drew glanced back over at the teenager who was at that moment receiving a dressing down from his father. Harriet's gaze travelled back to the treehouse. The remnants creaked and groaned in the wind. She'd been so intent on getting out of the tree, she'd failed to notice that even more of the wood had collapsed, landing in a tangled heap on the lawn. That could have been her or Simon.

Stop catastrophizing, she inwardly scolded herself.

"Mr Campbell--"

"Haven't you lot done enough?" Declan turned on Drew. "You've terrified and upset my son. He could have been killed and all because of her." He pointed a shaking finger in Harriet's direction.

"Dad, it's not her fault," Simon whined. "She was trying to help."

"I want you all to leave."

Drew glanced back at Harriet and she subtly shook her head. "We were hoping to have a conversation with Simon," Drew said. "Dr Quinn said he was pretty upset about something."

"My son has nothing to say, do you, Simon?"

Simon's shoulder's rounded over and he shrank in front of them. "I..."

"It's all right, Simon," Harriet said. "I told you, DI Haskell here can help."

"Harriet." The warning in Drew's voice was implicit. Not that she needed it. Harriet already knew she was on shaky ground. Simon was a minor and without his father's consent, Drew's hands were tied.

Simon glanced up at her, and then his eyes shifted to his father's face.

"We're going inside," Declan said. His grip tightened on his son's shoulders and Simon winced.

"You lied about, mum," Simon whispered. Tears glistened in his eyes. "You said she left me. That she didn't want me."

"Shut up, Simon," Declan said. There was a hitch in his words as he tried to manhandle his son towards the house.

"You said she never loved me," Simon's voice rose in pitch. "But that was a lie. Mum loved me."

"You don't know what you're talking about," Declan said. His face had gone white.

Simon pulled free of his father's punishing grip. "I can prove it." He gripped the phone tightly behind his back.

"Prove what?" Declan asked.

"You pushed her..."

"That's not true, Si. You know I'd never hurt your mother. I loved her."

"You pushed her," Simon said again. "And she screamed."

"Why are you lying? You know I'd never hurt her." Declan glanced over at Drew and Harriet. "Simon had nightmares after his mother abandoned us. With everything that happened, and the investigation..." Declan sighed. "He thought I had something to do with her leaving."

"I didn't imagine it," Simon said. "And I can prove it." Simon produced the phone with a flourish. "You pushed her on the stairs. And when I told you I'd seen it happen, you told me I was making it up. That I was a liar." Simon's face was white as he waved the phone at his father. "But I caught it all on my phone —" Simon never finished the sentence before his father lunged at him. The teenager yelped and stumbled back. Tripping over his own feet, he landed on the grass with a dull thud.

Drew was there before Declan could reach his son. He blocked him with his body, holding him back, preventing him from laying his hands on the youngster. "You ungrateful little bastard," Declan said, fury colouring his words.

"Mr Campbell, you do not have to say anything, but it may harm your defence..."

Harriet tuned out Drew's words, Her concern was for Simon, who was watching the events unfolding. "Simon, are you all right?"

"This is my fault," Simon said, a tremor in his voice.

"None of this is your fault," Harriet said. "I don't think you need to see this."

"Declan?" Beth's voice rang out from the back of the house. "What's going on? Declan?"

"Is there someone I can contact, Simon?"

He glanced up at Harriet as the tears started to drip down his face. "I want my mum..."

CHAPTER SEVENTEEN

"JOAN?" Nigel's voice carried through the house. Joab started, her heart picking up its erratic tattoo against her ribs as she scrambled to straighten up.

"In here," she called out, hating that her voice betrayed the fact that she'd been asleep. He would know it, and it would no doubt sour his mood for the evening. Swiping at the drool that had dried onto the side of her cheek, she straightened her cardigan and fluffed her hair as Nigel appeared in the living room door.

"You were sleeping," he said. It wasn't a question. More a simple statement of fact as he took in her appearance. "I suppose there's no dinner."

"I thought maybe we'd get a takeaway," she said quickly.

Nigel rolled his eyes. "Like you need one of

those." There was a glimmer of disgust in his eyes as he stared at her.

Joan's gaze fell to her lap. She twisted her fingers around the balled up tissue she held. "I've been doing much better lately, Nige. I lost two whole pounds this morning."

"You been watching those old movies again." Nigel cocked an arrogant eyebrow at her.

"No, I..." Joan trailed off. She looked over at the box of tissues next to her. There was a reason she'd fetched the tissues, but it wasn't so she could watch the old romantic movies she favoured.

"You know, I heard something interesting on the radio on the way home," Nigel said, ignoring her completely. He shrugged out of his wax jacket and kicked his boots off.

Joan studied his careful movements. Why he insisted on wearing the wax jacket and hiking boots baffled her. His attire would not have been out of place on a country gentleman. But Nigel was not that. In fact, the more she thought about it, the more Joan was convinced of how ridiculous he looked.

"Are you going to ask me what I learned?" He interrupted her thoughts with his question. Joan snapped her gaze up to his face. She'd made a mistake. The look in his eyes was one of irritation. It wouldn't take much for him to go from irritated to outright angry.

"Sorry, Nigel," she said sheepishly. "What did you learn?"

"Oh forget it," he snapped. He snatched his jacket up from where he'd draped it over the arm of the sofa. "Would it kill you to offer me a cuppa?"

"Of course, sorry, Nige. Would you like some tea, love?"

His grunt was the only acknowledgment Joan knew she could expect. Pushing to her feet, she made her way on unsteady legs to the kitchen. Pausing in the doorway, she glanced back at him. His hand slipped from his pocket and he dropped something onto the couch. The hairs on the back of Joan's neck prickled.

He turned and glared at her. "Any chance of that tea, Joany-Pop?"

"Of course."

Joan ambled into the kitchen. Picking up the kettle she filled it with water before she switched it on to boil. What had he dropped onto the couch? Curiosity burned inside her. As she opened the cupboard to grab the teabags, her stomach rumbled. Had she eaten today? Her eyes settled on the jar of biscuits.

"Do you ever stop thinking about food?" Nigel asked as he dropped onto one of the wooden kitchen chairs. Joan let the cupboard slam shut before she turned to face him. "

You know gluttony is a sin, Joan," he said. "One

of the seven *deadly* sins in fact. Perhaps a little bit of fasting wouldn't go amiss. It might get you back on track, spiritually and physically."

"Fasting?" Joan wrinkled her nose up in disgust.

"I've been recommending intermittent fasting to my clients," Nigel said. "They've been having such wonderful results with it. More focus, sharper responses. And best of all, those who need it are seeing weight loss as a little added perk." He leaned his hands on the table. His hair was a little darker than usual. Was he dyeing it? And was it her imagination, or was it styled a little differently?

She studied him a more closely. His face was animated. How long had it been since she had seen him like this? Her mind drifted back to the sight of him at the couch. If she could just slip inside...

"Are you listening to me, Joany-Pop?"

"Whatever you think is best, dear." She pulled in a deep breath and looked away. "What was it you learned on the way home?"

"There's no need for pretence, Joan. I know you don't give a shit." He slumped back in his chair.

Joan winced at his use of such crude language. If she spoke like that he'd have been only too happy to rinse her mouth out with soap. Rather than let him see how unnerved she was, she turned back to the counter and busied herself with preparing the tea.

"Of course I'm interested." Joan forced herself to

sound more upbeat than she felt. What was she missing? Something tugged at the dark recess of her mind but every time she tried to latch on, it slipped away from her.

"You remember a few years ago?" Nigel chuckled to himself. "Of course you don't. You've got a brain like swiss cheese." His dark chuckle made her squirm.

Her hands shook as she dropped the teabags into the cups. He appeared beside her and pulled open the cupboard. Joan shied away from him as he lifted the jar of biscuits down and carried it back to the table. "Do you think it'd kill you to get some nice biccies next time? Some HobNobs or the Fox's ones. Why should I have to suffer, just because you're a pig?"

Joan closed her eyes, trying to ignore his barb. She grabbed the kettle and set about pouring the water into his cup.

"Anyway," he said, talking around a mouthful of custard cream crumbs. "I was coming home."

Joan picked up the cup, only half listening to him as he prattled on behind her. Turning around she started across the floor.

"They said they found a body up at the Hole of Horcum. And I reckon it's that woman you tried to befriend a few years back. Gwen Campbell I think they said her name was."

The memory of the news report slammed into

Joan. Her hands shook, slopping tea over the table top as she set it down in front of her husband.

"For goodness sake, Joan, can you do anything right?"

"I'm sorry, Nigel. It's just..."

He glanced up at her and the look in his eyes softened. "I'm sorry, Joany-Pop. Are the pills giving you tremors again?"

Ducking her head, she tried to hide her face behind her hair. "Yes, Nigel. Perhaps, we could try a lower dose for a while? You know I haven't had any episodes for awhile now."

He shook his head sadly. And when Joan met his eye, she could see a glint of something darker lurking beneath. "I'm not convinced that's a good idea," he said. "I'm sure if you give it some time, the side-effects will settle down."

Disheartened, Joan nodded before taking the chair opposite him. "Did they say anything else about the body they found?"

Nigel smiled as he scooped another biscuit from the jar. "I changed the station. It's not good to listen to rubbish like that." There was an expectant look on his face.

"Is there something else, Nige?"

He sighed and stuffed the biscuit into his mouth. When he spoke, it was to shower crumbs over the table top. "Don't you think you should get on with dinner?"

"I thought we were having a takeaway."

He chuckled. "Waste of money. Anyway, I'm in the mood for some pie and mash. And you can't beat a bit of home cooking." He stood, and headed for the living room door. "Try not to take too long, I'm famished." As he reached the door he paused and looked back at her. "And don't forget to take your tablets."

"I won't," Joan said stiffly.

"Do you need me to supervise?" There was an edge to his voice as though he could see straight through her to the tumultuous emotions that coursed through her mind.

"Of course not, love. I can manage. You go and put your feet up. You deserve the rest. I'll pop dinner on and have it into you in no time."

The hardness faded from Nigel's eyes. "That's my girl," he said proudly.

He disappeared into the living room and a moment later Joan heard the volume on the television turn up. She sat for a moment, her palms face down on the table.

She knew what was required of her. Nigel's hold on her was absolute, but learning about Gwen had shaken her to her core. There was something she wasn't remembering. Something the medication was preventing her from drawing up from the dark corners of her mind. Something important. Going to the fridge, she took out the bottle of wine and poured a generous measure into Nigel's glass.

Carrying it into the living room, she glanced at the couch. Her phone sat half buried among the cushions. Had it been there all along or was that what Nigel had dropped there when she was in the kitchen.

"Thanks, love," Nigel said carefully taking the glass from her shaky hands.

"Is your phone not working?" The question seemed innocent enough, but the sour look on Nigel's face told her she'd made a misstep.

"Why?"

"I saw you leave my phone on the couch and—"

"Why would I need your phone, Joan?" Concern edged Nigel's voice.

"I thought maybe..."

"You thought what, love?" Nigel leaned forward in his chair. "Oh, Joany-Pop, have you started seeing things again?"

She shook her head vehemently. "No, Nigel. I saw you drop my phone back on the couch. I just thought maybe you needed it."

Setting his glass on the table beside him, Nigel got to his feet and place his hand on her shoulder. "I never touched your phone."

"Nigel, I saw you." She tried to keep her voice steady.

His mouth was set in a grim line. "I can't believe

we're back here. Has something upset you, Joan? Maybe I shouldn't have told you the news about that body on the moor."

"Nigel, you dropped my phone on the couch after you came in. I saw you..."

He glanced towards the couch and his concerned expression cleared. "Are you sure it was your phone you saw?"

"Yes."

"Are you sure it wasn't the remote control?" Nigel's mouth turned up at the corners. "I turned down the sound on the telly after you got up to the go to the kitchen. That's what you saw."

"But my phone is on the couch where you dropped it..." Joan could hear the uncertainty in her own voice. Maybe she hadn't seen him drop her phone after all.

"Joany-Pop, you know how messy you are. Your iPad and laptop are also on the couch. Or are you going to accuse me of putting them there too?"

"Well, no, but..."

"I know you're under a lot of pressure to get back to work." Nigel pursed his lips. "Maybe I should supervise you taking your medication."

Joan shook her head. "No. You're right, Nigel. I must have been mistaken. I'm sorry..."

He leaned over and pressed his lips to her forehead. "There's my clever girl. I knew you'd get there in the end."

Feeling deflated, Joan went back to the kitchen. Had she been mistaken about the phone? And if she'd been wrong about that, then maybe she was wrong about Gwen too.

Could you forget something like that?

Pain burrowed beneath her ribcage and she grimaced, grabbing onto the kitchen counter. No, Gwen had been her friend... Nigel made it sound as though they hadn't been close at all. When she tried to think about Gwen, the memories were overlaid with fear and terror.

She needed to remember. But that had been in the *before* time. And everything from the *before* time was a little wavy around the edges.

Suddenly certain about what needed to be done, she went to the medicine cabinet and took her pill bottles down. As she glanced back in the direction of the living room, her heart climbed into her throat. She popped the lids and took the requisite number of pills from each pot. Moving to the sink, she quickly stuffed them down the drain before filling a glass of water for herself. Sipping at it, she closed her eyes.

"All done?" Nigel asked.

Joan jumped, nearly dropping the glass in the process. Glancing over her shoulder she smiled at her husband.

"All done."

Turning back to the sink, she turned the tap on

full and watched the water swirl away down the drain washing away the evidence of her lie.

Thou shalt not lie.

If she didn't say anything at all, then it wasn't really a lie. God would understand.

She needed to know the truth. She needed to remember.

CHAPTER EIGHTEEN

"ARE you sure you're all right?" Drew asked, sitting in the chair opposite Harriet at the desk.

"I'm fine." Seeing the unconvinced look on his face, she added, "Really, it's just a scratch. I've had worse."

Drew's face darkened for a moment and Harriet knew he was remembering the first case they'd worked on together. He sniffed suddenly and then sneezed loudly.

"Shit, sorry."

Harriet eyed him speculatively. "You all right?"

Drew nodded. "Fine."

"Has he said anything yet?" Changing the subject seemed like the safest option. It had the instant reaction she had hoped for. Drew's expression cleared.

"Nothing. He's getting acquainted with the custody suite." Drew twisted his mouth into a grim line. "We jumped too soon on this one. We don't have the evidence to charge him with the murder of his wife. We don't even have a positive identification on the bodies from the moor."

Maz's excited shout cut Drew off mid-sentence. "It's them. They got an ID on one of the bodies."

Drew pushed to his feet and held his hand out. Without needing to be told, Maz passed the file over to his boss. Drew's eyes flicked quickly over the contents, his lips compressed into a tight line. "It's Gwen Campbell," he said finally. He caught Harriet's eye. "We got lucky with a dental match, otherwise, we'd still be waiting." He returned his attention to the file. "But they don't have anything on the second set of remains."

Maz shook his head. "They'll need DNA for that and it's going to take some time."

Drew dropped the file onto his desk. "Anything on the phone we got from Simon Campbell?"

Maz glanced in the direction of the office across the hall where Jodie Meakin, their computer analyst worked. "I can check..."

"Go," Drew urged. "If there's nothing on that phone..." Drew didn't have to finish the sentence. Everyone knew just how much was at stake. If they'd arrested Declan too soon, there was a real chance he could walk away with murder.

Harriet returned her attention to the scattered files on the desk in front of her. The moment they'd arrived back in the office, Harriet had settled in with every scrap of information the team had been able to gather about the Gwen Campbell case. It wasn't an insignificant amount of information to peruse, but Harriet was determined to do it. If she could find something here that would help...

"Didn't you say you had a meeting this evening?" Drew asked, cutting through her silent contemplation.

Glancing at her watch, Harriet was shocked to discover the time. Misha would be waiting for her. Her automatic thought was to cancel the arranged meet-up with her student, but guilt made her hesitate. Cancelling in the past had been one of the reasons she'd fallen so far behind. And Misha was on the edge. Harriet didn't need a Ph.D in psychology to know that the young woman was extremely vulnerable. One mistake now, and she might walk away from her chosen educational pursuits entirely. That wasn't something Harriet was comfortable with.

"You're right," Harriet said. I've got to go." She gathered up her papers reluctantly.

There was a look on Drew's face that she couldn't quite pinpoint. "You're not going to be here when we interview Declan?"

Harriet paused, her fingers tapping softly against the files as she contemplated her next move. "If you need me here—"

As though he could read the conflict going on

inside her head, Drew shook his head. "You should go. I take it this is one of those meetings you've been putting off with your students?"

Harriet nodded. "And I really don't think I should postpone this one."

"Then go," Drew said. "I've been doing interviews like this for a long time. As much as I'd like you here, I'm sure we'll muddle through without you."

Harriet smiled at him. "You'll do just fine. I'd only get in the way, and ask too many meandering questions anyhow."

"You mean you'd ask all the questions we didn't know we needed?"

Picking up her handbag, Harriet returned his warm smile. "You'll do just fine, Drew. If Declan Campbell had anything to do with his wife's death, I know you'll get to the bottom of it."

Drew hesitated. "You don't sound convinced that he's our man."

Leaning on the edge of the desk, Harriet splayed her fingers out over the files that remained. She wanted nothing more than to sit back down and continue with the work she'd started. There was something about the case that bothered her, but because she couldn't pinpoint exactly what that might be, she'd been loathe to mention it to Drew. Now that he had asked her outright, well, that was a different matter. But she still couldn't give him the answers, she knew he would need.

"Let's just say, I'm keeping an open mind," she said cautiously. "There are a lot of loose threads in this."

"And you want us to be certain we're pulling the right one."

Harriet nodded, relived that Drew understood her. "Yes."

"Anything in particular you think I should be looking at?"

With a small sigh, Harriet shook her head. "I only just started to go through the files." Drew's face fell. "But..." She grabbed one of the top folders. "Press him on his whereabouts the day his wife went missing. Simon was very clear that his mum and dad fought. But Declan insisted he'd left the house that day without speaking to Gwen."

"And you don't think Simon could be mistaken about when the fight happened?"

Harriet shrugged. "It's possible. Eye witness recall is notoriously unreliable. But you don't have to rely on Simon's memory."

Drew's expression was grim. "No, once we get into the phone we should have a clearer idea of what we're dealing with." Drew's face screwed up again and then cleared a moment later.

"You sure you're all right?"

"I'm fine. It's just this dusty office."

Harriet raised a brow at him. "You don't sound so convinced."

"Well, I am. It's just dust, Harriet. All the files came out of storage and that place is filthy."

Glancing at her watch, Harriet realised she was going to be late.

"Go," Drew urged. "If anything crops up, I'll let you know."

"Good luck," Harriet said. As she hurried for the door, guilt gnawed at her. She was leaving Drew with a lot of work. Piles of files and evidence that had been gathered during the initial investigation. Not to mention, Drew's previous involvement with the case had ended with him having to excuse himself because of Freya. It was a lot for him to deal with.

She caught sight of the flicker of concern in his eyes as he began to sift through the paperwork.

Harriet was leaving him with the prospect that the case would not be the open and shut crime they'd initially thought. She'd introduced doubt to the situation. She could only hope she'd done the right thing.

CHAPTER NINETEEN

STANDING outside the door to the student bar, Harriet paused. In all the years she had worked at the university, she had never once set foot in the place. It felt too much like an intrusion. It was a sacred space where the students came to blow off steam and rid themselves of the weight of the world. Although some might argue that it was nothing more than a place to get drunk and shake off inhibitions.

Pushing open the door, she scanned the interior. Misha sat in a corner booth. Crossing the floor, Harriet was surprised to see the table in front of her student was empty of the promised research. Harriet took the empty seat opposite Misha, all the while ignoring the curious glances from those present.

"You came." Misha sounded surprised as she glanced up. "I wasn't sure you'd make it."

"I'm sorry, things ran over at—" Harriet inter-

152

rupted herself. It was better if Misha didn't know the details of her work with the police.

"Don't worry about it," Misha said brightly. "I'm just glad you're here." A look of pleasure crossed her delicate features as she gestured to the glass in front of Harriet. "I wasn't sure what you liked to drink, so I got you a gin and tonic."

Harriet smiled politely and moved the glass aside. "I'm not sure that would be appropriate." She took a notebook from her bag.

"Oh." Misha traced the path made by a droplet of condensation on the side of her glass. When it reached the table, she used the top of her finger to pull it out into a spider-web pattern. "I only did it because I know it's your favourite drink."

There was a coyness to Misha's voice that made Harriet pause. Cocking her head to the side, she cautiously contemplated her response. "What makes you say that?"

"Louise..." She stopped and corrected herself. "Mum wrote about it in her journal."

Harriet looked at the glass. So much time had passed, even so, she remembered Louise as though the intervening years had never happened. Pushing the thoughts aside, Harriet tightened her grip on her pen. "How do you want to start?"

"What was she like?" Misha's question caught Harriet off guard.

"Excuse me?"

"Mum. What was she like? I mean, you knew her better than anyone. It's all well and good reading about her, but it's not the same as knowing her." Misha hesitated, looking suddenly much younger and more vulnerable. "Do you know what I mean?"

Harriet nodded. "I can understand that it must be very difficult for you." She drew in a deep breath. The young woman was clearly looking for a connection to her past, but Harriet could not be the one to give it to her. "Have your grandparents not spoken to you about her?"

Misha shrugged. "They don't like to talk about her. I suppose it brings up too many painful memories for them." She met Harriet's eyes. "I can understand that, you know? It can't have been easy for them to lose their only child."

"No, I don't suppose it has been easy for any of you." She cleared her throat, and suddenly wished she had something to drink. Her gaze darted towards the glass on the table. "Misha, we really should..."

"She really cared about you," Misha blurted out. "She writes about you quite a bit."

"We were colleagues."

Misha leaned across the table. Her hand darted out, her slender fingers closing over Harriet's. "Tell me what happened. I've read everything I can get my hands on about what went down, but—"

Harriet pulled her hand away. "Misha, is that what all of this is about?"

Chagrined, Misha looked towards the wall. "I just want to know her and there's nobody else I can ask."

"You brought me here to discuss your research..."

"I do need help with that," she said. "But...I don't know. I saw an opportunity, so I took it. You can't blame me. My mother is this spectre that hangs over our family. She's always there, but nobody will talk about her." There was a trace of bitterness in her voice. "You know, I found some old VHS tapes, family holidays and the like. When I tried to watch them, my grandmother took them away and hid them."

"Why would she do that?" Harriet asked, genuinely curious.

"She said they were painful reminders of everything they had lost." Tears brimmed on the edge of Misha's lashes. "I remind them of her as well."

Harriet could understand why. Misha shared a strong resemblance to her mother, especially her eyes.

"I'm sorry you feel you can't speak to your grandparents. But this really isn't appropriate, Misha." Shaking her head, Harriet got to her feet. "When you're ready to discuss your research you can make an appointment with Martha."

"Please, Harriet..." Misha's face coloured. "I mean Dr Quinn."

Seeing her pained expression, Harriet felt her

heart constrict in her chest. "Misha, this isn't something I can discuss with you. We were colleagues. It wouldn't be right for me to break that kind of confidence."

"But she's dead. You wouldn't be breaking anything."

Harriet shook her head. "I'm not sure what you think you know. Your mother and I, we weren't exactly friends. Not the way you seem to think we were."

Misha's hand darted out, she tried to catch Harriet's hand again, but missed. "I won't mention her again, but please, don't leave. We can discuss the research."

The frantic note in Misha's voice caused alarm bells to go off in Harriet's mind. "Did you bring the research with you?"

When Misha glanced down at the table, Harriet had her answer.

"Misha, what is all of this about?"

"I just..." Misha spread her hands wide in front of her. A helpless gesture that sat uneasily with Harriet. Everything she had seen of the young woman told her that Misha was anything but helpless.

"I should go."

"Harriet, please... You don't understand, I can't—" Misha cut off and glanced down.

"You can't what? If there's some kind of problem."

The next words came out as a whisper. "Not like

this. I can't. I'm sorry..." There was a desperation to her voice that caused the hair on Harriet's arms to stand to attention.

"I really should go," Harriet said, pushing away from the table.

"Please, Dr Quinn, don't leave." Misha's voice followed her as she hurried out of the bar. "Don't leave me!" Once outside, Harriet gulped down a deep breath. Misha's behaviour had taken her by surprise, and that concerned her.

How had she not seen the signs of an unhealthy attachment before now? It made perfect sense. Misha's troubled past, not to mention Harriet's connection to her mother and her sudden demise. Pushing the thoughts away, Harriet decided that taking a step back from Misha would be the best option for everyone. She could make the recommendation to Dr Baig in the morning.

Satisfied that she'd made the right call, she contemplated returning to the office, but instead decided that going home and getting an early night would be the most sensible thing she could do right now.

CHAPTER TWENTY

PUSHING open the side door that led into the stone church, Joan paused in the entryway. As she exhaled, the air in front of her face turned white. The building was freezing and she drew her coat more tightly around her frame. The cold didn't bother her, really. Not here, anyway. As she closed the door softly, the space below her ribs tugged at her, making her wince.

When she'd awoken that morning, Nigel was already gone. His side of the bed had been cold, the sheets oddly smooth as though he'd never lain within them.

The cup of tea he'd left for her on the bedside locker had long since lost its warmth. He wouldn't have been happy to know she'd poured it down the sink. Nigel's motto was, 'waste not, want not'. And anyway, Joan had been happy to make her own tea, especially as the fog she'd grown so accustomed to inside her head had lifted. Not completely gone, not by a long shot, but enough to give her hope. Enough to make her think she could venture down to the church. Just a quick trip out. Nothing more than a leg stretching exercise.

For the first time in so long, Joan felt hopeful.

Crossing the flagstone floor, footsteps echoing, she made her way to the small bank of candles. Ignoring the gnawing sensation in her abdomen, she fished a couple of coins out her pocket. She slipped the money into the box and quickly lit a candle. Retreating to the nearest pew, she sat on the hard wooden bench. The pain in her stomach slowly receded to a dull ache.

The silence of the church slipped around her like a cloak. The weight of it, which for someone else might have been oppressive was, for Joan, a comfort. In here, everything seemed simpler. There was nothing between her and her God. The time she carved out to spend in the chapel was sacred. Joan wouldn't allow anyone to interfere, not even Nigel.

And now that she was here... it confirmed, at least in her own mind, that her decision to stop taking the medication had been the right one.

Basking in the silence, she allowed her mind to wander. Since she'd seen the news report about the body being discovered, she'd been plagued by a deep sense of unease.

"One step at a time," she whispered to herself.

She was still shaky, and the short walk to the chapel —she wasn't comfortable with the idea of taking the car out just yet— had left her feeling exhausted. But it was progress.

Now, if she could only just remember her friendship with Gwen. Burying her face in her hands, she closed her eyes and tried to conjure a memory. Her brain responded sluggishly.

There was something she was supposed to remember. Fear gripped her as she struggled to recall the first true friend she'd had in years. With her eyes closed, her mind was a jumble of images that refused to come together and form a cohesive picture.

Rain on the windscreen. A storm... The sound of screaming.

"Joan?"

She jerked in the pew and her eyes snapped open. Focusing on the woman standing in the aisle next to her, Joan fought against the blind panic that descended on her mind. It passed as quickly as it had arrived and she recalled that she was sitting in the church.

"It *is* you, Joan. It's so good to see you." The tall, willowy woman next to her reached out and attempted to pat Joan's arm with mittened hands.

Joan shrugged away, noting the look of hurt that crossed the woman's face.

Joan knew her. There was a familiarity about the

face that tugged at the recesses of her memory. The cream gilet she wore, with the silver fur trim around the neckline, fitting snugly against the woman's slender frame. The honey blonde hair falling around her face in careless waves.

"Charlene?" It was a guess, but the name had popped into Joan's head as she studied the woman next to her.

Colour suffused Charlene's cheeks. "You remember! Oh, wow, when I approached you, I was so sure you'd forgotten me."

Joan returned Charlene's smile with what she hoped was a warm smile of her own. When Charlene didn't run away, Joan assumed she'd succeeded.

"I know we only met once or, I think maybe twice..." Charlene popped one hip to the side as she spoke. "I wanted to say what a big fan I am of your work. But I was a little nervous..."

Charlene blathered on blithely, offering Joan the opportunity to study her a little more closely. Being so close, Joan could tell that the woman's makeup had been applied heavy-handedly. Not that Joan could really say anything; she couldn't even remember the last time she'd worn makeup. Getting up and dragging herself into the shower most mornings was hard enough without adding any extra work to her routine.

A hazy image formed in Joan's mind. Charlene had been one of the women who attended the slimming club meetings. The same meetings where Joan had met Gwen for the first time.

Charlene's nose was thinner now, with a cute button tip that Joan didn't remember from the last time they'd met, although her memory was still hazy. Above the nose, Charlene's perfectly shaped eyebrows were perfectly shaped and a couple of shades darker than her hair. Joan was unable to tear her gaze away from those eyebrows, which she noted didn't move, despite the young woman's animated chatter. It took her a moment to realise they had been micro bladed.

Joan brushed her cold fingers over her own paltry eyebrows, conjuring a memory. Gwen had suggested they should both go and have the procedure done. Now that she'd witnessed the result, Joan was glad they'd never kept the appointment. When she didn't try to force herself to remember, the memories returned with ease.

"You know, you really should come back to the group, Joan. I've found the accountability really helped me to shift those last few stubborn pounds. I'm the lightest I've ever been."

"Well, you look wonderful," Joan said quietly, wishing the woman would just bugger off and leave her to her solitude.

"You're too kind," Charlene said with a giggle. "I've got a new goal now."

"You want to lose more weight?" Joan interrupted.

"Well, yeah, obvs." Charlene frowned. At least Joan thought it was a frown, she couldn't be entirely certain due to the frozen state of Charlene's face. Charlene leaned on the edge of the pew, closing the distance between them. "I have to. You see, I started one of them Instagram accounts. You know, to show off mine and Mikey's new house. Actually, you should follow me. If you did that, it'd be amazing. I've got nearly sixty-thousand followers now."

Joan stared at her uncomprehendingly. She had never once understood the allure of social media. Gwen had loved it.

A vague memory stirred in the back of Joan's head, but Charlene's continued chatter pushed it back.

"So, when I started to grow my account professionally, I got a manager and everything. And they said I'd need to lose a few pounds. You know how the camera adds ten pounds and the trolls are so cruel sometimes." Charlene's eyes misted and she sniffed softly.

"I'm sorry to hear that," Joan said. She wasn't really, but it seemed like the correct thing to say.

"Thanks." Charlene sniffed again. "Its been really hard, actually. And talking to you has been a real help."

"Why don't you just quit?"

Charlene's face morphed into one of shock. "Quit?"

Joan nodded. "If it's so difficult, you could just walk away. It's only social media."

Charlene stared at her for a moment before starting to laugh. "Oh, that's a good one. You really had me going there for a minute."

Joan continued to stare at her but she didn't add anything else. As far as she was concerned, why *couldn't* Charlene just walk away from it?

"You know, if you wanted, I could put a word in with my manager for you."

"Why?" Joan didn't bother to hide the bluntness of her question.

"Well, to see if there were any opportunities for you. I know its been a while since you..." Charlene trailed off. "You know, since you..."

"Released a book?" Joan offered.

"Yes, that," Charlene said, sounding relieved that Joan hadn't forced her to say anything more uncomfortable. "I could find out if there was anything he could do for you from a publicity standpoint."

Joan raised her hand to her lips and chewed at the frayed edge of her thumbnail. The word 'publicity' had the ability to tighten a knot of worry deep in her belly.

Charlene wrinkled her nose with distaste as her gaze tracked Joan's movements. Realising it was her behaviour that Charlene was so disgusted by, Joan let her hand drop away from her mouth.

"That's very kind of you," she said, trying to keep her voice even. "But that really isn't necessary." She'd come here to be alone in the peace offered by the chapel. Charlene had spoiled that. A dull ache had started in the back of Joan's skull. If she didn't come up with a good excuse soon, she was positive she would snap at the young woman.

"Oh, it's no trouble," Charlene said. "Everyone was so sorry to hear about your *illness*. Just give me your number, and—"

The loaded way in which she said the word started a buzzing in Joan's head. She didn't wait for Charlene to finish the sentence. Snatching her bag from the pew, she pushed out past the shocked woman, almost knocking her down in the process.

"Joan!"

There was a pitch to the woman's voice that Joan hadn't thought was possible from a human. Beating a hasty retreat towards the door, she contemplated apologising but the anxiety that welled inside her chest kept her feet moving forward.

Hurrying around the side of the stone building, she put as much distance between herself and Charlene as she could. The thought of having to deal with other people, with the public, brought her out in a cold sweat. They all knew about her. They had probably laughed and laughed when they'd heard about her mental breakdown. She could see it now. The jokes, the barbs. Nigel was right, she was nothing more than a local mockery. She couldn't turn back the clock. And she couldn't go back to her old life. *Wouldn't* return to that life. Not now, not ever.

She collapsed back against the wall and, closing her eyes, let her head fall back against the cold damp stone. Why couldn't Charlene have just left her alone? Gwen would have understood. She'd always known when to stay quiet, allowing Joan to collect her thoughts without making her feel overwhelmed.

Guilt wormed its way beneath her skin. Charlene was trying to help. She was being nice. And instead of being gracious, Joan had overreacted. What would Nigel say?

Joan didn't need to think about what Nigel would say. She could already hear his voice inside her head, berating her for her irrational actions.

The pain in her stomach returned with a vengeance. Her eyes settled on the gravestones in the churchyard and her stomach suddenly rolled. Bile crept up the back of her throat. Her heartbeat, which had started to settle, began to gallop in her chest again. Clutching at the front of her jumper, she felt clammy sweat clinging to her skin.

Nigel's voice filtered through the panic in her mind. Was he here? Had he come looking for her? He would help her...

On legs that threatened to buckle beneath her,

Joan turned away from the graves. With her hand pressed to the stone wall, she put one foot in front of the other as quickly as she could. Nigel would help. His laughter drifted to her, carried on the wind.

The sound of car tyres crunching on gravel.

Joan focused on keeping her body moving.

Rounding the side of the church, she reached the path that led out of the churchyard. The sound of a car engine fading in the distance mingled with cawing crows overhead. But there was no Nigel.

Had she imagined him? Fear tightened the band on her chest. Darts of pain travelled from her abdomen, shooting up into her chest. It felt like someone had lodged a cactus below her sternum. As she reached the road, reality wrapped itself around her. She had imagined him. Nigel was not here.

Besides her, the only other person on the pavement was a woman pushing a buggy up the hill towards the village. Joan swallowed her terror. If Nigel discovered that the hallucinations had returned...

Wrapping her arms around herself, she prayed for the pain in her abdomen to go away.

She wouldn't tell him. She'd go home and everything would be all right. He didn't have to know.

CHAPTER TWENTY-ONE

AS SHE APPROACHED HER OFFICE, Harriet's phone rang in her bag. Pausing, she fished around in the contents, until finally, her fingers closed over the phone. Tugging it free, she answered the call without bothering to check who was calling her.

"Hello, Harriet." Dr Connors' familiar voice caused her mind to freeze. She stood in the middle of the corridor. Despite being surrounded by other students and staff members hurrying hither and tither, she was transported back to her own living room the night he had barged in on her.

"What can I help you with?" She was surprised to find her voice was steady and betrayed none of the discomfort she felt.

"Ever the professional," Jonathan said. "I was just calling to congratulate you." There was bitter edge to his voice.

"Congratulate me for what?"

"You know what," he hissed. His voice dipped and Harriet could imagine him standing with the phone pressed tight to his mouth as he spoke into it. "You think you've won, but you have no idea what you've done." She couldn't be certain, but it almost sounded as though there was a slight slur to his words.

"They came back with a decision," Harriet said, a hollow feeling opened in the pit of her stomach.

"You always liked to play the innocent victim," he said. "But I know there's more going on in that head of yours. You've never fooled me."

"Jonathan, have you been drinking?"

"What do you care?"

"This is not what I wanted," Harriet said. "But the mistake you made..."

"Like you never fuck up," he spat at her. "Little Miss Perfect. You're as screwed up as the rest of us."

"I'm going to hang up now," Harriet said.

"You'll be sorry for this," he said. "If it takes the rest of my life I will see you pay for what you've done to me."

"Sober up, Jonathan." She ended the call. Her hands trembled as she slipped her phone back into her bag. Her feet carried her forwards and she pushed open the door to her office. Martha glanced up from her computer, her stern expression fading as she took in Harriet's appearance.

"What happened to you?" There was a softness to her tone.

"It doesn't matter," Harriet said, moving woodenly to the door to her office. "Do I have any appointments this morning?" She paused as she reached the office door that stood ajar.

"Misha McDermid is waiting for you in your office," Martha said, narrowing her eyes at Harriet. "I wanted her to wait out here, but she was in a bit of a state and, well..." Martha trailed off as she shrugged. "Are you sure you're all right?"

"Just a personal matter," Harriet said, brushing aside the older woman's concern. "I'll be fine."

Martha tutted her disapproval before she returned her attention to the computer. "I've sent you a list of speaking engagements Dr Baig would like you to look over and approve."

Harriet said nothing as she stepped into her office and closed the door softly behind her. Misha lay on the couch, her back turned to the room, her breathing soft and rhythmic. Harriet couldn't see the young woman's face, but there was something about the set of Misha's shoulders that suggested she wasn't asleep. But for some reason she wanted people to believe she was.

"Misha, what can I help you with?" Harriet remained where she was inside the office door.

The young woman jerked, and raised her head. Her eyes were bleary, and she scrubbed at them with her knuckles. "Dr Quinn, I'm sorry. I think I dozed off."

"Is there something I can help you with?" Harriet asked again. "I wasn't aware we had an appointment for this morning."

Misha struggled to straighten up on the couch, very nearly sliding off it in the process. Harriet's eyes flicked to the piles of papers the young woman had clearly disturbed in order to lay down on the sofa in the first place. Had Misha been going through the papers? The thought left Harriet feeling uncomfortable.

Moving away from the door, she approached her desk and set her bag down. She could feel Misha's eyes tracking her movements.

"You're angry with me?"

"Should I be?" Harriet raised her eyes to Misha's. She kept her expression mild, despite the uneasiness that plagued her.

Misha sighed and planting her elbows on her knees, she buried her face in her hands. "I've screwed everything up."

"What makes you say that?"

"Last night," Misha started to speak, and then paused. A moment passed and Harriet kept her mouth clamped shut. The urge to comfort the young woman was overwhelming. But she couldn't allow her feelings of guilt surrounding the death of Lousie

McDermid to colour her reaction to Misha. It would do neither of them any favours.

Misha looked up at her finally. Behind her eyes, Harriet could see a flicker of an emotion incongruent to her expression. It was gone in an instant as Misha glanced away towards the floor.

"I came here to apologise. My behaviour was unacceptable..." She pulled in a shaky breath, tears glistening on her cheeks. "It's just, I never knew my mother, and I hoped you would help me fill in some of the blank spaces I had."

Harriet grabbed the box of tissues from her desk and crossed the floor to Misha. Passing the tissues to her student, she perched on the other end of the sofa. "You need to understand, Misha, it wouldn't be appropriate for me to discuss that part of my past."

"I know you can't tell me the details surrounding her death," Misha said looking up into Harriet's face. "I understand why you can't do that for me. But I'm not asking for details. I just want to feel close to her..." She trailed off. Grabbing a handful of tissue paper from the box, she blew her nose noisily.

"And I can understand that," Harriet said. "But I don't think I'm the person you should be asking. Your grandparents would be much better candidates. They can tell you things I could never have known about Louise."

"As I said in the bar, they don't like to talk about her," Misha said. "It makes them sad. I've always found it easier just not to talk about her around them."

Harriet clasped her hands in her lap. She could feel Misha's pain, it rolled off the young woman in waves and lapped at Harriet despite the distance between them. "Misha, you need to know that this isn't at all appropriate. I'm your lecturer, your supervisor."

"I know that," Misha said. She cast a sideways glance in Harriet's direction. "I really do need help with my research. I wasn't lying about that."

"And I would happy to help you with it," Harriet said, a bitter taste coating her tongue. "However, I feel it's my duty to inform you that I will be speaking to Dr Baig about our conversations thus far."

The colour drained from Misha's face. "You can't do that," she said. "They'll kick me out of the university."

"No they won't," Harriet said. "But they will assign you to a different lecturer, which I think will be for the best."

"For who?" Misha asked passionately. "Who will that serve? I only came here because of you. I don't want to study with anyone else." Her voice rose to fever pitch.

"Misha, we need to do what's best for you. And I really think this will help you to focus on your studies in a way that will--"

"She was right, you know." Misha pushed to her

feet suddenly. She towered over Harriet, two spots of colour sitting high on her pale cheeks.

"Misha, please. You need—"

"I don't need anything from you," she said, leaning in close. "Louise said you were a stupid bitch and she was right."

Harriet's tongue stuck to the roof of her mouth. Seeing Misha so angry transported her back to the last argument she'd had with Louise. It was uncanny how alike the two women were, even down to the way Misha's face contorted in rage.

"I know it was your fault," Misha said, her voice dropping. "I've got the proof."

"Proof of what?" Harriet finally managed to find her voice.

"You're the reason she's dead." Misha straightened up. She pushed her hair back from her face, but the look of rage never faded from her eyes. "It should have been you." Without another word, Misha snatched her book bag from the ground and strode out of the room. The door to Harriet's office slammed into the wall and the unmistakable sound of plaster cracking made her jump.

A moment later, Martha stood framed in the doorway. "Dr Quinn?" There was a note of hesitation in the other woman's voice. "Are you all right?"

Harriet swallowed hard. "I'm fine, Martha, thank you."

"What happened?"

Harriet closed her eyes, Misha's words ringing in her ears. "Could you arrange a meeting with Dr Baig? I think this is something he needs to hear about from me."

"Of course."

Harriet listened to the sound of Martha's light footsteps as she padded back to her desk. She pulled in a deep breath, feeling some of the earlier tension leave her body. She had been right to turn Misha away, especially with everything else going on. While she could understand the young woman's desire to connect with that part of her mother's past, Harriet knew she could not be the one to give it to her. It would help no one to dredge it all back up.

It had been the right choice to make, no matter how much it pained her.

CHAPTER TWENTY-TWO

PUSHING her chair back from her desk, Olivia got to her feet. If she spent another moment sitting down, she was going to lose her mind. Scanning the room, she noted Maz's absence and a stab of jealousy caught her in the gut. It wasn't fair.

Swallowing the thought, she concentrated on her breathing. It *was* fair. Maz wasn't the one who had screwed up royally by pursuing a potential suspect alone. No, the only person she could blame for the predicament she found herself in was herself.

Heading for the hall, she glanced into Jodie's office. It had been a bustling place not so long ago, but one by one, the nerd squad had been whittled down and now, only Jodie remained. Not that Olivia minded. The place was much quieter with only the tap-tapping of Jodie on her keyboard.

There was still the hum of machinery and as

Olivia entered the room the warm smell of technology, that reminded her of opening a brand new laptop, washed over her. Behind a bank of monitors that NASA would have been proud of, she spotted Jodie.

"Fancy a coffee?" Olivia stood on tip-toe and craned her neck to see the tech at work. The other woman's face was mere inches from her screen and if she heard Olivia she never made it known. Bemused, Olivia made a beeline for her.

"Whatcha looking at?" Olivia asked, pausing behind Jodie's ergonomic chair.

Jodie jumped with a loud gasp. Launching herself backwards in the chair, her gaze snapped up to meet Olivia's.

"Where did you come from?"

"I called to you from the door, but you seemed a little pre-occupied."

"I was," Jodie said. Her gaze wandered back to the screen in front of her as she spoke.

"Well, what's so interesting?" Olivia looked over her shoulder but the screen was covered in rapidly moving lines of text. "What is that?"

"It's a forum," she said. "I've been tracking mentions of Gwen Campbell online since the news broke."

"Let me guess," Olivia said. "She had a smile that could light up a room? Or maybe, she was the kindest, most generous person they've ever known."

Jodie glanced back at her. Her eyebrows arched over her the frames of her blue glasses. "If I didn't know any better, I might think you sounded a little bitter."

Olivia laughed. "Nope. I've just heard it all. The minute someone dies, everyone starts tripping over themselves to tell you what a beautiful soul and wonderful humanitarian they were. It's all crap though. They don't mean it. It's just a chance for them to show off how wonderful they are. Another form of social one-upmanship. For once it'd be nice to see people share what they really thought."

"Like this perhaps?" Jodie clicked a couple of buttons and the words on the screen increased in size.

> THEEEASTERBUNNY76: Gwen was a vapid b*tch. The only real thing about her was her sense of entitlement. I watched her IG stories just so I'd know what brands she worked with so I could avoid 'em.

> ZellieBellie: Totes wit u THEEEASTERBUNNY76. She was fake AF! She got everyting she deserved. Glad we'll neva have 2 c her ugly mug preaching kindness bullshit on IG again.

"Where did you get this?" Olivia couldn't believe her eyes. The messages kept coming hard and fast.

She took a step back, half afraid that the vitriol being dripped through the screen would somehow infect her.

"It's a website I discovered while I was crawling the web results," Jodie said. "Some of the things on here, you wouldn't say to your worst enemy."

"Who are these people?"

Jodie shrugged. "A lot of them post anonymously, I could track them down but that's going to take time. It's pretty common. A lot of the big influencers have some kind of thread where people post about how much they hate them."

Folding her arms over her chest, Olivia stared at the screen incredulously. "You mean people actually deliberately go to these places just so they can, what? Moan about someone they saw on the internet?"

Jodie nodded. "That's about right. I tracked some of the posts back to before Gwen went missing and I found something interesting."

"Let me guess, more hatred?"

Jodie shook her head. "Not exactly. Plenty of hate. But there was a user called SinEater81 defending Gwen every chance they got."

"Try and say that name fast with a few drinks under your belt," Olivia said with a smile. Jodie stared blankly at her and Olivia shrugged. "Nevermind. What's so special about this Sin Eater?"

"Well, about a year before Gwen's disappearance, Sin Eater never mentioned Gwen. They didn't go into the threads about her and didn't interact with any of the other users regarding her. That all changed a few months before Gwen went missing, SinEater81 suddenly starts popping up in the threads defending Gwen every chance they got. They even *started* threads just to talk about how great Gwen was."

"Right, so a bit of a fan then," Olivia mused aloud.

"That's what I thought too," Jodie said. "And then this happens." A couple of rapid clicks later and a new set of messages appeared on the screen.

> SinEater81: If I have to watch one more plea for information about the saintly Gwen, I'm going to vom. Silly cow is probably laying low somewhere hoping this goes national so she can get more publicity for her IG.

> SinEater81: She was lying scum! Far too fond of making up stories just to ruin people's lives. I hope she got everything she deserved.

Jodie continued to click through the forum posts. Each time the user SinEater81 mentioned Gwen their anger increased.

"And then there was this," Jodie said. A moment later another set of messages appeared on the screen.

SinEater81: Maybe Gwen should have paid closer attention to her commandments. Thou shalt not bear false witness. If she had maybe her killer wouldn't have needed to dump her in the devil's punchbowl. #RIHGC

The message was followed by a picture of a laughing devil surrounded by flames.

"What does the hashtag mean?" Olivia asked, leaning closer to the screen as though that alone would provide her with the answers she sought.

"Nearest I can tell, it's an acronym for Rot In Hell and I presume the GC is Gwen Campbell."

Olivia let out a low whistle. "We need to find out who these people are. The worst offenders at least. And especially this Sin Eater. What's up with that name anyway?"

Jodie clicked on the keyboard. "From what I could find, Sin Eater's were people hired to ritually eat food that was placed on, or near a deceased person. The food would somehow absorb the sins of the dead person and when the sin eater consumed the food the deceased person was absolved of their sins. Thus, allowing them to go to heaven." Jodie arched an eyebrow at the screen. "Sounds disgusting."

"Agreed," Olivia said. "Can you print all this off--" She cut off as Jodie handed her a file of printouts.

"Already done. And I've sent the information to

you digitally, too. You know, in case you want to keep looking yourself."

"This is really great work, Jodie." Olivia was already on her way out of the office as she spoke.

This could be the opportunity she needed. Everyone was so busy. Perhaps, if she showed enough initiative, DI Haskell would allow her some time away from the desk.

As she crossed the hall, Olivia knew the chances of her boss letting her go back into the field were practically nil. But those were still better odds than she'd had yesterday and she was willing to take the chance.

CHAPTER TWENTY-THREE

SETTLING TOBY IN HIS HIGH-CHAIR, Libby paused at the kitchen island and glanced down at her phone. The temptation to log onto *Rattle* was all consuming. But the last time she'd been there... Libby shuddered at the thought and folded her arms over her chest. She wasn't going to go back there in a hurry.

Toby shoved a chunk of his crustless cheese sandwich off the edge of his tray. Bert, their one-year-old french bulldog snatched it out of the air and gobbled it down before Libby could say a word.

"Tobes, I've told you before," Libby said, moving around to the front of the high-chair so her son could see her. He was leaning over the side of his tray giggling as he watched Bert lick his slobbery chops. "No more dropping your food."

Toby straightened up to watch her as he grabbed

another chunk of the sandwich. He crushed the white bread between his chubby fingers. Margarine slid out coating his hand as he raised it to his mouth and took a nibble. After a moment sucking on the soggy bread, he thrust his little fist towards her offering her a piece of his lunch. "No thank you, sweetheart. Mummy made that sandwich for you."

Libby smiled and ruffled her sons brown hair gently. He looked so much like his father. It was uncanny. She couldn't see a hint of herself in his rosy cheeks, or his bright eyes.

Her phone dinged and Libby grabbed it from the counter.

Really enjoyed this morning. I can't wait to see you tonight.x Just receiving a message from him was enough to put a smile on her face.

She contemplated tapping out a reply and then thought better of it. He was probably already with a client and he'd lectured her in the past about distracting him while he was at work. Picking up one of the bread crusts from the plate on the counter, Libby chewed on it as she scrolled idly through Instagram.

An image caught her attention, causing the bread to catch in her throat.

RIP Gwen.

Libby's heart dropped as she scanned the comments. Each message was a variation of the same set of condolences. After all, there was only so many ways you could say how sorry you were for the death of someone.

Flipping open Google, Libby quickly typed in the name Gwen Campbell. The screen loaded and she was presented with a veritable cornucopia of news articles surrounding the discovery of human remains on the moors. It didn't take her long to find the confirmation she'd been seeking. The headline read, *Body of missing Influencer Gwen Campbell unearthed.*

Libby fell back against the kitchen counter. She hadn't been close with Gwen, but she had known her. After all, when you attended the same slimming club it made the world feel like a very small place.

For a moment, guilt pulled at her. She, like most everyone else, had assumed Gwen had done a bunk. The rumour mill had been in high gear when Gwen had disappeared. There was a story circulating that, despite being married, Gwen had been involved with another man. Not that there had been any kind of solid proof about it, but that hadn't quelled the speculation.

Unable to resist, Libby opened her bookmarked pages and watched as the familiar Rattle screen loaded. Her fingers moved with the surety of a deeply ingrained habit. There was already an active thread about Gwen. Libby hesitated for only a heartbeat before she clicked into it.

The familiar names covered the screen. While

she'd never met any of these people in reality, they spoke with the kind of conviction that only come from personal knowledge. That alone was enough to make Libby feel uncomfortable. How could they know so much?

> MardArse5108: Silly cow really thought she was better than anyone else.

> PrecociouslyPink: If I have to hear one more time about the #BeKind tag, I'm going to lose my shit. It's not as though anyone was nasty to her.

Libby wasn't entirely sure she would have agreed with that sentiment. Rattle had said plenty of nasty things about the Influencer when she was alive.

> TwizzyWhizzy47: Has anyone heard from SinEater81 recently? She's conspicuously quiet about all of this. I'd have thought she would have had a lot to say, considering her feelings about Gwen to begin with.

Several messages followed where other members expressed their shock. Libby scrolled through the messages until she found MardArse's latest entry.

MardArse5108: As for Gwen, I was sorry to hear what happened to her. But I kind of think maybe she brought it on herself. She was always posting about her and her kids.

PrecociouslyPink: You don't think she it was one of those dark web paedophile rings that killed her, do you? I mean, you read about some of the crazy things they'll do to get children to sell.

CharCharBinks: OMG, I read an article that said they take the children to a forest in Germany and chase them so they can drink their blood. It keeps them young or something...

PrecociouslyPink: I read that too! Hilary Clinton is their leader.

CharCharBinks: No, she's too old. It's Taylor Swift.

Libby scrolled down the page, but the conversation had devolved into a witch hunt about which celebrity drank the blood of children in order to stay young. It wasn't until she reached the last page that the message board returned to the topic of Gwen.

TwizzyWhizzy47: They've just said on the news that there was another set of remains found with Gwen's. You don't think it was Evie, do you?

Libby's heart dropped. Who would do such a thing? Gwen had brought her to group once or twice. She had been such a happy little girl...

Tears threatened to blur Libby's eyes. She glanced up at the little boy sitting in his high-chair. Oblivious to the cruelty of the world, he continued to drop pieces of his sandwich on the floor.

Setting her phone on the kitchen counter, Libby moved back to her son. Ignoring the margarine and bread squished in his chubby fists, she scooped him up and held him close. Drinking in the smell of baby powder and the soft warmth that babies shared, she sent up a silent prayer that the members of *Rattle* were wrong.

But Libby wasn't that naive.

CHAPTER TWENTY-FOUR

"GUV."

Drew knew from Maz's voice that whatever he was about to say would not make him happy. Raising his face, he met Maz's gaze head on. "What have you got?"

Maz pulled a face and paused next to the desk. "It's not good news."

"Well, spit it out. No use in keeping me in suspense." Drew could hear the nasally quality to his voice and he hated it. He sneezed and Maz looked at him in surprise. It seemed it had not been the dust after all.

"You all right, guv?"

Drew nodded. "Fine. Just a bit of a cold." The pain in his head wasn't exactly making him feel in tip-top shape but there was nothing he could do about it. "Go on, hit me with the bad news."

"The phone is a dead end."

Drew felt his already fragile patience fray further. "What do you mean it's a dead end?"

Maz looked down at the file clutched in his hands. "There's nothing they can do with it. The whole thing is corrupted. The simcard is useless. And the phone memory..."

"Go on," Drew urged.

"Well, someone wiped it. They think maybe Simon did it, or..."

"Or Declan Campbell knew about his son's secret and wiped the video himself," Drew finished the thought for his sergeant. With a sigh, he dropped back in his chair and ran his hand through his hair. It was getting too long to be comfortable. But there simply wasn't time to visit a barber... At least that was how Drew consoled himself. It had nothing to do with the fact that he hated having to get his hair cut.

"Ms Meakin has one last thing to try but to be honest, guv, she's not sounding too hopeful."

"If we have nothing we can't hold him."

"We could try talking to him again." Maz shifted nervously from one foot to the other.

Drew shook his head. "What for? It's not not as though the last time went well." They'd spent more than two hours sitting with Declan and his solicitor, each question receiving the same answer of, 'no comment'. Going back in there again with nothing would amount to *Groundhog Day*. Declan's solicitor had known from the off that they had nothing. He could already imagine the smug expression of the man if they returned to the same line of questioning with nothing new to show for the time that had passed.

"Shit," Drew swore, causing Maz to jump.

"Haskell!" The monk's gruff command caused the attention of the others in the squad room to glance up from their work.

"Guv, I'm sorry. I can..."

Drew cut his sergeant off with a shake of his head. "You've done your bit," he said.

Crossing the floor, Drew tried to gather his thoughts. He'd screwed up. Going to Campbell's house had been impulsive. He'd known it at the time, but there was something about seeing the final resting place of Gwen and her daughter that had caused something to snap inside Drew. He was tired of always being too late. For once, he wanted to get ahead of a situation. It wasn't going to bring back Gwen or her baby, but it would still give him a small sliver of satisfaction.

Slouching into the monk's office, he shut the door behind him. The monk sat behind his desk, his attention fixed on Drew's face. He could tell from the set of the other man's shoulders and the tic that had started in his right eye that DCI Gregson was anything but pleased with his work.

"What the fuck were you thinking?" Gregson

barely waited for Drew to settle into the seat opposite before he launched into his attack. "Dragging Campbell in here when we have nothing. Have you lost your mind?"

"It wasn't my intention to bring him in," Drew said. "It's not as though I had a choice."

"Of course you had a choice! There's always a choice." Gregson scrubbed his hands over his face as he leaned back in his leather chair. He sat like that for a moment, his attention fixed on the ceiling above his head. "Please tell me we have something. Anything."

Drew stared down at his hands clasped loosely in his lap. "So far, sir, we have nothing."

Gregson blew out a harsh breath and returned his attention to Drew's face. "What do you think of Campbell? Do you think he's good for this?"

Drew wanted to say yes. He wanted to be certain, but he'd spent the night going through the tissue paper thin evidence against Campbell that had been gathered back in 2016. A good solicitor would rip it apart before the ink had even dried. And Campbell's solicitor was one of the good ones.

"I'm not so sure," Drew said quietly. He waited for the inevitable explosion, but it never came.

"This just keeps getting better and better..." Gregson muttered.

A knock on the door behind Drew pulled both of their attention.

"Come," Gregson said, his voice thick with anger.

Olivia poked her head around the door. "Sir..." She paused and looked between the two men. "There's a Beth Smith here. She says it's important."

"What does she want?" Gregson asked.

Olivia looked nervous. "She wouldn't say. Just that she wanted to speak with DI Haskell."

The monk sighed. "Well, you better go and find out."

Drew got to his feet, but Gregson stopped him before he could leave. "If we've got nothing to hold Campbell then you know you'll have to cut him loose."

Drew nodded. "I know."

"Then you better be certain that he's not responsible for this, Haskell. I'm telling you now, if you let him go and later you discover you made a mistake the press will hang, draw, and quarter this team in the court of public opinion. And that's not something we can afford to have happen."

"I understand, sir."

Gregson studied him for a moment longer, before he gave a quick jerk of his chin towards the door. "Go. See what she has to say for herself."

Drew didn't need to be told twice. Escaping the office, he took a moment to gather himself, before he crossed the floor and made his way to the stairs. Olivia caught up to him as he reached the stairwell.

"I put her in Interview One," she said. "It's the quietest place in here right now."

"Why's that?"

"The press have been camped outside since they released the statement about the identity of the remains."

"Camped outside? Here?" Drew couldn't keep the surprise from his voice.

"Well, yeah. They found out you'd brought Declan Campbell in and now they're all waiting for a statement from the force."

"Shit," Drew swore beneath his breath. This was the last thing they needed. Not that he was wholly unsurprised. Gwen Campbell had been a bit of a local celebrity. And her decision to run for a place on the council had created a stir.

"This is not going to end well," Drew said more to himself than Olivia.

"Guv, you had to bring him in. If you hadn't then people would have questioned the police's actions."

"I know," Drew sighed. "Right, we'll see what Ms Smith has to say for herself and then we'll reassess."

STEPPING INTO THE ROOM, Drew noted the nervous manner in which Beth straightened up. She let her hand drop away from her lips, the evidence of her emotions obvious in the ragged state of her manicure.

"Where's Declan? Can I see him?" Beth's rapid fire questions didn't surprise Drew. How many times had he encountered something similar?

"Mr Campbell is helping us with our enquiries," Drew said, as he grabbed a chair and dragged it around the side of the table. He set it down at an angle, allowing him to sit with Beth without making her think she was being interrogated.

She snorted derisively and returned her hand to her mouth to chew at her nails. "We both know that's not true. You think he killed Gwen, don't you?"

Drew smiled thinly. "I can't discuss the particulars of the case with you, Ms Smith. Is there something I can do for you?"

"Yes," she said. "You can release Declan. He didn't hurt her. He would never hurt anyone."

"You seem very sure of that," Drew said.

"Of course I'm sure," she said, her voice becoming a little shrill. "We're having a baby together. I know him. He's a good man. He would never hurt anyone." Tears glittered in her eyes and she swiped them away unconsciously. "I can't even get him to kill spiders. He insists on releasing them into the garden."

Drew nodded and tried to keep his expression suitably sympathetic. "We have to follow every lead, Beth."

"If you mean Simon..." She shook her head and glanced down at her hands. "I don't mean to sound cruel, but the boy is troubled."

Drew bit his tongue. What did she expect? The boy's mother was dead, murdered, possibly by his own father. If that wasn't a recipe for dysfunction.

"You think I'm an insensitive idiot, don't you?"

"Nobody thinks that."

She sighed. "I can see it in your eyes. I'm the wicked step-mother in this story, DI Haskell. I know how the story plays out. But I'm telling you now, it's not true. I love that boy. I have for a very long time, but that doesn't change the fact that he's troubled."

"Any and all information you can offer us, Beth, will help us to get this matter cleared up as quickly as possible."

She nodded and swallowed hard. "You know about the phone."

Drew stilled. They hadn't mentioned the phones existence to anyone. Declan knew of it, a fact Drew regretted. His solicitor had been quick to jump on it, demanding to know what information they had. The fact they hadn't been able to recover anything from it, yet, didn't sit comfortably with Drew. It made things far more complicated than they should have been.

"You seem surprised that I know about it," Beth said. She studied him from beneath her lashes.

"What exactly do you know?"

She glanced down at her hands. "There's nothing on the phone," she said softly.

"Simon seems to think there is."

She swallowed hard. "Well, he would. He thought he had it hidden."

"But you knew where it was?" Drew prompted.

"We all knew where the phone was. Declan let him keep it... I told him he should insist on Simon throwing it away, but he thought it would be better to let him keep it."

"Beth, what do you know about the evidence on the phone?" There was a hard edge to Drew's voice and it caught her attention.

"I didn't do anything to phone if that's what you're thinking," she said quickly. "But I knew there was nothing on it." She looked away.

"How did you know that?"

"Because Simon had a fight with his dad about six months ago. He threatened Declan. Said he had proof that Declan knew what happened to his 'real' mum." She clenched her hands together until the knuckles whitened beneath the pressure of her grip. "So, Declan demanded to see the proof. Simon was so proud when he produced the phone. He really believed he had something." There was a bitterness to her voice. "He showed us the video, but there was nothing on it."

Drew shifted in his chair. "What do you mean there was nothing there?"

"He recorded an argument between Declan and Gwen, but it was nothing really. The audio was really poor and the video itself was so grainy, I could barely make out the person arguing with Gwen. And before it ends, Gwen leaves."

"You just said the audio and video quality was poor, how can you be so certain Mrs Campbell left?"

Beth leaned her elbows on the table. "Because Simon went to the garage after her. And you can see the car drive away, DI Haskell. The video ends with Simon sobbing."

"And you're certain it's Gwen who gets in the car and drives off?"

Beth hesitated. "Well, who else would it be?"

"So that's a no, then?"

Beth glared at him. "She got in the car and drove off, DI Haskell. I'm not sure what else you want me to say."

Drew leaned back in the chair. There was no way to know if Beth was telling the truth unless they somehow managed to recover the video. And as time passed, that prospect kept getting smaller and smaller.

"And how sure are you about this?"

Beth's expression soured. "I know what I saw, DI Haskell."

Drew sighed and climbed to his feet. "We're going to need a statement saying everything you just told me."

"And then can Declan come home?"

"Mr Campbell will be released as soon as we're satisfied."

As Drew left, Beth's voice followed him into the hall. "He didn't hurt her, DI Haskell. He wouldn't do that."

Olivia followed him into the hall. "Get a uniform to take a statement from her regarding the video."

"Do you think she's telling the truth?"

Drew ran his hand down over his face. "Only one way we can know for certain."

"And if we can't recover the video?"

"Then we've got nothing to hold him on and we let him go."

"But, guv, everyone thinks he did it."

Clenching his fists, Drew dropped his chin towards the floor. "None of that matters, DC Crandell. We work the evidence, no matter where it leads."

He left, his long stride carrying him away from the interview room and the rapidly growing mess the case was creating.

CHAPTER TWENTY-FIVE

SITTING AT HER DESK, Harriet tried to concentrate on the task in front of her. But the more she tried to focus on the words of the case study, the more her brain wandered.

What had Misha been thinking? Walking in to find a student curled up, feigning sleep, well, it certainly wasn't considered normal. But Misha was a relatively easy problem to deal with. Jonathan, on the other hand, was a more complicated animal.

The phone call had left Harriet feeling shaken. She didn't want to admit it to anyone else. There was a part of her that felt ashamed over the situation that had spiralled out of control. If she had just seen the truth of Jonathan's personality sooner, then maybe this could all have been averted.

But she hadn't. And Harriet knew he was a persistent man. He'd meant it when he'd promised to ruin her life. But what could a disgraced psychiatrist do?

Probably quite a lot, Harriet thought. It wasn't a comforting realisation to come to. She would keep away from him. That wasn't exactly difficult. Especially now that he'd been dismissed. Of course he would still have friends at the hospital where her mother was held and that would be awkward.

No, once he sobered up and his temper cooled, he would lose interest in her. She was certain of it. In the meantime, she would ensure that she remained busy enough to avoid him at all costs. She wouldn't be the naive fool she had once been.

Of course, that also meant taking the proverbial bull by the horns where Misha was concerned too. Climbing to her feet, Harriet crossed to the door that led to the reception area.

Martha glanced up at her over the rim of her tortoiseshell glasses.

"Any chance Dr Baig has got back to you with a suitable time for an appointment?"

Martha pursed her lips and then returned her attention to the computer screen. She shook her head as her gaze travelled down over the email list. "Nothing yet, although..."

Harriet waited as Martha continued her silent appraisal. When she lifted her face, a sly smile had slid over her lips. "He's free currently."

Harriet raised an eyebrow at the other woman.

"Do I want to know how you could possibly have that piece of information?"

Martha's smile turned into a grin that changed her appearance entirely. Her smile lit her eyes, smoothing the permanent frown lines that sat between her eyebrows, lending her an overall younger air. "I have my ways," she said secretively.

She glanced over at the wall clock and her grin faded around the edges. "Although, if you don't hurry and leave now, you'll miss your chance for the day entirely."

Harriet didn't hesitate. Swinging back into her office, she snatched her bag and coat. Sliding the coat on as she passed Martha in the reception area, she paused.

"You don't think I was too harsh on Misha, do you?"

"I wouldn't—"

Harriet cut her off before she could deny knowing anything about the situation. "We both know you hear everything that's said in my office. And I appreciate you looking out for me." It wasn't a lie, she did appreciate it. Martha was one of her harshest critics, but over time something had changed between them.

If Martha was surprised by her admission, she never let it show. Instead, she paused and mulled the previous question over before responding. "No. You weren't harsh at all. There's something not quite right with that girl."

Martha's answer caught Harriet off guard. "What do you mean?"

Martha shrugged. "I know she had a troubled past but there's something else." Despite her pause, Harriet knew there was something the other woman wasn't saying. Martha stared down at her hands as they rested on the edge of the desk. If Harriet could have reached into the other woman's head and plucked out the truth it would have been easier than waiting in silence.

"You don't have to worry, Martha, anything you say will remain here."

Martha glanced over at her. "She's trouble," she said finally. "You always look for the best in others, Dr Quinn, and I think that makes you vulnerable to someone like her."

Harriet bit her tongue, suddenly unsure of an appropriate response. She'd known there was something about Misha that made her uneasy, but she'd dismissed it as nothing more than feeling overwhelmed because of past events. But what if that wasn't the real reason for her feeling so out of her depth?

"Thank you, Martha," Harriet said. "I'll consider what you've said."

Martha shrugged dismissively. "Do what you like," she said. The edge was back and Harriet realised that without intending to, she had managed to insult the other woman again.

With a sigh, she headed for the door. She paused, with her hand on the handle and glanced back at the older woman working at her desk. "I appreciate your candour," Harriet said. She paused, trying to choose her words carefully. "I really mean that. I don't take your words lightly. You've given me something to chew on. Thank you."

Martha looked up from her work. Her expression was closed, but there was colour in her cheeks and she wasn't glaring anymore, so Harriet took it all as a positive sign. She left quickly before she said anything else that could be misconstrued by the other woman.

TEN MINUTES LATER, Harriet stood outside Dr Baig's office. His assistant had given her a secretive smile, letting Harriet know just how Martha was so knowledgeable about the department head's movements.

She knocked, and a moment later was granted entry. Closing the door softly behind her, Harriet was surprised by Dr Baig's decor.

The walls were lined with stark white book-shelves. She'd expected a more classic choice from the department head, something more in keeping with the university's history. Instead of dark wood panelling and equally dark bookshelves, his office was light and airy, and altogether modern in its appointment.

The walls were a warm white. Drew, if he were here, would have made some kind of remark about the beige walls being an extension of *Dr Beige's* personality. Suppressing the inappropriate thought before she gave her amusement away, Harriet returned her attention the room. A few sparse splashes of colour prevented the room from looking too clinical. But even they were limited.

The shelves, unlike her own congested bookcases, were sparse and minimalist to the extreme. As she studied the few items that made up the display nearest to her, Harriet wondered how Dr Baig ever got any work done without having his reference material close to hand.

"Harriet, so lovely to see you," Dr Baig's greeting cut through her own thoughts as he exited a small side room off his main office. He was wearing a heavy camel coloured coat that cut him off at the knees. To her mind, it made him look like a small boy who had raided his father's closet. "To what do I owe this unexpected pleasure?"

Even as he spoke, he wrapped a scarf around his neck, leaving her in no doubt as to his true intention.

"I wanted to have a quick word about one of my students." Harriet gave him what she hoped was a warm smile.

"Oh?" Dr Baig, moved to his desk. "Perhaps, we could discuss them another day. I'm sure Kathy would be happy to pencil you in for a chat, maybe later this week?"

Harriet had already started to shake her head before he'd even finished speaking. "I'm afraid that won't do. This is not something that can wait, Dennis."

He seemed taken aback by her use of his first name, but he recovered quickly. With a wave of his hand he directed her to an uncomfortable cream leather chair opposite his white desk.

Harriet sat and waited as he settled himself. There was a frown line between his brows that hadn't been there a moment before as he clicked through the screens on his computer.

"I don't see anything here to make me think there's an urgent discussion we need to have." He glanced up at her. "Has something happened?" The accusation was implicit and Harriet stiffened.

Clutching her hands together, she dug her short nails into the palm of her hand in an attempt to settle her anger. "That's why I'm here. In light of our conversation at Christmas, I would like to request that Misha Collins be assigned to a different supervisor."

Dr Baig dropped back in his seat as though her words had physically impacted on him. "And why would you want that?"

"Because it's my opinion that Ms Collins had developed an unhealthy attachment towards me."

The colour slowly drained from Dr Baig's face. "What did you do to encourage her?"

Harriet stilled. Shock settled over her as his words sank in. "Excuse me?"

"You and I both know unhealthy attachments don't just form out of thin air."

"They do when one of the people involved has a troubled background." Harriet tried to catch herself before she allowed her anger to overcome her. "Dr Baig, what you fail to realise is, I used to be acquainted with Misha's mother."

Dr Baig had laid his hands flat on the desk. "I was aware."

"Then you must be aware of the circumstances surrounding the situation. Misha believes I can shed light on her mother's character. She asked to meet last night in the student bar. I went, thinking we would be discussing her research, as she'd led me to believe would be the case. But..." Harriet blew out a breath. "When I got there, she made it plain that wasn't what she wanted to discuss."

"Harriet, what you do during your own time is your own business. And I think I've been more than fair when your outside interests have clashed with your commitments to the university."

"I'm not sure what my working with the police has to do with this situation. I'm asking you to

207

transfer Ms Collins to another supervisor because I think professional distance is necessary for her benefit. I wouldn't want to see her throw her prospects away for something I can not give her."

Dr Baig sat back in his chair and steepled his hands in front of his body. "I hear you, Harriet, really I do. But you must know, I can't just swap students around willy-nilly because you find it difficult to separate your personal and professional life."

Sagging back in the chair, Harriet stared at the man opposite her. "That's not what's happening here."

Dr Baig pulled a face that said he was unconvinced by her. "That's not how it looks to me." He leaned forward. "Look, I can see if anyone has any room to take on another student. I can't guarantee they will, but I can ask. However, I think, for your sake, it would be prudent to find a way to work with Ms Collins."

"Dennis, considering our discussion at Christmas, I thought it would be wise to come to you first--"

"And I appreciate that, I really do. But I really don't think you have anything to worry about. It sounds to me like Ms Collins is just a young woman who is reaching out to you. Think about it, Harriet, if you turn her away, how is that going to make you feel?"

"Look, I've asked you to find another supervisor

for her. And I've made my feelings on the matter known."

Dennis nodded. "I understand." He sighed. "I'll see what I can do. And in the meantime, will you continue to work with Ms Collins?"

Harriet's smile was thin. "If you're asking me whether I'll do my job or not, then you should already know the answer to that."

"Of course I do," Dennis said, pushing to his feet. "I was merely confirming..." He glanced towards his watch. "If there's not anything else, Dr Quinn, I really should go."

Going to the door, Dr Baig trailed her. "I really do appreciate you coming to me about this, Harriet," he said as she stepped into the reception area. "I'll see what we can do to get this situation settled as swiftly as possible."

"Thank you." Harriet tried to school her features into a neutral expression. Dr Baig smiled indulgently at her, as though she were a small child who had done something vaguely interesting.

He hurried out of the office without a backwards glance, leaving Harriet to feel as though she had been 'managed'. It wasn't something that sat well with her. Not that there was anything she could really do about it. Only time would tell if Dennis actually had listened to her at all.

And what if he hadn't? What then? Harriet shook herself free of the dark turn her thoughts were intent on taking. Misha was a troubled student. But Harriet was aware of the situation now and she had done the right thing by informing her superior.

Everything would be fine. So if that were true, why did she feel that coming here had set a chain of events in motion. Events that only time would show if they were for good, or ill.

Unsettled, Harriet decided to focus on something else and Drew's case was the perfect distraction. Throwing herself into her work in the past had always helped settle her. This would be no different.

CHAPTER TWENTY-SIX

STEPPING INTO THE INTERVIEW ROOM, Drew felt unsettled. It wasn't normally like this when he interviewed suspects. He'd watched the earlier conversation with Declan, replayed the tape in the hopes that he'd find some kind of chink in the man's armour, but there was nothing. Well, nothing Drew could use, anyway, and that frustrated him more than he could show.

When Gwen had disappeared, the officers who had investigated had been convinced of Declan's guilt. They had conveyed that to everyone else on the Force and it had created an atmosphere of certainty. When he'd taken up the case, Drew had been sure Declan was his man. And now...

Blowing out his cheeks, he turned to face the man sitting at the desk with his head in his hands.

"We've been over this, DI Haskell," Roger Blackwell, Declan Campbell's solicitor said. The fact that Declan could afford to hire a shark like Blackwell spoke volumes about the change in his standard of living. When Gwen had been alive they had mostly lived off the money she had made from her work as an influencer. But she wasn't raking in the kind of cash that some of the larger internet celebrities could command. "My client has nothing else to say."

"There are a few things I'd like your client to clear up for me," Drew said addressing the solicitor before he turned his attention to Declan. "Can I get you something to drink before we start, Mr Campbell?"

Declan shook his head, but kept his gaze fixed on the table top.

"That was quite the situation this morning. Your son is a spirited lad," Drew said amiably.

"Where is Simon?"

"Your son is being looked after," Drew said, keeping his voice light. "You don't need to worry about him. He's in safe hands."

There was a bleakness to Declan's eyes. A misery that words couldn't convey. "Why would he say those things? How could he believe I would hurt his mum?"

"Declan," Blackwell's warning was clear. Not that Declan seemed to hear him.

"I just don't know who would put something like that in his head." He glanced at his solicitor.

"Mr Campbell, we discussed this," Blackwell said smartly. "You've got nothing to say on the matter."

Declan shook his head. "I wold never hurt his mum," he said. "Why would he say otherwise?"

"Your son is hurting," Drew said carefully. Despite trying to tread lightly he received a warning look from the solicitor. "We had a look at your finances."

Declan's head snapped up. "Why would you do that?" He turned to his solicitor. "Why would they do that? What does that have to do with anything?"

"We spoke about this," Blackwell said placatingly. "It's just normal procedure, nothing to be concerned about."

"But they have no right..."

"Actually, we have every right," Drew said softly. "Before Gwen went missing, your business wasn't doing too well."

Declan shrugged. "So? It was a new venture. It was hard to get it off the ground."

"You were behind on your payments," Drew said. "And then magically you weren't."

"Is there a point in all of this, DI Haskell?" Blackwell's tone was one that brooked no argument. Drew had a feeling that he was a man used to getting his own way quite a bit.

"Well, I'd like to have a chat with Declan about what happened."

Blackwell shook his head. "My client has been

through enough. This is nothing more than a fishing expedition and we both know it. You should charge my client or release him. But holding onto a grieving man when you have nothing to detain him with is unnecessarily cruel."

"I'm doing my job," Drew said. "I'm sure Declan would agree that he'd like me to do everything in my power to find out what happened to his wife."

"My client had nothing to do with his wife's death. We all know it."

Drew returned his attention to the broken man in front of him. "Mr Campbell, is there a reason your son would make the kinds of accusations he has?"

Declan stared blankly ahead. "I don't know why he'd do this. He knows how much I love him." He turned his gaze on Drew. "I've never given him any reason to make him think I would hurt Gwen, or Evie--" Declan's voice broke over the mention of his daughter's name.

Nodding stiffly, Drew pushed onto his feet.

"Are you going to release my client?" Blackwell asked.

"I'll get back to you," Drew said stiffly.

CHAPTER TWENTY-SEVEN

DRUMMING her fingers against her leg, Joan studied Nigel from the corner of her eye. He sat in his chair, head thrown back, mouth partially open. The soft snores he emitted could be heard above the soft murmurings from the television. His half-empty glass of white wine sat on the table next to him.

Lifting her laptop onto her lap, Joan tried to concentrate on writing a sentence. Just one. That was all she needed to get started.

But every time she tried to catch the words, her brain conjured other images. Violent images. Blood and terror. Rain on skin. The cold shock of mud on her hands as she tried to regain her balance. She'd barely begun to write her story, so why had her mind chosen to throw such a jumble of scary images together?

Joan had always wanted to write. Difficulties

when she'd been young had very nearly made that dream an impossibility. But she'd fought through her problems and come out the other side stronger. Not that Nigel seemed to believe she was stronger.

She glanced over at him as a news report about Gwen came on the television. The reporter droned on about the dump site and a video of the moors appeared on the screen. Sweat dampened Joan's palms as she watched.

She swallowed hard, glanced down at the computer screen, and was surprised to discover she'd been busy typing with her eyes closed. Some of the words were badly misspelled; a product of her inability to touch type properly. She'd tried to learn in the past. Nigel had told her it would help speed up her writing but no matter how hard she tried to learn the technique, her brain and fingers refused to cooperate correctly.

Instead, when she was writing she preferred her method of hen pecking at the keys with just her two index fingers. It might not result in a speedy draft, but at least the manuscript wasn't littered with errors.

Unlike the mess she was now faced with. Grumbling to herself, Joan tried to make sense of the words.

A dark road at night. Rain drumming against the windscreen as the car pulls into a parking spot. Taking the keys from the ignition. The engine falling silent. The rain suddenly loud, thrumming against the roof. And something else... A moan.

Turning in the seat, the driver glances towards the boot of the car. Another soft cry.

Joan stared at the words, surprised by what she had written. It made no sense. It didn't fit with her outline at all.

Her head snapped up as Nigel snorted and shifted in his chair. Setting her laptop back on the couch, Joan rubbed her palms against her soft tracksuit bottoms. The news report had moved on from Gwen. She was grateful for small mercies. Evidently, the discovery of Gwen's body was messing with her head.

Nigel had fallen silent and she glanced in his direction. His eyes were still shut. But was that a small gap in his short stubby lashes? Was he watching her?

"Fancy a cup of tea?" Her voice was filled with forced cheerfulness.

Nigel jerked awake and glanced blearily at her. It took him a moment to focus on her face, but when he did, he sat up a little straighter.

"What is it? What's wrong?"

Joan started to shake her head, but Nigel's pursed lips stopped her. She knew that expression. His ability to read her like a book left her feeling uneasy. If she lied to him now, he would know, wouldn't he?

He shuffled to the front of his seat. His eyes narrowed as he studied her. "Joan?"

"It's just..." She gestured helplessly towards the television screen. She deliberately kept her attention away from her book. Having somebody read the text before she was ready felt like a violation. Not that Nigel had ever taken notice of her boundaries. More than once she had caught him reading her work before she was ready to show it to the world.

"What?" He snapped, glancing over in time to see the news flip over to a discussion about an upcoming football match.

"They were talking about Gwen," she said quietly, glancing down at her hands. Her nails were chipped and ragged.

"Ah..." Nigel's voice had lost its censure. Surprised, Joan tilted her head up to look at him.

He met her gaze and smiled sadly. The first real show of emotion since the news had broken about the discovery of Gwen's remains.

"Did you want a cup of tea?" Joan asked.

Nigel climbed to his feet and stretched. "I'll make it. You stay here." His gaze shifted over to the laptop next to her. "You keep on working."

Surprised by his sudden shift, Joan sat back among the sofa cushions. He was being unusually nice. She picked up the computer and sat it on her lap. It was better to do as Nigel asked. That way he couldn't find fault in her. But the laptop was quickly forgotten, so caught up was she in her own thoughts.

The pain in her abdomen still nagged at her but she did her best to ignore it. She'd suggested to Nigel that perhaps a trip to the doctor was in order but he'd just dismissed the idea.

She listened to the sounds of Nigel moving about in the room next door. Ordinary noises that others might never take any notice of. But it put Joan on edge. She was not used to him being kind. And the fact that his kindness had come on the heels of her admission over watching a news piece on Gwen... that had been most surprising of all.

Why was she working so hard to poke holes in Nigel's behaviour? Just because it was unusual, did not mean she should question it. Perhaps this was a new leaf he was turning over? Perhaps, like her, he was tired of the constant arguments that created a miasma of misery that permeated every inch of their house. Poisoning them both as they went about their daily lives.

Yes, he wasn't the man she'd fallen in love with, the man she had married. But that did not mean he could not change, that he could not grow. As she was.

Joan thought about the pills she had washed down the sink that morning. When she'd done it the first time, guilt had wormed its way beneath her skin. She was after all, lying to Nigel. And he wanted what was best for her, didn't he? But the more she got rid of the tablets, the better she was beginning to feel. Her mind was clearer, and... Joan looked down at what she had written on the computer earlier. Concern nipped at her, but she quickly pushed it aside.

The *buzz buzz* of Nigel's phone as it rang on the table next to his chair pulled her attention. Getting to her feet, Joan crossed the floor and stared down at the name pulsing on the screen.

Libby.

Who was Libby and why was she calling at this time of night? Joan contemplated answering the call. A memory tried to break through the surface of her mind. This wasn't the first time a strange woman had called so late in the evening.

Gwen. When she closed her eyes, Joan could see Gwen's name flashing on the screen. The memory was gone as quickly as it had arrived. Hearing the noise in the kitchen stop, Joan moved back to her seat and sat down.

Had Gwen called Nigel in the past? Was that what she was remembering? Joan glanced over at the dark laptop. Where the two things somehow connected?

She shook her head. That was nothing more than her overactive imagination swinging back into over-drive. And she needed it, now more than ever.

Nigel carried a steaming mug in the sitting room. Setting it down next to her, he smiled and produced two small biscuits from behind his back. "I thought you might fancy something sweet to keep your blood sugar up while you work," he said.

Stunned by his turnaround, Joan took the offered biscuits. "Thank you, Nige..." She held the biscuits in her hands and stared down at them. Her gaze wandered over to his phone which had since fallen silent. The sensation of wanting to cry overcame her, but she knew there would be nothing there. The medication made her eyes too dry and she hadn't been off them long enough to feel any of the physical positive benefits she expected.

Nigel caught her eye. "Something the matter?"

Joan shook her head and tried to summon a smile. "Thanks love. This is, this is really lovely."

"Well, you've been really trying lately," he said. "I think maybe you've even lost a couple of pounds. The rolls when you sit are getting smaller." His smile was beatific as he pointed to her midriff. "Like I always say, how do you eat an elephant, Joan? One bite at a time. Or in your case, less bites." He chuckled to himself.

It took her a moment to catch his meaning. And when she did, Joan looked down at her stomach. Was he right? Was she starting to lose weight? If she was, it was only because she'd stopped the meds, she thought. Setting her second biscuit on the edge of her chair, she nibbled delicately at the first.

"Nigel, who is Libby?"

He stared at her for a moment. A hardness settled over his features.

"Has somebody been snooping again?"

"No!" Joan shook her head. "It's just your phone..."

Nigel glanced in the direction of his chair and his expression shifted to one of irritation. "It's nothing, love. Just one of my clients. You know how they can get sometimes. They're all so needy."

Joan smiled and stared down at her biscuit. Nigel continued to watch her and she nervously nibbled at the edge of the biscuit.

"Go on then," he said. "Try the tea. I know how fussy you are."

Nervously, Joan picked up the cup. She studied the liquid as it sloshed against the sides. If she spilled...

Nigel made encouraging noises as she lifted the mug to her lips and took a tentative sip. The tea scalded the inside of her mouth. Joan winced. She started to set it back down, but he cleared his throat and caught her eye.

"Is there something wrong with it?" There was a sharpness to his tone that hadn't been there a moment ago. Nigel sat down and grabbed the tv guide.

"No, love, it's perfect. Thank you." She hesitated, her fingers tightening around the handle. The shake in her hands now had nothing to do with the medication she took.

Nigel shook his head and returned his attention to the tv guide in his lap. "You try to do something nice. But some people... There's just no pleasing them."

Despite the show he made of staring at his magazine, she could still feel his attention fixed on her. It pressed against her, an oppressive force that threatened to bury her beneath its weight.

Fixing a smile on her face she took a larger mouthful and swallowed the pain of drinking something much too hot. Nigel lifted his head and studied her. A broad smile spread over his face as he watched her drink the tea. If he knew of her discomfort, he never let it show.

"That's my good girl."

Hearing his praise, Joan swallowed more of the burning liquid and ignored the pain that spread down through her throat into her chest. Beneath the scalding heat, there was a bitterness to the tea. She wanted to ask Nigel if he'd used a different tea bag, but knew that if she did he would assume she was questioning him. And that was not worth the argument that would ensue. And anyway, Joan already knew there was only one type of teabag in the cupboard. They were probably just off...

As she finished the last of the drink, the tremors in her hands were so bad she nearly dropped the cup as she set it back on the small table next to the couch. Settling back against the couch cushions, she ran her tongue over the small water blisters that had risen inside her lips.

Surprisingly the pain she'd initially felt had faded and was now just a vague nuisance that tugged at her.

"You get some work done," Nigel said.

He pushed onto his feet and headed for the kitchen. Joan tried to ask him where he was off to, but he was already out the door before she could form the words. Her eyelids felt heavy as she stared down at the computer screen. The cursor blinked repeatedly, mesmerising her as she stared at it.

The cushions sucked her down. Gone was the soft comfort. It was replaced by a strange feeling of being held in place. Held down.

Time slowed to a crawl as she stared at the glaringly white screen. She sank further and further into the sofa cushions. Somewhere in her mind, Joan wondered if she kept going would she eventually be swallowed whole?

By the time the laptop slipped from her grasp and hit the floor at her feet, Joan was too far gone to notice, or even care.

CHAPTER TWENTY-EIGHT

HARRIET SAT behind the steering wheel and stared out at the moors stretching out before her. It was beautiful. Not even the white forensics tent and police vehicles could completely mar the scenic view. Climbing from her car, she pulled her coat more tightly around her body.

The wind tugged at her playfully. It whipped through her hair, tugging curly strands free from the clip she'd used to wrestle it into some semblance of order that morning. Moving around to the boot of the car, Harriet flipped it open and pulled out a pair of walking boots. Experience of working with Drew had taught her that when you attended a crime scene, a sensible pair of shoes was a necessity. Well, especially if you did not want to end up on your arse in the muck.

Considering the muddy puddles that littered the ground in the car park, Harriet had a feeling the moors would not be forgiving of anyone who came unprepared. Sliding her feet into the boots, an image of Bianca flooded through her mind. She could already imagine the grin her friend would have worn if she could see her now.

Closing her eyes to try and push the grief aside -- at least until she had a moment when she could address it properly-- Harriet focused on the feel of the cold metal from the Mini's body beneath her fingers. The wind pulled at her, stinging her cheeks and bringing tears that had nothing to do with the pain of her loss, to her eyes.

Drawing a steady breath into her lungs, she bent down to secure the laces on her boots. Thinking of Bianca had reminded her that she was overdue a visit to Tilly. She would have to make a concerted effort to check in on the little girl. Harriet had not been much older than Tilly was now when her life had collapsed around her ears. While her experience was not exactly the same, she better than others, could understand the emotions the little girl would undoubtedly be experiencing. And she owed it to Bianca to keep an eye on Tilly.

Bianca had been there for her when she'd needed someone. The very least she could do was offer some comfort to her daughter.

Straightening up, Harriet chucked her shoes into the boot and slammed it shut. She gave herself a moment to settle her composure before she headed for the main road.

It took her a moment to cross. Despite the police presence, many motorists still felt it necessary to practically come to a stop in order to get a good look at the events unfolding. Their rubbernecking created a small traffic jam that wound through the moors like a steel snake.

Just how many of them had made an unnecessary journey past this spot just so they could catch a glimpse of the scene? Harriet wasn't sure, but she did know human nature. The moment people would have heard on the radio about the situation, it would have drawn some of them out onto the moors. And for some it would act as proof that their lives were not so terrible after all.

Despite the progress in technology and infrastructure, humans were still quite primitive in their behaviour. In medieval times you attended the market square to watch a hanging, or worse. A morbid day trip for those seeking entertainment to cure them of their boredom. After all, your own ills paled by comparison, both literally and figuratively, to those whose necks were planted squarely on the chopping block.

Nowadays, you did not have to leave the comfort

of your home in order to get your fix of degrading or macabre entertainment. You only had to look to your smart phone, or television for a smorgasbord of human misery and excess, trotted out in easy to consume videos and reality television.

The moment she found a break in the cars, Harriet took her opportunity and darted over the road. Pausing on the gravel that lined the roadway, she studied her surroundings. Despite the traffic, the area was relatively quiet. She would have to ask Drew or one of the other team members about the level of traffic the area suffered from under normal circumstances.

As far as her surroundings were concerned, the moors were a perfect place to stash a body. It wasn't the first time a killer had chosen the exposed and abandoned area of natural beauty to conceal a crime. The public were only too familiar with the heartfelt pleas from a mother whose child was still lost to the lonely landscape. An innocent victim, one of many, who had fallen prey to a vicious pair of predators.

But this particular spot, Harriet noted, was close to the road. She studied the path that wound further into the moorland. A well worn path, testament to the number of visitors who made the pilgrimage.

Thrusting her hands deeper into her pockets, Harriet huddled in her coat and wished she had brought with her a pair of warm gloves.

"Excuse me, Ms, you can't be here." A gruff male

voice carried over the wind to Harriet. Turning, she spotted the uniformed officer who strode purposefully towards her. His booted feet crunched over the gravel. His expression was severe as he reached her. "This area is closed to the public," he said. "You need to go."

"I'm Dr Harriet Quinn," she said. "I work with the major crimes team. DI Haskell is leading the investigation and--"

"I'm sorry, Dr Quinn. DI Haskell isn't here right now and you can't stay."

Harriet hid her frustration behind a smile and allowed the police officer to direct her back to the parking area over the road. She was aware that Drew was not at the crime scene. She'd come here, alone, in order to get a feel for the area. Seeing the crime scene, or at least the general area would help her to create a useful profile of the person they were searching for.

And Drew was feeling the pinch in regards to the case. The media was crawling all over it. You only had to put on the television or radio in order to hear something about the tragic discovery of Gwen Campbell's remains. Shock had drifted away quickly, aided by the media's stoking of public resentment and anger.

It was just that kind of behaviour that led people to question why it had taken the police so long to find the young mother's body. Much to Harriet's chagrin, they conveniently, forgot just how large the moors truly were. As for how difficult it would be to find a body out here? It was a needle in a haystack scenario. Only in the case of the moors, you were dealing with multiple barns filled with haystacks and no idea which particular barn the haystack you needed was located in.

Harriet had wanted to something to ease the burden Drew was carrying. If she could bring him something useful then it might mitigate some of the guilt he was feeling over his bringing in of Declan Campbell.

"Dr Quinn?" The voice was familiar and Harriet turned in time to see a man hurrying over the uneven ground towards her. There was something familiar about the man and it took her a moment to recognise the CSM.

"David Farley," he held his hand out to her. His cheeks were pink, eyes bright, and his hair was wind ruffled. Splashes of mud marred the legs of the white coveralls he had tied off at his waist.

"I remember," Harriet said. She took his hand and was surprised by the warmth of his grip. "You worked with us on the case in Darkby."

The mirth in David's eyes momentarily dimmed, like a dark cloud passing over the sun.

"A terrible case. I'm just happy we were able to assist in getting a result." The darkness his eyes was gone as quickly as it had arrived. "Are you here with

DI Haskell?" He glanced past her towards the empty stretch of car spaces.

"No." Harriet shook her head. "I thought I would take a look at the place myself. It's easier when you can have a feel for a place. Photographs don't always capture the essence of a scene. Not that there's anything wrong with the crime scene photographs," she added hurriedly. "They're always very thorough."

David cocked an eyebrow at her, an amused smile playing around his mouth. "Good to hear," he said. "I thought we might have to completely rethink our approach to the recording of a scene."

"Gosh, no," Harriet said. "Really, it's perfectly fine. Excellent even, I wasn't trying to imply that you were doing anything less..." Catching his grin Harriet realised, belatedly, that he was teasing her. She returned his smile with one of her own. "Oh, you're not being serious," she said relieved.

David's laughter was infectious. A rich sound that warmed Harriet all the way down to her toes in spite of the chill in the air.

"Its been one of those days and I'm a little more distracted than I should be."

"Don't worry about it," he said. "It's just an annoying habit I've got."

Harriet cocked her head to the side. "How so?"

"Well, if you ask the others who work with me, they'll all tell you the same thing. I vex them all constantly with my bad jokes."

Harriet wrapped her arms around herself. "There's nothing wrong with trying to bring levity to a situation. Especially one like this. In fact, studies have shown that a sense of humour is an important weapon to deploy when looking after your mental health."

"I'll bear that in mind the next time my colleagues rib me over my dad-jokes."

Harriet smiled along with him before she turned towards her car. "I better get off--"

"I thought you wanted to take a look at the scene?" There was an eagerness to David that hadn't been there before.

"I'm not allowed," Harriet said. "Without DI Haskell here to accompany me, I'm just another nosey civilian."

"I could show you," David said.

"Really? Wouldn't that be against the rules?"

David shook his head. "We're just clearing up. I've already sent someone to take down the tent. We'll be out of here before dark. So, if you wanted, I could show you the scene. I mean, only if it would help."

"That would be wonderful," she said.

"Anything I can do to help, Dr Quinn."

"Honestly, call me, Harriet." David's smile brightened as she spoke.

"Well, all right then, Harriet. Just give me a few minutes to sign off on my paperwork and I'll take you down."

"I really appreciate this," Harriet said, following him back towards the main tent. "This will really allow me to assist DI Haskell."

There was a slight stiffening in David's shoulders that Harriet noticed. But the wind chose that moment to tunnel over the moor and sweep through the car park making them all shiver. Harriet put his reaction down to the chill in the air.

DAVID WAS as good as his word and fifteen minutes later, he was leading her over the road. He'd given her one of the white coveralls to wear and a pair of latex gloves. She snapped them on as she picked her way carefully down the path behind him.

"I thought you said you were finishing up?" Harriet asked as David waited for her.

He nodded. "We are."

"But we still have to wear the forensic coveralls?"

He grinned at her. "Protocol. You never know, you might turn out to be the perfect good luck charm and you'll see something we missed. The defence would have a field day with that," he said. "Plus, it's an extra layer of clothes. And out here you need every scrap of cover you can get."

Harriet had to agree with him. Where as before when she'd crossed the road the bitter cold had bit at her fingers, but now with the latex gloves the worst of the cold was kept at bay.

She paused on the path as it took them further from the road. "It's just out of sight of the main road," she said. "Not much cover, but still, better than nothing."

David stood next to her, his gaze travelling over the expanse of scenery. "Do you think they chose this spot because it's not visible from the road?"

Looking back over her shoulder, Harriet stood the place where the white tent stood. "Possibly. It's not exactly an opportunistic burial site. The killer had to know about the path."

"Well, it's not exactly a secret," David said.

Harriet looked at him in surprise. "I didn't know about it."

David's laughter seemed to bubble up from his centre. "Lots of people come up here to hike. The Hole of Horcum is a popular spot."

"Do you come up here?" Harriet ran her gaze over the man next to her. Unlike Drew, who was built more like a rugby player -- at least that was how Martha had described him when she'd overheard her discussing the DI with another colleague -- David Farley was slim, wiry even.

"I come out here quite a bit," he said. "But my real passion is rock climbing. I try to get out whenever I have some free time."

Harriet tried to hide her surprise. "Rock climbing?"

"Yeah." He chuckled. "Don't look so shocked. It's wonderful fun. Freeing."

Harriet shook her head and tried to imagine anyone deliberately going out of their way to climb a rock face. She couldn't imagine anything worse. Not that it was a surprise to her. Athleticism had never been one of her strengths. The only thing she'd ever successfully climbed had been the professional ladder. And she was happy to leave it at that.

"I think I'll just have to take your word for it," she said, returning her attention to the scene. "I don't think you're correct though."

"What do you mean?"

Harriet did a slow turn on the path until finally she was facing towards the big dip in the moors that had earned the nickname 'The Devil's Punch Bowl.'

"They're not overly familiar with the path."

David glanced at the ground as though he expected the answer to have been hidden in the bracken. "Why would you say that?"

"Because look at the size of the moors. Is this where you would bury a body?"

"Well, no... I suppose not."

"You're familiar with this area. Are there other spots that would be much more conducive to keeping a body hidden?"

David's expression had turned thoughtful. "Well,

yes. If you just went twenty feet in any direction off the path the chances of the body being discovered drops dramatically."

"Exactly," Harriet said triumphantly. "The killer is someone who has a rough working knowledge of the area. But not enough to stray off the beaten path."

David screwed up his face. "But a body would be heavy to carry. Maybe they dumped it here because it was easier than taking it any further?"

Harriet pursed her lips. "It's possible. But they went to this much trouble." She gestured to the track they had walked down to the deposition site. "And as you said, they could have left the path but they chose not to. To me, that suggests somebody unfamiliar with the terrain."

Harriet fell silent. Closing her eyes she tried to imagine the killer standing where she was now. But rather than get a clear picture of the person responsible, Harriet felt the chill seep into her bones.

"Are you all right?" David asked. His voice cut through Harriet's silent contemplation. Surprised, she turned to face him, a smile fixed on her face.

"Sorry. Sometimes I get lost in my thoughts."

David returned her smile with a shy one of his own. "Don't apologise. I do the same. Drives everyone batty."

Harriet laughed in spite of herself. "Always nice to know you're not alone."

He nodded.

"What do you know about the actual burial site?"

He sighed and shifted so that his body was directed down the track. "This wasn't where she died, if that's what you're wondering."

"And the second body?"

Grimacing, David shrugged. "Until the forensic anthropologist comes back with a report, I'm afraid there's not much I can tell you. We believe it's the remains of a small female child. But we don't have a cause of death."

"Will you be able to determine the cause of death?"

"For the older of the female bodies, yes."

Harriet paused, uncertain if she should ask the question that hovered on the tip of her tongue. As though he could sense her curiosity, David cocked an eyebrow at her. "Go on, Harriet. Ask me anything. I want to help." There was a layer of sincerity that Harriet hadn't expected from him. As though the work he did was less of a job and more of a vocation. And perhaps it was. Drew was much the same. For him it was not a job but a calling.

"Why don't you refer to them by their names?"

He smiled sadly and ducked his chin so that his gaze was fixed on the ground beneath his feet. "Force of habit really. When we get a call we don't always know the identity of the victim. In fact, more often than not we have no clue as to who they were in life. It also ensures we don't colour our perception of the scene. If we go into it with preconceived notions of who the victim is it could impact our recovery of the evidence. When we know nothing it makes it easier not to overlook crucial pieces of the puzzle." The unspoken hung between them, but Harriet could tell there was more he wanted to say.

With a sigh, he met her eyes head on. "Plus, and perhaps this sounds silly, it makes it easier when I don't have to think of who they were. When it's just a body, doing my job is infinitely more painless. A body tells a simple story of biological factors and events. A person is much more complicated and far more heartbreaking."

"It's a heavy burden to carry," Harriet said sympathetically.

"I try to focus on just dealing with what's in front of me. That way I can't be led astray." He puffed out his cheeks and shrugged as though struggling to rid himself of unnecessary emotion. "Listen to me waffling on. You don't need to hear my whole life story."

"No, but it's nice to understand all the same."

He eyed her speculatively. "Aye, I suppose considering the job you do it's easier."

She tilted her head and let her gaze wander over the countryside. "I wouldn't say it makes it easier. More that it's a necessary evil."

"Shit, I didn't mean to sound insensitive."

Harriet looked over at him and was surprised to see a genuine look of panic on his face.

"You didn't," she said with a crooked smile. "Well, maybe a little. But it's understandable."

"I've screwed it up. I'm always putting my foot in it."

"David, it's fine. Don't worry about it."

He sighed, his shoulders drooping. "We should know the cause of death for the older-- for Gwen Campbell, in the next day or two."

"And the smaller body?"

"The remains were badly damaged. We might never have a clear picture of what happened unless it left a definitive mark on the skeletal remains we have recovered."

"It's a beautiful place," Harriet said, speaking more to herself than David.

He moved up next to her. "You think maybe that had something to do with placing them here?"

"Perhaps," Harriet said. "And then again maybe it was just convenient." Not that she really believed that.

BY THE TIME they had trekked back up to the car park, Harriet was more than ready to get home so she could take another look at the files she had on the case. Stripping out of the Tyvek suit, she felt the wind as it passed through the layers of her clothes.

"Thanks for this," she said. David held an evidence bag out to her and she placed the suit inside.

"I don't know if you'd be interested in continuing our conversation over a drink?" The hopeful note was back in his voice.

Looking up at him, Harriet paused changing her shoes. "I've got some work to--"

David shook his head. "Sorry, I shouldn't have sprung this on you." He grinned at her. "It's just I can't remember a time when I enjoyed doing a walk-through on a crime scene so much."

Warmth flooded Harriet's face and she returned her attention to unlacing her boots. It would be easier to politely turn him down. As she worked the knot free, Harriet imagined what Bianca would say to her were she here.

And then there was the situation with Drew. While there had been a time when she'd entertained the idea that something might happen between them, his relationship with Melissa had put paid to that notion completely. It occurred to her then that she'd been silent for far too long. The tension stretched between them growing more and more awkward with every second that ticked by.

"Uh, yeah, I'd like that," she said finally unhooking the knot at the same time.

David's face was wreathed in a smile. "Do you want me to pick you up, or..."

Harriet had already started to shake her head. "No, I can meet you somewhere." It was easier that way, for both of them. If it became to strained, they could both escape back to their respective cars and go home without the other feeling obliged to escort them.

"Great. Sure. I look forward to it." David's grin had grown and he turned to walk away before he stopped himself and returned to face her. "Sorry, I guess we should arrange something."

Harriet returned his smile with one of her own. He was nervous and seeing it reinforced her decision to agree to his invitation. Grabbing a pen and a piece of paper from her bag in the boot of the car, Harriet quickly scribbled her number and handed it over. His fingers brushed against hers as he took it. There was no *frisson* of passion. No spark to speak of. Not that Harriet believed in that kind of thing, but she'd watched her fair share of romcoms down through the years.

"That's me," she said, indicating the paper. "I've got some work to do this evening, but if you're free tomorrow night, you can let me know."

"Perfect," David said. "I'll let you know."

Harriet chucked her boots into the car and gripped her keys in her hand. David jogged back up the carpark towards the main forensic tent leaving her with her thoughts. There was a small voice in the back of her head that warned she was making a mistake, but Harriet pushed it away. Bianca's death and Misha's sudden appearance in her life had shown Harriet that life was for the living.

And even if nothing came of the situation with David, it would, Harriet thought, be nice to have another friend to call upon.

CHAPTER TWENTY-NINE

SLAMMING the papers onto his desk, Drew dropped back into his chair. "We've got to let him go," he said addressing Maz. "Better to do it now and garner some goodwill." Drew's headache was worse and he was starting to feel like death warmed up.

"Are we giving up on him as a suspect?" Maz asked.

Drew stared down at the mountain of paperwork gathered on his desk. "We're not giving up exactly. We're going to broaden our approach. We can't allow the opinions of the initial investigation to cloud our judgement here, or we'll miss something."

Maz nodded, but he looked unconvinced. Not that Drew could blame him. There was a reason they looked to the partner first. Time had taught them that nine times out of ten it was the significant other. But in this instance, Drew couldn't shake the feeling that he was allowing his past feelings to interfere with the evidence as it appeared in front of him.

And something had changed in Campbell's monetary situation after Gwen disappeared. It was a loose thread that needed to be pulled on.

"I want Harriet to--" Drew sneezed violently cutting his words off mid-speech.

"Are my ears burning?" Her voice cut through the noise in the room. Spinning in his chair, he glanced up at her. Her hair was wilder than usual and there was colour in her cheeks.

"I was going to say that I wanted you to take a look at the transcripts from our interview with Simon Campbell." Drew sneezed again.

"You're sick?" She seemed surprised.

"No." Drew's tone was belligerent but he didn't care. Ignoring the smile that crossed Harriet's face, he shuffled the papers on his desk.

She sat opposite him and began to unpack a notebook and pen from her bag. "So, you spoke to Simon?"

Drew paused his rearranging. "We got an appropriate adult to sit in with him, but he's not as sure anymore about his story."

Harriet flipped open her notebook and stared into the middle distance for a moment. "He's probably struggling with the idea of potentially losing both his mother and father."

"But if his father killed Gwen--"

Harriet shook her head and met Drew's gaze head on. "Think about it from his point of view, Drew. He's still basically a child."

"He's a teenage boy," Drew countered.

"Exactly. He lost his mum a few years ago. That's a blow for a young boy. And then his father moves on with his life. Starts a new relationship, there's a baby on the way. It's a lot to take on board."

"You think he was making it up?"

Harriet looked down at her notes. "It's possible." She tapped her fingers lightly against the desk as she gathered her thoughts. "I think it's more likely that he's misremembering what really happened. In some ways it would be easier for him to believe that some-body else kept his mother from him. And because he's angry with his father he's a suitable candidate."

"But?"

"But," Harriet smiled at him, "Simon has had time to think about the ramifications of his accusation. His mum is gone. If he persists with his story, that his father and mother fought, that it turned physical, resulting in Declan pushing his wife down the stairs..." Harriet spread her hands on the table, palms up. "He knows it will cost him his father too. His last connection to a time in his life when he was happy. It's a lot of responsibility to place on his shoulders."

Drew nodded. He'd already considered that the weight of so much responsibility would take its toll on the boy.

"If we could see the video then we could say definitively."

Drew nodded. "I know. That's the frustrating part."

Harriet tucked a stray strand of hair back behind her ear. "Where were you?" Drew asked.

She looked up at him, surprise etched into her features. "What do you mean?"

"You didn't come from the university," Drew said.

"How could you possibly know that?"

Drew grinned at her her. "I'm a detective, Harriet, detecting is my job."

She narrowed her eyes at him. "I went to take a look at the scene."

Surprise rendered Drew momentarily silent. He could feel Maz surreptitiously watching them from the other side of the desks.

"You went on your own?"

"I knew you were busy here," she said. "I thought I'd make myself useful and get a feel for the scene."

"They're still working out there, right?"

Harriet's attention was fixed on her notepad and her response was noncommittal. "Yeah."

Frustrated, Drew cleared his throat. "Harriet, are they still working at the scene?"

She snapped her attention up to him. "They're almost finished. Mostly just packing up and..." She paused and turned to face him. "What is it? What's wrong?"

"If they've let you in then the site is not secure anymore," Drew said, irritation coloured his words. "I'm going to string the uniform up by--"

"The uniform is still there," Harriet interrupted him. "He wouldn't let me near the scene."

Relieved Drew settled back into his chair. "Well, that's a relief. I had visions of the press crossing the cordon and pictures of Gwen Campbell's remains turning up in the late papers."

"No. You don't have to worry about that happening. They've already moved the remains."

"I can take you up there if you'd like to get a proper look at the scene?"

"No need," Harriet said. "I've got everything I need."

"It's no trouble," he said. It took him a moment to register the information she'd just shared with him. "Wait, how do you know they've moved the remains already?"

"I met David Farley up there. He took me around the scene. It was really helpful actually."

Despite the headache that had started to pound behind Drew's eyes and the fact that his brain felt as though someone had wrapped it in cotton wool, it was anger that swelled in Drew's chest.

"David Farley showed you around the crime scene?" His voice dropped. From the corner of his eye, he spotted Maz as he glanced sharply in their direction. "The CSM let you into the scene without consulting someone here?"

"Yeah. He said because they were basically done, it would be all right." Harriet seemed to register Drew's anger as she looked over at him. "Why, is there a problem?"

"Oh, I don't know," Drew said snappily. "Just a CSM making arbitrary decisions to let a civilian into a closed crime scene."

"Drew..." Harriet stared at him, her expression a mask of confusion and hurt. She glanced down at her papers. "I'm sorry. I assumed that because *you* let me go to the scenes, and he said it was fine, there wouldn't be a problem."

"I'm the SIO," Drew said. His voice rose an octave, growing hoarse as it strained due to his head cold. "It's different if *I* give permission. It's my arse in a sling if something goes tits up and you touch something you shouldn't." He was being unfair. Harriet had never been anything other than careful at the crime scenes he'd taken her to. Deep down he knew it would have been no different today. And yet...

"Drew, I would never endanger a crime scene. You know that." This time Harriet didn't even bother to hide her indignation. The hurt was still there but it was masked somewhat by the other emotions that had come to the surface. "It's never been a issue in the past."

248

"God, you can't even see how problematic for me this is, can you?"

Harriet gathered up her items and hastily shoved them into her bag. "I'm sorry you feel like that," she said primly. "I think it's best if I leave."

"I think you're right," Drew snapped.

With a backwards glance that betrayed her hurt and confusion, Harriet left. Getting up from his desk, Maz moved around to Drew and paused next to the desk.

"What?" Drew snapped. The ache in his head was getting worse.

"What was all that about?" Maz asked.

"None of your business," Drew said. "Any word on getting that video pulled from the phone?"

Maz shook his head. He opened his mouth as though he planned to say more and then as he caught Drew's eye he thought better of it. "I'll get on it, guv."

"Great," Drew growled. As Maz slinked off, guilt tugged at Drew's consciousness. It had been an over-reaction. Never once in the time he'd worked with Harriet had he ever thought she would behave inappropriately at a crime scene. And if David Farley had given her the go ahead to be there... Well, he was the crime scene manager for christ's sake. The man had worked enough scenes to know what he was doing. "Shit," Drew muttered beneath his breath. He'd well and truly stepped in it up to his eyebrows.

"Haskell!" DCI Gregson's voice rang out over the

chatter of the other officers as they worked. Closing his eyes, Drew wondered if he could legitimately pretend not to have heard his boss. Not that it would wash with the monk.

Getting to his feet, Drew pulled a fresh tissue from his pocket and blew his nose before he ambled over to the DCI's office. He didn't have any Lemsip at home and he would have to swing by a pharmacy and pick himself up a packet. Might even treat himself to a beer, or two.

Stepping into the monk's domain, Drew took the seat opposite the desk and waited for the boss to look in his direction.

"What crawled up your arse?" The monk lifted his head out of the paper's that lay in a tangle over the surface of the desk.

"Sir?"

"You and Dr Quinn. I saw you two have words and then she hightailed it out of here. What's going on between you?"

Caught unawares, Drew shook his head. "Nothing, sir." He caught the warning in Gregson's face and decided to amend his statement. "Not nothing, exactly. She went up to the deposition site and the CSM let her go over the scene."

"And?" Gregson asked, raising an eyebrow in Drew's direction.

"Well, to be frank, sir, I didn't think it was right.

What if she made a mistake. The chain of custody in regards to evidence is--"

Gregson cut him off with a shake of his head. "You never led me to believe she was untrustworthy in the past."

"Well, she wasn't," Drew said, sniffing loudly. The heat in the DCI's office was unbearable. Why hadn't he noticed it before? Sweat beaded on Drew's brow and his shirt clung to his clammy skin. "But Dr Quinn has always had one of the team with her when she reviewed a scene in the past."

"And you don't think Farley is a suitable replacement for you?"

"I didn't say that, sir," Drew argued.

"Do you not think he's up to the task of being CSM?"

"Well, no, I think he does a fine job as CSM. We've never had any issues--"

"Good. I happen to agree with you. So what was the real issue?"

"Well, it's chain of command really. I think as SIO I should have been informed--"

"Then lucky for both of us, Farley contacted me and sought permission. Not that he actually needed it, they were finished down there. But he did check to ensure Dr Quinn was working the case with us. And I personally gave permission for Dr Quinn to walk the scene."

Drew felt all of the fight go out of him. He

flopped back against the chair as a bead of cold sweat rolled down the side of his face. "That's that then," Drew said flatly.

"Go home, DI Haskell," the monk said. "Or better still go to a doctor. You look like shit, man."

"I'm fine, sir. I've got..."

The monk was already shaking his head before Drew managed to finish his sentence. "Get Arya to do it. I want you to go home and get some rest."

Limp limbed, Drew stood and turned to the door.

"And, Haskell?" Drew glanced back at his boss. "When you're feeling more like yourself maybe think about apologising to Dr Quinn. I'm not the biggest fan of her profession but she's proven herself to be a team player. And we need people like her on our side. Especially when so many people out there think we do more to prioritise the safety of criminals over the general populace."

"Yes, sir," Drew said quietly. He was suitably chastised and all he wanted to do was escape the heat of the office and crawl under a rock somewhere and get some sleep.

Gregson nodded. "Off with you then."

Drew did not need to be told twice. He escaped the oppressive heat of the office and crossed the floor to his desk. From the corner of his eye he caught sight of Melissa signalling to him from her office, but Drew ignored her. The last thing he needed right now was to have her find some reason to invite herself over. Not when he felt like death warmed up.

By the time he reached his chair and grabbed his coat, Drew's teeth had started to chatter. Olivia swung around to face him, her mouth already open to ask a question. But she took one look at his pallor and changed her mind. "Never mind, guv," she said, swinging back to her computer.

"Shit," Drew muttered beneath his breath as he made a break for the doors. "I must look as bad as I feel."

As he made his way down the stairs, his phone started to ring in his pocket. Slipping out the side door of the building, he crossed to his car. Pulling the phone from his pocket, he studied the name that pulsed on the screen in time with the vibration. Melissa.

With his bed calling to him, Drew contemplated answering but ultimately decided against it. Tomorrow was another day.

CHAPTER THIRTY

HURT, Melissa watched from the window of the office as Drew sent her call to voicemail before he slid the phone back into his coat pocket. If it had been the illustrious Dr Quinn, would he have ignored her, too? Melissa doubted it.

This wasn't like her. She wasn't the jealous type, especially not in a situation like this. Drew was with her. He had chosen her. And they were having fun. Melissa had forgotten just how much fun Drew could be. It was a little different now. Drew was sometimes weighed down with guilt over the past. And Melissa sometimes found it difficult to pull him out of his moody reveries. But she was willing to put up with it, for now at least.

No she wasn't jealous. Drew had made it clear that he was all in with her. It could not have been more clear cut in her mind. And yet... here she was watching him ignore her call. She sighed and turned away from the window.

And it wasn't the only thing. He'd lied to her the other night about wanting a chance to catch up on his paperwork. Instead, he'd invited Dr Quinn over to his for a quiet little dinner for two.

Pinching the bridge of her nose, she squeezed her eyes shut. She wasn't the jealous type and Drew was not the kind of guy to jerk her around. That left only one option... Dr Quinn.

In spite of Occam's Razor telling her the only possible remaining answer to her problem had to be Dr Quinn, Melissa found it difficult to believe that the good doctor was deliberately making a play to come between her and Drew. It was possible she was doing it unconsciously, although Melissa found it hard to fathom that a woman who made her living crawling inside the heads of the most damaged and depraved beings could do anything unconscious.

If it wasn't Dr Quinn, then what was she missing? Grabbing her coat, Melissa slipped it on and gathered up the last of her files. With her personal belongings in hand, she left the office. If Drew had ignored her because he planned to meet up with Dr Quinn then she would get to the bottom of it.

And if she were wrong? Well, Melissa was confident that she knew what would put a smile back on

Drew's face. With a wave to Olivia and Maz, Melissa sauntered out of the office. One way or another she would get what she wanted.

CHAPTER THIRTY-ONE

JOAN SAT UP ABRUPTLY. Sweat soaked her skin, causing her T-shirt to stick to her back. The only light in the living room came from the white glow of her computer screen. She blinked rapidly, trying to clear her vision but the nightmare came back.

Even now, she could feel the cold, wet dirt as it stuck to her body. She'd begged him not to do it, but he didn't listen. He never did... Joan tried to separate reality from fiction. Her writing had a terrible habit of bleeding into her dreams and terrifying her. And she was writing about a murder.

Closing her eyes, Joan could see the scene laid out before her. On her knees, she'd begged for her life. Rather than listen he'd swung the shovel towards her, catching her along the side of her face. Blood, warm and wet trickled along her cheek.

Sitting on the couch, Joan ran her finger up the side of her face and into her hairline. Hr heart stalled in her chest as her fingers found something. It was real... The scar was a raised patch of skin covered by her hair. The kind of scar you would only have from being hit with something heavy.

Panic surged through her as the nightmare, with all of its terrifying emotions, washed over her. Getting up suddenly, Joan's slippers tangled in the carpet and she fell. Her arms windmilled as she tried to grab onto something, anything.

Her head smacked off the edge of the coffee table and as the world turned black she was certain she heard a man and woman laughing...

CHAPTER THIRTY-TWO

PARKING the car in front of Dr Quinn's house, Melissa stared up at the dark building. She could make out a dim light reflected through the glass in the front door. It was the only sign that suggest Dr Quinn was at home.

Climbing from the car, Melissa locked up and sauntered across the road. Pausing on the doorstep, she took a deep breath before making the decision to ring the bell. Coming here was a risk but it was one she had to take.

As the sound of the bell echoed through the house, Melissa turned and stared at the residential street. A few car spaces below hers, headlights flared to life and a small black five door sedan pulled out. It inched carefully down the street, only accelerating once it reached the end of the road.

The door behind Melissa swung open and warmth washed over her.

"DI Appleton?"

Was that surprise she detected in Dr Quinn's voice? Had she been expecting someone else? Brushing the paranoid thinking aside, Melissa turned her best, hundred-watt smile on the petite woman framed in the light from the hall.

"Dr Quinn, I'm sorry to bother you so late but I was hoping I might get a chance to pick your brain over a couple of things?"

Pleasure and something that more closely resembled caution swept through the doctor's eyes. And then, both emotions were gone, hidden behind a cold blue wall of her eyes.

"Of course, come in." She stepped back, allowing Melissa the opportunity to slip past her into the hall.

Dr Quinn paused and carefully locked the door. She slid a bolt into place and then gestured for Melissa to move ahead of her down the hall. The chequered tiles beneath Melissa's feet gave way to flagstones in the kitchen. The room wasn't particularly large, but the lack of decor made the space seem empty. To Melissa's mind, the bland, characterless quality of the house was just an extension of the woman who owned it.

From what Melissa had seen of Dr Quinn, she did not have much of a personality. Instead, she reminded Melissa of some kind of chameleon, constantly shifting to fit the mood of the room she wound up in. What Drew could see in her, well, that was his business.

"Can I get you a coffee, or a tea?" Dr Quinn paused in the doorway to her kitchen. She seemed uncertain, not that Melissa minded. There was a smugness to Dr Quinn when she floated in and out of the office. Seeing her caught on the back foot made a pleasant change.

"Tea would be great," Melissa said. She smiled brightly and dragged out one of the stools that sat beneath the breakfast counter. Planting her elbows firmly, Melissa studied the doctor as she moved around the space. "You've got a lovely home," she said.

The doctor glanced back over her shoulder, surprise drawing her brows comically upwards. "Thank you. I keep meaning to do more with it but I never seem to find the time."

Melissa kept her smile fixed in place. Was it all an act with Dr Quinn? She came across as harmless and non-threatening but how could she have so successfully climbed the career ladder whilst maintaining that level of virtue?

"We can sit through here." Dr Quinn inclined her head towards a door that led off the kitchen. "It'll be more comfortable in there."

"Sure." Melissa followed her. As they crossed the threshold into the living room, she was surprised to find such a warm, inviting, if not a little cluttered, space. The hardwood floors added a richness to the space but Melissa could see they were scuffed and neglected. There were a number of laden down bookcases that stretched to the ceilings. And where she could see wall space, it was mostly lost beneath vibrant pictures and paintings.

The heavy wooden coffee table in the centre of the floor, which looked as though it had been crafted from one solid piece of polished timber, was half buried beneath paperwork. Several glass-cloche covered ornaments, which would not have looked out of a place in a Victorian gentleman's curio collection, were dotted around the room.

Against the back wall sat a large stuffed couch. Two large jewel covered throws lay over the back. Scattered papers peppered one half of the sofa. As Dr Quinn set the mugs down on the coffee table, she hastily attempted to tidy up the sheets of paper. Melissa watched as she haphazardly jammed them into file folders. It was a hopeless endeavour and Melissa smiled tightly as Dr Quinn managed to carve out a small area for her to sit.

"I'm sorry about the mess." Dr Quinn paused and looked around the space as though seeing it for the first time in a while. "Things have been a little busy."

"Don't worry about it," Melissa said. "We all let things get on top of us from time to time." She thought of her own immaculately appointed apartment. Josephine came around three times a week, ensuring she would never find herself in such a predicament.

Dr Quinn flopped down onto the opposite end of the couch. "Well, what can I help you with DI Appleton?"

"Please, call me, Melissa." She smoothed down the front of her Phillip Lim tailored trousers. "Considering the work we do together, we shouldn't stand on ceremony with one another."

"All right then," Dr Quinn said. Her impenetrable gaze met Melissa's, leaving her to feel exposed. "What exactly would you like my help with?"

Melissa placed her hands together in her lap, the way her mother had taught her. Unconsciously, or not as Melissa supposed, Dr Quinn mirrored the movement. Melissa had done a few courses in psychology as part of her training and she recognised the move for what it was, an attempt at manipulation. Mirroring her actions in order to make her feel more at ease. Of course, there was a chance, Dr Quinn was doing it without thinking. But Melissa suspected there was nothing the good doctor did without first thinking deeply about it.

Fixing her smile in place, she relaxed her shoulders. She contemplated lying. It would be easier to feel her way into the real conversation she wanted to have. That way, she could feign innocence if it went sideways. But Melissa was not a fan of subterfuge, unless her work required it of her.

"I think we should talk about DI Haskell." Melissa was gratified to see the dart of guilt that passed through Dr Quinn's eyes. But the emotion was fleeting and was gone in an instant.

"I'm not sure that would be appropriate," she said. Her back stiffened. Gone was the ease of a few moments ago. Instead, Dr Quinn looked like a woman ready to bolt at a moment's notice. "Drew, I mean, DI Haskell is not here. And I don't make it a habit to discuss my friends behind their backs."

Melissa ignored the pointed looked Dr Quinn threw her direction. "The insinuation is that I do make a habit of discussing my friends behind their backs, is that it?"

"I didn't say that." The doctor spoke softly. Out of the corner of her vision, Melissa saw that she had started to pick at her fingernails. A nervous gesture, no doubt. For all her education and emotional intelligence, it seemed she had just as many tells as the rest of the world. It comforted Melissa to know the woman opposite her was human after all and not the god-like creature Drew often portrayed her to be.

"Because I don't," Melissa added. "I came here tonight because I've known, Drew a lot longer than you." Melissa's smile turned sympathetic. "I'm not saying you don't know an aspect of his personality, just that I've seen more than just the professional side."

Dr Quinn nodded but remained silent. Her cup remained untouched on the coffee table. Melissa took the opportunity to reach for hers. It was important to put the doctor at ease. If she sensed any of Melissa's discomfort, she would start to suspect an ulterior motive.

Sipping at her tea slowly, Melissa contemplated her next move. Resting the cup in her hands, met Dr Quinn's inquisitive gaze. It was all too easy to just sit in the woman's company. Despite the silence that stretched between them and Dr Quinn's obvious nervousness, she still managed to create a kind of calm. Melissa found herself wanting to confide in the doctor. And it was that dark desire which frightened her.

"He's changed, you know?"

Dr Quinn cocked her head to one side, her expression open, inviting even. "You've known him for a long time. I would expect you, more than anyone, would notice these changes."

Melissa sipped again at her tea. "I know some change is normal. Expected even. But..." She stared down into her cup.

"But there's something bothering you?"

"Well, yeah. I know he's been through a lot. And anyone who's faced such a traumatic event, well it's going to leave a scar."

"It would be odd if it didn't." Some of the tension in Dr Quinn's shoulders eased.

"Did you meet Freya?" Melissa already knew the answer, but she wanted to hear it from the horse's mouth.

"Yes," Dr Quinn said. The fidgeting started up again. "But it was a fleeting meeting. I didn't know her."

"She was brilliant," Melissa said. "Smart, funny, and beautiful. Triple threat." Melissa's laughter sounded forced to her own ears. She needed to be careful not to overdo it. She owed it to Drew to at least be tactful.

"But she's dead and you're not," Dr Quinn said. The blunt manner of her delivery took Melissa by surprise. For a moment, she didn't know how to respond and Dr Quinn took her silence as an invitation to continue. "Drew needs stability in his life. Someone he can rely on. Someone he can trust..."

"He can trust me," Melissa snapped.

The smile on Dr Quinn's face suggested she didn't believe Melissa. That alone infuriated her.

"That's not why I'm here," Melissa said, changing tack. "The change in Drew is connected to his work."

Dr Quinn surprise manifested in a physical movement as she sat back on the couch. "DI Haskell is an excellent investigator."

"In that, we're in perfect agreement," Melissa

said. "He's one of the best. Far better than me. But something has changed."

Dr Quinn sipped from her own cup. "I don't see a change. I know he's suffering from a cold..."

Melissa's laughter was sincere. Was she for real? Could she really not see what Melissa was trying to say to her? For someone who was supposedly so smart, she wasn't behaving like it. "You wouldn't, Dr Quinn..."

"Please, call me, Harriet..."

Melissa smiled. She had no intention of ever calling the doctor by her first name. It was too easy to slip into complacency like that. All too easy to forget what you were dealing with. She'd spent time working undercover, she knew all the slippery slopes one could find themselves on. No, first names were for those you could trust to have your back one hundred percent. And as far as Melissa was concerned Dr Quinn was not one of the chosen few she could trust.

"What I'm trying to say is that the change in Drew is because of you."

"I'm really not sure how I'm supposed to take that," Dr Quinn said.

However you want, Melissa thought. Instead, she said, "I'm sorry if I've upset you. It's just, I think it's important for the team... for the sake of the public we serve that Drew is at his best."

"And you don't think he's at his best because of

me?" Puzzlement caused a frown to appear between Dr Quinn's brows.

"How can he be?" Melissa set her cup aside and pressed her elbows to her knees, allowing her to lean forward. "You're very good at what you do. Probably the best I've ever had the pleasure of working with."

"Thanks... I think." She cleared her throat. "I've only ever tried to give my best to the work." Dr Quinn sounded so uncertain. Melissa's heart flipped in her chest.

"And it shows," Melissa said. "But and I don't mean to sound harsh, Drew has a tendency towards being lazy." She knew the moment the words left her mouth that she'd made a misstep. Dr Quinn's expression instantly became guarded and the tension returned to her body.

"I'm not sure I'd agree."

"I knew that was going to sound wrong," Melissa said, struggling to backtrack. "Drew is an excellent detective, but I don't think he's trying as hard as he could."

Dr Quinn's eyebrows rose towards her dark hair. "He's hardly slept since he picked up this case. He refuses to go home to rest, despite the fact that he's clearly very sick. And you think he's not trying enough?"

"I'm really messing this all up," Melissa said. "Drew was a different kind of investigator before he met you. But since you've joined the team, he doesn't question things as much as he used to. Instead, he relies on you to do the questioning. When a new lead comes in, he wants to wait and see what you'll think of it instead of acting on his own. During the briefings he refers to you, rather than sharing his own thoughts with the team... Please tell me you see what I'm saying?"

Dr Quinn remained silent for several moments. Melissa's heartbeat thudded in her ears, deafening her.

"I didn't realise I was having such an effect," Dr Quinn said hesitantly. "It's not as though I have anything to refer to. I didn't know DI Haskell before..."

Melissa shook her head. "No, you didn't. And I'm not blaming you, Dr Quinn. You're just doing your job. But Drew is beginning to take a backseat and that concerns me."

"The role of a DI is to utilise the various strengths of their team."

"But that shouldn't happen at the expense of their own expertise," Melissa said. "Look, people are beginning to take notice. Drew hasn't confided in me what his plans might be for the future. I don't know if he wants to continue to aim higher. But right now, his constant second-guessing of his own investigative skills means even if he wants to, he won't get the chance to go any further..."

Dr Quinn remained silent. The moment

stretched between them and for the first time since she'd arrived, Melissa began to feel nervous. Had she said too much? What if Dr Quinn decided to go straight to Drew with everything she'd just said? He wouldn't understand what she was trying to do for him. He would see it as a betrayal of his trust instead... Had she just screwed everything up between them? The idea that she might have destroyed their fledgling relationship cut Melissa to the core, far more than she'd thought was possible.

"I realise all of this has probably come as a shock," Melissa said. "And I'm going to throw myself on your mercy here and ask you not to say anything to Drew..."

Melissa could read the doctor's expression as a woman who was torn by her loyalty to Drew. What was it about this man in particular that could make him inspire so much loyalty and confidence in those around him. Melissa felt his pull, the gravity he exerted on those in his orbit. And if he discovered what she had done... Melissa couldn't bear the idea of being on the outside. Exiled from his warmth...

"You've put me in a predicament here," Dr Quinn said finally.

"I realise that," Melissa said quickly. "But I had to say something. All I want for Drew is to see him succeed. And I know he's capable of more. You have to know that."

Dr Quinn nodded. "I know you care about him."

Melissa stared down at her own hands. "I really do."

"I'm not going to promise anything." Dr Quinn stood. "You've given me a lot to think about."

Surprised by her abruptness, Melissa got to her feet. "It wasn't my intention to offend you."

"And you haven't," Dr Quinn said. "I've got an early start in the morning. And a lot of work to get through tonight."

As she was shown to the door, Melissa ran through the options in her head. There had to be something else she could say. Something that would guarantee Dr Quinn did not throw her under the bus. But Melissa's mind was blank.

Pausing with her hand on the door, Dr Quinn turned to face her. "I appreciate you coming here, Melissa. I know it can't have been easy."

"I just want what's best for DI Haskell."

Dr Quinn's smile was gentle. "And I don't doubt it. But I think you'll discover that Drew is not a man who takes kindly to being managed, even by those with good intentions."

Taken aback, Melissa opened her mouth to respond but was unable to find the words necessary.

"Have a safe journey home." Dr Quinn ushered her out onto the doorstep. Before Melissa had the chance to so much as utter a word, the door was firmly closed in her face. The sound of the locks turning and the deadbolt sliding home left her in no doubt as to what Dr Quinn thought of her and her visit.

Feeling enraged, Melissa made her way down the path. Crossing the street, she climbed behind the wheel of her car. The voice in her head rubbed her nose in the fact that she had screwed up. And make no mistake, she had messed up. Dr Quinn was a shrewd operator. The whole innocent act, was just that, an act. And somewhere along the way, Melissa had shown her hand. Now she was at Dr Quinn's mercy as to when she would reveal their conversation to Drew.

Slamming her hands against the steering wheel, Melissa swore violently. Tear stung her eyes as she started the engine and pulled out into the street. Dr Quinn had won this battle, but she would not win the war. Melissa intended to make sure of it. She would slip up somewhere and when she did, Melissa would be waiting.

CHAPTER THIRTY-THREE

BARRY, or Footworship85 as he'd named himself online, logged onto Only Fans. He scrolled through the list of people he subscribed to until he came to Mistress Holly. Excitement swelled in him as he realised she had a new video. Granted, the food porn videos she made weren't exactly his favourite, but she was known to do things with her feet and that definitely got his motor running. Glancing over his shoulder, he checked to make sure the door to his office was closed. Getting to his feet, Barry crossed the floor and flicked the lock. The last thing he needed was for his toddler daughter, or worse yet, his wife to come and check on him. She wouldn't understand. The last time he'd broached the topic of him worshiping her feet in a pair of stilettos, she had called him a freak.

Not that he could blame her. Even he thought he was a freak. But the heart wants, what the heart wants. And his heart wanted to worship the feet of every goddess out there.

Rummaging in the bottom drawer of his desk, he pulled out a tube of lube and set it on the desk next to him. Pulling the box of tissues closer, he settled back into his chair and put on his headphones.

"Mad Hatter's Tea Party." The title flashed on the screen and he felt his heart drop into his stomach. It was going to be another food video.

The video started, Holly's plump, pouty smile caused the blood in his veins to pump a little harder. Her breathy voice whispered through his headphones and goosebumps rose along his arms in response. Barry watched as she took the can of squirty cream and ran the nozzle of it over the tan skin of her chest.

Glancing over his shoulder again, he unzipped his jeans and pushed them down his hips as Holly crawled towards the camera. The PU leather of his office chair was warm beneath the bare skin of his arse. Closing his eyes, he tried to imagine Holly crawling across the creamy coloured carpet of his office.

"Today we're going—"

Her voice cut off mid-sentence. The camera angle shifted, the sudden switch jarring him out of the fantasy. The camera work was a little shakier than he was used to, reminding him of some of the found-footage movies that had grown in popularity recently. The picture on the screen was blurry which struck him as odd. Holly was normally slick, and the editing on her videos was second to none. And he should know, considering it was his job to edit videos professionally.

The picture came into focus, showing a black rubber mat on the floor. The camera skimmed upwards, lingering over a pair of perfectly shaped feet. He straightened up, his eyes glued to the screen. Holly's toenails were painted shell pink. Barry knew they were Holly's feet because he'd taken enough screen captures of them during his time as a subscriber to her channel. They were perfect in every way. The high arch, the wrinkles and creases, her perfectly shaped toes. Not too long, not too short. He felt like Goldilocks in the three bears' house whenever he managed to catch a glimpse of Holly's feet. They were just right.

His arousal intensified. Grabbing the bottle of lube, his hand dipped below the desk. The sound of laboured breathing surrounded him, travelling through the headphones so that he was cocooned in it.

He'd started to work himself towards fever pitch, his heartbeat hammering in his head as he drank in every inch of her beautiful feet. The camera zoomed in, and he groaned. The image shifted, the camera angle moving upwards. Through his half-closed eyes, he spotted something that seemed out of place. His eyes widened.

The zip-ties around her ankles had dug into her flesh, reddening the skin in a way that left him feeling cold. He wasn't into BDSM. The idea of inflicting pain on someone so beautiful turned his stomach. No, Barry was a lover, not a fighter. The camera continued its journey up her body. It moved over her shapely legs, to her thighs.

Holly was sitting on a chair. The familiar background juxtaposing the very unfamiliar vision of her that filled the camera screen.

"Holly has been a very naughty girl..." The strange electronically modulated voice so close to him, he could practically feel their breath against his ear, forced him to glance over his shoulder. "Gluttony is a sin, isn't that right, Holly?"

"Such a greedy girl. Holly takes the money she makes from all of you and uses it to buy material things." The camera angle shifted so that Holly fell out of focus, and the handbags, and shoes lining the closet shelves came into view instead. "Her idolatry for these false gods..." The jerky movement as the person moved across the floor to the shelves. A gloved hand snaked out, the snap blade coming into view as the one holding the camera swiped at a bag Barry knew his wife would have given a kidney to own. The leather of the bag gave way beneath the sharp knife. It tumbled from the shelf, hitting the floor with a dull thud.

The camera moved on, the person holding it cutting another bag to pieces. It went on like this before they stopped and set the blade down and swung the camera back around.

The screen went black, and Barry thought the film had ended. He glanced down at the comments and was gratified to find he wasn't the only one off-put by the strange video.

What was Holly thinking? Nothing about this was a turn on.

The screen lit up, the camera panning upwards so that Holly's chest and head came into view. Barry gasped, his arousal withering as he took in the sight in front of him. She was bound to a chair. Her dirty hair was matted to her head, her upper body streaked in food and what looked suspiciously like blood and vomit. Her brown eyes were wide and filled with terror.

But it was the item wedged into her mouth that sealed the air in his lungs. Her mouth was open, clamped in place by something that looked as though it should have been used for some kind of medical procedure. Saliva covered her chin, her usually lush mouth bruised and bloodied.

The camera shook as the camera operator moved closer to Holly. "You know you've sinned, don't you, Holly?" The whispered voice sent a shiver down Barry's spine.

The bound woman shook her head, her eye

make-up was streaked, mascara having dried into thick black trails on her cheeks. The camera shook again as the person holding it took a moment to set it on the holder. They pulled it close, so close to Holly's face that Barry could practically see her tonsils when her attacker forced her head around towards the camera.

"I'm here to show Holly the error of her ways," the whispered voice said.

A tube came into view, a funnel attached to one end. The gurgled scream was cut off as Barry ripped his headphones off. He fell from his office chair, his jeans sliding down around his ankles so that they tripped him. He retched, barely managing to grab his small rubbish bin from beside the desk. Acrid vomit burned his throat, and his eyes streamed.

He glanced up at the screen, but it only brought a second volley of vomit racing up from the pit of his stomach. Squeezing his eyes shut, Barry scrambled for the mouse. Grabbing it, the sound of Holly's gurgled screams could still be heard pouring from the headphones. Salty tears, snot, and the bitter taste of vomit combined as he tried to click out of the video. Through one half-shut eye, he moved the cursor over to the exit button. His last glimpse of Holly, which was burned into his retina, as she writhed against her bonds forced his brain to shut down.

The screen went black, and Barry hit the floor.

He drew his knees to his chest as he curled into the foetal position next to his desk.

CHAPTER THIRTY-FOUR

SinEater81: Did you see on the news! They released Gwen Campbell's husband.

CremeEggFanatic: Sick prick needs locking up. Imagine doing that to your baby? Getting shut of Gwen were one thing, but not the little 'un too. That is unforgivable.

Mard-Arse5108: You don't think they let him out cos he was innocent?

SinEater81: Not a chance. Bastards guilty as sin. Everyone knows it. I heard he killed her for the money.

TheGreedyTruthx0x0: Wot!!! Like as in life insurance? Where'd you hear that SE?

SinEater81: Prolly that too. But yeah, everyone knows it. Just an open secret. He were in financial difficulty up the wazzoo and got involved with some group that promised him a boatload of cash if he looked other way. And then she goes and cocks it up by announcing she's running for council. He had no choice...

Mard-Arse5108: Shit! Remind me never to get on your bad side, lady! How do you find out all this shit?

SinEater81: :D :D :D You've got nowt to worry about. None of you lot do. You're my people.

CHAPTER THIRTY-FIVE

"JOAN, CAN YOU HEAR ME?" Nigel's voice drifted through the darkness. She tried to sit up, but a hand against her shoulder prevented her from succeeding. "Don't struggle, Joany-Pop. You had a bit of a fall. Knocked your head pretty hard."

"Where am I?" Her eyes fluttered open, but the bright light overhead blinded her and she closed her eyes again.

"At home, silly," Nigel's familiar, condescending tone wrapped around her.

"My head..." Joan moaned. Nausea caused her stomach to roil uncomfortably. Grabbing out at Nigel, Joan managed to roll onto her side as acrid vomit climbed her throat and flooded into her mouth. She clung to the edge of the sofa as she heaved again. The effort of vomiting caused pain and pressure to build behind her eyes and in her head. She moaned again, a sound like that of a wounded and dying animal. "Hospital..."

"You'll be fine," Nigel said sternly. He unpicked the grip she had on his arm. She heard him tutting as he straightened up. "Look at the mess you've made."

"I'm sorry," Joan said, the pain in her head subsiding a little as she stopped heaving.

"Why would you do something so stupid?"

"I fell," she stammered. "I think..."

"I know you fell," he said. "I came home to find the house in darkness and you on the floor. For a moment I thought you were dead. Imagine how I must have felt."

Joan closed her eyes, anything to help ease the pain that threatened to drown her under the weight of it all. "I'm sorry, Nigel."

"You're always doing such stupid things," he said. He sighed, and Joan was only barely aware of the sound of him walking away.

Her stomach rolled again and she turned onto her side, but there was nothing left inside to vomit. The movement caused sparks of light to explode behind her eyes. Groaning, she covered her face with her arm. It helped to block some of the light out. At least there were still some small mercies to be had.

Something wet and cold slapped down onto her face and Joan jerked. Fear spiked her adrenaline. Her eyes snapped open, but she was still in the dark. It took her pain addled brain a moment to realise Nigel had brought her a cold, wet washcloth.

"Use that to clean yourself up," he said. Irritation coloured his words, and Joan shrank away from him. Shame burned two spots of colour high in her cheeks as she mopped at her face with the cloth. When she opened her eyes, it surprised her to see the cloth was stained red.

"I'm bleeding." Her voice was flat and it wasn't a question, but Nigel was only half paying attention to her.

"That's what happens when you throw yourself on the floor," he said. "Even small children have the good sense not to smack their heads on the furniture."

"I didn't mean it," she said. "I tripped."

"And why would you trip? You've never tripped before?"

Joan bit her lip. Better Nigel didn't know the truth. Whenever she'd fallen in the past, she'd never bothered to tell him. Well, there was that one time, but he hadn't believed her then. She had a vague memory of him demanding to see the bruises. And even then he hadn't been satisfied. His rough treatment had left more bruises than the fall had. But this was different. She'd never blacked out before.

She struggled into an upright position. Gritting her teeth against the nausea, she waited for the room to stop spinning before she opened her eyes fully.

"I think maybe the tablets made me--"

"Oh, here we go again." Nigel huffed out a breath. He glanced in her direction, a dark glint in his eyes. "Anyone would think you didn't want to get better, Joan."

"Of course I want to get better," she said. "How could ask me that?"

"Because from where I'm standing, you keep making excuses for reasons why you shouldn't be taking your medication."

"That's not fair," she said. "I'm taking them."

"And what would you call this kind of behaviour? Falling over. Trying to make me feel guilty because I want to be with the woman I married." He sighed and shook his head sadly. "Perhaps this isn't working out, Joan."

"No!" She tried to stand, but the world shifted suddenly. The pain, which had up to that moment subsided into the background, flared back to life as soon as she tried to get off the floor. She dropped back down onto the carpet and cradled her head in her hands. A memory tugged at her and she tried to latch onto it, but it slipped through her fingers like sand.

"I'm going out," Nigel said. "I need some time to clear my head."

"Please, don't go," Joan whispered, anything more would have been too painful. But if he heard her, he gave no indication of it. Instead, a moment later Joan heard the sound of the front door slam. It was so loud the pictures rattled on the walls and she winced. She remained on the couch and time passed slowly.

When the pain in her head had once again receded into the background, Joan contemplated moving. Gingerly, she got up from the floor. Testing her legs, she was pleased to discover they were capable of supporting her. She shuffled from the living room and made her way into the kitchen. Gathering a wash bowl and cloth, she returned to the living room.

It took some time to scrub the vomit from the carpet. As she worked, the pain behind her eyes threatened to overwhelm her, but she fought against it. Whenever it got too bad, she pressed her head to the floor and waited for the worst of it to subside.

Finally, she was satisfied that Nigel would not be able to find fault with her work. Climbing the stairs, she made her way to bed. As she sat on the side of the mattress, she contemplated the tablets she was supposed to take. Nigel would be furious with her if he found out she was skipping doses. Then again, Nigel was already furious with her, anyway. Setting the tablets back on the bedside table, she climbed into bed and pulled the duvet over her head.

In the dark, she allowed her tears to flow freely. Nigel hadn't always been so cruel, had he?

When they'd been newly wed, things had been better. He'd been loving and attentive. Sure he'd had his oddities. She had never understood his desire for taking pictures of her in various states of undress. She'd gone along with it all. Her desire to please him had been all-consuming.

As she thought about Nigel, the memory of her husband was overlaid by another. Declan Campbell... It hadn't been her imagination. She'd seen his picture on the news. They'd released him from police custody.

Joan's eyelids grew heavy as her thoughts swirled in her mind. Her brain still felt as though it was made mostly from cotton candy making it difficult to full comprehend the situation at hand. Declan's face morphed into Nigel's. He smiled cruelly as he closed the boot of the car on her and she screamed to be released.

CHAPTER THIRTY-SIX

"HOW DID WE GET THIS?" DC Martina Nicoll parked the car outside the lavish townhouse. "I would have thought something like this would have been right up Haskell's alley."

Ambrose swallowed the last of his chips and shrugged as he sucked the salt and vinegar from his fingers. "They're all tied up in the Gwen Campbell case. Rather them than me," he said. "This us?"

Martina nodded and peered up at the building in front of her. "Fancy place."

"Aye." Ambrose was already out of the car. He pulled the collar of his coat up around his chin in an attempt to protect himself from the worst of the rain.

"How's Julie and the new baby?" Martina asked as she followed him out into the rain.

"Great," he said quickly. "You know they tell you

sleep deprivation is hard but I think this job prepares you for it."

"You mean Julie is doing all the night feeds and you're lying on your arse in bed?" Martina grinned at him.

"I do my share." He paused. "Apparently I don't know how to put a nappy on proper. Last week I changed the nappy before I left for work and screwed it up. Jake did something called a 'poonami', whatever that is." Ambrose grinned. "I mean don't get me wrong. I'm proud of my boy. But all the same I'm glad I wasn't around for it neither."

"Poor Julie," Martina said. They paused at the door to show their identification to the officer waiting.

"Julie said it was in his hair an all."

"Ok, yuck. And you owe your wife a night off."

"I'd do it in a heartbeat but she's having none of it."

"I'm going to tell her you put the nappy on loose on purpose," Martina said.

"You bloody well won't!" He glared at her. "Are you trying to have me killed?"

Martina didn't bother to try and hide her smile. "Well, you know what to do." As she spoke they dressed in the waiting Tyvek suits. Once suited and booted, they picked their way carefully up the stairs.

"What information do we have on this?"

Ambrose's voice was muffled from behind the mask he wore.

"Female, deceased. It was called in by an anonymous tip. They've already tracked the call to a residential address in Uttoxeter. Uniforms are going to call there and get some more details. It seems unlikely that the call came from the killer though."

"Can't rule it out though," Ambrose said as they arrived at the top of the stairs. A figure emerged from the room. He pulled off his mask and grinned at Ambrose.

"Good to see you again, DS Scofield. You look good for a man getting no sleep."

"Oh, he's getting all the sleep. Poor Julie on the other hand..." Martina trailed off but ignored the wicked look thrown her direction by her sergeant.

David Farley's laughter echoed in the upper hallway.

"What have we got?" Ambrose asked, his tone brusque.

"It's pretty grim in there." The smile faded from David's face as he glanced back over his shoulder. "Why anyone would want to do something like this..." His voice dropped away. "You know, you should probably ask Dr Quinn to take a look at the file. I'm sure she'd tell you something about the scumbag you're looking for."

"That bad, 'eh?" Martina's chest squeezed as she

glanced into the room beyond that bustled with activity.

"Worse. Whoever did this really wanted to make her suffer. If you've got some vicks to dab on your nose I'd use it."

"Already did it before we got suited up," Ambrose said gruffly.

Martina shot a look at her sergeant and his brows disappeared beneath the hood of his suit. As David turned away for them and gestured for them to follow him onto the plates Ambrose leaned towards her.

"It's got to be bad if the CSM is warning us." Martina nodded but remained quiet. This was the part of her job she hated the most. It was an expected part of the work, but just because she expected it, did not make it easier to deal with.

"Mind your step it's pretty messy, even with the plates we've laid down."

Martina followed David closely as he led them into the apartment. The room was lit with bright overhead spots. As they left the main area and headed into the bedroom, Martina got her first glimpse of the crime scene.

The smell was what got to her first. Despite the mask and the menthol she'd dabbed below her nose, together they were no match for the putrid smell of vomit and excrement. Her stomach churned uncomfortably as David led them to a doorway.

Pausing, Martina tried to get her brain to focus on the external details of the space. It looked like some kind of walk-in wardrobe that had been transformed into a studio space. The rubber mat beneath the plates was covered in food and other substances that she struggled not to identify.

She catalogued the space, all the while trying to keep her brain from piecing the horrific scene that was set up in the centre of the room.

"Fuck!"

Hearing Ambrose swear next to her was all it took for Martina's brain to put the pieces of the scene together.

Her gaze fixed on what remained of the young woman opposite. Her face was twisted into a grotesque mask of horror and pain.

Martina turned away and took a few steps back across the plates. Pausing in the living room of the apartment, she ignored the speculative glances thrown her direction.

"DC Nicoll?" Ambrose's voice followed her.

Swallowing past the saliva that flooded her mouth, Martina tried to compose herself. Tears stung at her eyes but she blinked them away.

She felt the presence of Ambrose at her back. "You all right?"

Nodding, she swallowed again and wished she was outside in the damp air. Anything would be better than the oppressive stench of the apartment.

"Whoever did that--" She cut off and squeezed her eyes shut. It was the wrong thing to do; the image of Holly Thomas was burned into her retinas and bloomed in the darkness behind her eyelids. She opened her eyes and looked up at Ambrose. "That's the work of a monster."

Nodding, he glanced back at the room. "You fit to go back in, or do you need--"

Before he could finish, Martina had already started to shake her head. "I can go back." She straightened her shoulders. "I can do this."

"You don't have to." The unspoken hung between them. They both knew if she ever wanted to progress beyond her current rank she would have to face this and probably worse in the future. And she could not be seen to shy away from the gruesome reality of the work they did.

"Thanks, guv, but I can do this." She smiled up at him, momentarily forgetting that she was wearing a mask that covered her expression. "I mean it. I'm fine. Really."

Ambrose studied her for a moment longer and then with an abrupt nod turned on his heel and headed back to the room. "Come on then. We've got work to do. And Farley is right, see if you can have Dr Quinn look over the files. If she can shed some light on this, we might stand a chance of getting ahead of it."

Nodding, Martina followed him, albeit at a

slower pace. As she reached the doorway, the low drone of the CSM's voice caught her ear.

"He wanted her to suffer. Used a tube to force feed her until her gut ruptured. I'm hoping the forensic pathologist tells us that she suffocated before that happened but to be honest, I'm not holding out much hope."

Martina stepped into the room and made a silent promise that no matter what it took, she would find the bastard responsible.

CHAPTER THIRTY-SEVEN

JOAN AWOKE in the middle of the night tangled in the sheets. She was sweaty and feverish, and it took her a few minutes of lying in the dark to realise Nigel hadn't been trying to kill her. She was safe and sound in her own bed. Swinging her legs out of bed, she waited for the dizziness to subside before she stood. The pain in her stomach had returned and it was worse than ever. Even breathing hurt.

When she felt strong enough, she pulled on her dressing gown and made her way downstairs.

The house was empty and silent. As she paused in the living room door, she half expected to find Nigel asleep on the couch but he was nowhere to be found. It had been like this for days now. He was spending more and more time away from home. Away from her.

Her laptop sat on the table where she'd abandoned it the night before. Crossing to it, she hit a key and waited for it to wake up. It took a couple of seconds but when the screen came to life, Joan was surprised to find a word document open. Her eyes travelled down over the pages of writing and her stomach churned.

She didn't remember writing it. But it was on her laptop. She scanned the paragraphs filled with gruesome descriptions of murder and chaos. The strength left Joan's legs and she dropped into the chair. She couldn't have written this... could she? It sounded like her. And yet...

She swallowed around the lump in the back of her throat.

There had to be a mistake.

"Nigel!"

Silence closed around her. She'd driven him away. The tears came, but Joan's head felt clearer than it had in days. What if she had written this and Nigel had found it?

No. She stared down at the words. She didn't write this. She couldn't write this. Even if it did sound like her. Even if it was written on her laptop.

What if Nigel was right? What if her stopping her medication was causing breaks to occur? Reading back over the words triggered a memory to surface in Joan's mind.

She was slumped in the passenger seat. The icy rain had soaked through her jumper. And it was still falling outside. Joan squeezed her eyes shut, hoping that would make the memory clearer. Rain slid down the windshield blurring her eye line as she watched Nigel... No, it wasn't Nigel.

Joan took a deep breath. The dark silhouette took a moment to become clearer in her mind. Declan Campbell. She'd seen Declan Campbell manhandle his wife. But there was more than that. In her memory there was something wrong with Gwen. Something wrong in her movements. She wasn't moving at all and Declan was lifting her from the boot of her car.

Burying her face in her hands, she prayed for Nigel to come home.

CHAPTER THIRTY-EIGHT

HARRIET PAUSED in the doorway to the office and studied the people working. Since her argument with Drew and the subsequent visit she'd received from Melissa, she had decided to stay away but she couldn't keep it up, especially when Olivia had called and asked her to drop by.

There was no sign of Drew. Harriet heaved a silent sigh of relief. They had not spoken since the argument and it was strange to say the least.

She caught Olivia's eye and the officer waved her over. Grabbing a spare swivel chair, Harriet joined her at the desk.

"I wasn't sure if you'd come in," Olivia said quietly. "Since you went AWOL, the DI has been on one."

Ducking her head, Harriet studied the desk. "I didn't think I was welcome after the other night."

"Honestly, I think you should ignore him. He's been a miserable git since you left. Partly due to the 'man-flu', he caught from one of the PC's out at the Hole of Horcum but also because you haven't been around."

"Well, while that's a nice thought, he could have called if he wanted me to come in."

Olivia snorted. "Have you met DI Haskell? He's too stubborn to do something like that. Take it from me, if you want to make nice, you'll have to be the bigger person."

Suppressing a smile, Harriet's gaze snagged on the reams of paper scattered over the desk. "So what is all of this then?"

"This is what I was hoping you could help me with." Olivia's expression was apologetic. "Jodie found a forum where a bunch of people get together and bitch and moan about famous people."

"And what does that have to do with the Campbell case?"

"They had a lot to say about Gwen. Jodie has been tracking them since the news broke. Needless to say none of these people have had a good word to say about her."

Harriet picked up the first piece of paper and sceptically looked at it. "And you think maybe one of the users is Gwen's killer?"

"Well it's the best lead we've got. These people really did not like Gwen."

Harriet scanned over the sheets of paper, noting the vitriolic posts. "It's certainly possible. Although, many of these people are posting the more outrageous slurs because they feel safe behind their keyboards."

She continued her perusal. "I think you should be looking for, not necessarily the worst offender, but the person who is inciting the worst of the hatred."

"You mean somebody whipping the others into a frenzy?"

Harriet nodded. "Exactly. They'll probably throw out a few interesting tidbits and then sit back and watch the feeding frenzy." Pursing her lips, Harriet met Olivia's gaze. "The person who murdered Gwen was not a stranger. She knew her killer."

"How can you be so sure?" Olivia asked.

"The pathologist and anthropologist's report suggest blunt trauma to the side and back of the skull. They've said she was facing her attacker and that her injuries are consistent with a fall. Probably down a stairs."

"And that tells you she knew her attacker?"

Harriet nodded. "She was facing them. She wasn't afraid of this person, which tells me this was somebody she thought would not hurt her or Evie. A mother would not willingly expose her child to danger."

"But she could have been caught unawares."

"It's less likely. And if that's true and you're also

correct about these forum entries then somebody who knew Gwen will be able to offer personal information about her in order to get the others suitably riled up."

"I'll ask Jodie if she can narrow her search parameters with this."

Harriet smiled. "I can keep going through these if you'd like?"

Olivia glanced towards the door. "That'd be great, but I actually think someone is looking for you."

Following the officer's line of sight, Harriet spotted DC Nicoll hesitating outside the door. As soon as she caught Harriet's eye, she raised her hand in acknowledgment.

Crossing the office, Harriet stepped out into the hall. "Nice to see you again."

"Likewise," Martina said. "I'm sorry to drag you away from work but I was hoping for a quick chat, if you had a free moment."

Harriet glanced back at the office. "I'm a little tied up at the minute."

"This won't take long. I could buy you a cup of coffee in the place next door."

"Well, how can I refuse? I'll grab my bag and coat and follow you down."

. . .

A FEW MINUTES LATER, ensconced in one of the small booths in the corner of the coffee shop, Harriet smiled at the woman opposite. "What can I help you with?"

"Obviously, what I'm going to tell you is confidential."

"Obviously," Harriet said.

"We got an anonymous tip off about a murder. When uniforms arrived at the scene they found a young woman, deceased in her own apartment."

"The person who called it in, were they connected?"

Martina shook her head. "Poor bloke is so traumatised he could barely talk to the uniforms that called at his house."

"People can fake their emotions," Harriet said.

"I don't think they'd fake incontinence," Martina shot back.

Surprised, Harriet glanced down at her cup. "No. I suppose that would be a stretch. I don't think you brought me here to discuss the functions of the human body."

Shaking her head, Martina withdrew a file from her bag. "I wanted your opinion on this." She glanced at their surroundings. "I'm going to ask you to be very discrete with this. I've included some of the crime scene photographs and they're quite..." Martina cut off and Harriet could see the troubled expression that crossed her face.

Careful to keep prying eyes from seeing the contents, Harriet opened the file. It took her a moment to comprehend the images laid out before her. When she did, she closed the file again and took a moment to breathe through her nose.

When she opened her eyes, it was to find Martina studying her carefully from the other side of the table. "It's bad."

With a small nod, Harriet opened the file again. This time, she was a little more prepared for what awaited her. She tried to view the images with a critical eye. "It says here there was no forced entry to Ms Thomas' apartment."

"Not that we could find," Martina said. "Either Holly let her killer in, or..."

"Or they already had a key." Harriet flipped over each picture after she finished studying it. It was easier to concentrate with the images face down.

"Cause of death?"

"The pathologist is giving asphyxiation as the official cause of death." Martina drew in a slow breath. "A tube was inserted into her throat and food was poured down it causing her stomach to rupture," Martina said quietly. "They found evidence of an ulcer in the wall of her stomach and that weakness meant it couldn't stretch as much as it should have otherwise. The perforation along with vomit and aspirate in her lungs was the cause of death."

"Does the pathologist think the killer had medical experience?"

Martina shook her head. "No, he said the tube was inserted crudely. He knocked out one of her front teeth and chipped another in the struggle." She buried her head in her hands.

"What is all of these other things in the background?"

Martina didn't lift her head and instead, answered with her head still buried in her hands. "She was an influencer and made videos for her Only Fans community."

"So all of this was for work?"

Martina nodded. "We were thinking that maybe one of her fans managed to find out where she lived and paid her a visit but..."

"But you couldn't find anything that might support that theory?"

Martina lifted her head. "We've got nothing."

"Well, the lack of forced entry combined with the level of overkill involved I think you're looking for someone known to the victim."

"The boyfriend was away in London for a few days. He's got the receipts to prove it. And by all accounts they were very much in love."

Harriet closed the report. "The person you're looking for has a very controlling personality. I'd look for people who Ms Thomas in the recent past cut ties with."

"There is more," Martina said. "The killer filmed the murder and sent it out to her Only Fans page. They referred to her gluttony and the sins she committed."

Harriet sat back in her chair. "I suppose the murderer was careful to keep themselves out of sight of the camera?"

"And they used an electronic modulator to change their voice. We've got somebody looking at it, we're hoping they can clean it up some."

"You're looking for someone that Holly slighted. She made them feel small, insignificant. They believed they held control over her life and somehow she turned the tables on them. They perceived her behaviour as greedy and so they transformed her from the golden goose into one used to make foie-gras."

"Do you know how big a list that's going to be?"

Harriet nodded. "I'm sorry I can't be more help. If it helps, you're looking for a man."

"How can you be so sure?"

"There's a sexual element in the level of control used. Power and control killers are always male."

"But the religious aspect?"

"It's interesting but it doesn't change my opinion that you're looking for a man."

Martina's smile was tentative. "Thanks for this."

"I'm just sorry I can't give you more. But I'd need

more information than I think you can share with me."

Martina ducked her head. "This is off the record so to speak. But if Ambrose can convince the DI to bring you in you'll be hearing from us."

"Well, I hope you won't need my help and that you'll find your killer sooner rather than later."

Martina grimaced. "You and me both. How likely do you think it is that this bloke will kill again?"

Folding her arms over her chest, Harriet hesitated.

"I know you can't work in definitives but your opinion is important."

"Then I think you're looking at someone who will almost certainly kill again. I'd hazard a guess that this probably isn't his first kill either. There's an arrogance to this murder that tells me he's growing in confidence. There will be a cooling off period but I would imagine another woman is going to enrage him again and he will feel compelled to exert the ultimate control over them."

"How long of a cooling off period could we potentially be looking at?"

Harriet shrugged. "It's hard to tell. Someone like this could very easily be triggered. It could be weeks, months. Maybe even days. This is a very dangerous person and how soon they'll offend will depend on what triggers them and their motivations."

Martina's phone started to ring and she smiled

apologetically. "I have to go. You've been a real help, Dr Quinn. Thank you."

"Any time," Harriet said, gathering her things. She followed Martina to the door. "And if you get the approval to bring me in, I'd be happy to help."

Martina grinned and hurried to a car parked at the other side of the road. "I might have to hold you to that."

Harriet waited until the officer had driven away before she made her way back to the office.

Pausing at the bottom of the stairs, she decided to make a note of her thoughts over Martina's case. As she searched her bag for the diary Drew had given her for Christmas she was surprised to find it missing.

"You're here." Drew's voice pulled her from her reverie.

Harriet found Drew studying her from the steps. "Olivia asked me to come in."

He nodded and glanced down at the ground. "I wanted to apologise for the other day..."

"You were very rude."

"I was," he said. "In my defence, I wasn't feeling very well. And I've been under a lot of pressure..." He huffed a sigh. "I'm not trying to make excuses. I'm sorry. I was an ass."

Harriet smiled. "I'm sorry to."

"What for?"

"I should have called you before I went to the crime scene."

"You don't need my permission. Farley knows what he's doing." There was a gruffness to Drew's voice that hadn't been there before.

"Are you coming up?"

Hesitating, Harriet contemplated making her excuses before heading back to the university. Seeing the hopeful look on Drew's face she changed her mind. "I can come up for a while."

"Great. Did Olivia tell you, Declan Campbell is having a memorial service for Gwen. He asked us if we'd like to come."

Harriet's eyebrows rose. "Really, even though you brought him in?"

Drew nodded. "I was surprised to but apparently it was Beth's idea. I'm going to go. Will you come?"

Harriet hesitated. The conversation she'd had with Melissa weighed heavy on her mind. Then again, what could it hurt, she was a part of the team. And going could provide her with some valuable insight. "Of course. How's Melissa?"

"She's fine," Drew said with a smile. "She's been bringing me chicken soup to try and make me feel better."

Harriet smiled broadly. "How thoughtful."

"That's Melissa," Drew said as he moved ahead of her up the stairs. "I was just about to put on a brew. Do you want one?"

"I'd love one."

"Great, I'll bring it to the desk."

She watched him hare off down the hall. An uneasy feeling settled in the pit of her stomach. She'd put David Farley off the other night after the situation with Drew. It had seemed like the correct thing to do. And going for drinks was the very last thing on her mind.

But perhaps once everything settled she would call David and rearrange. After all, Drew had Melissa. Perhaps it was time she too branched out.

CHAPTER THIRTY-NINE

WHEN THE KEY turned in the front door, Joan was sitting in the dark at the kitchen table. The laptop had gone dark again. She'd been glad when its ghostly glow had faded. Glad not to have to read the words that were now indelibly inked inside her head.

A cup of cold coffee sat forgotten in front of her as she stared off into the shadows of the room. Her head still hurt, but a couple of paracetamol had taken the edge off it.

Nigel crept down the hall. The sound of his stockinged feet padding over the tile floor pulled Joan from her thoughts. Turning towards the door, she watched his silhouette framed in the light from the hall.

"Joan?" There was surprise in his voice. The kitchen bulbs blazed brightly as he flicked the light switch. For a moment, Joan thought she was blind.

She snapped her eyes shut, gratified that at least her automatic reflexes still worked in spite of her aching head. She waited a breath before she opened her eyes a crack.

Nigel stood at the end of the table, concern etched into his features as he studied her. "You're still up? Why aren't you in bed?"

Was that a note of accusation she detected in his voice? She pushed the thought aside, she didn't have time to ponder over it. Instead, she laced her cold fingers around the cup in front of her and lifted it to her mouth. The coffee was bitter against her tongue, but she swallowed it down. She needed to be clear headed for this conversation. If coffee could sober a person up, then it was bound to help her, too.

"What's wrong?" Nigel took a step closer. Joan shook her head. The cup shifted against her mouth and some of the cold coffee dribbled down her chin. "Is it your head?"

It had been so long since Joan had heard genuine sympathy from her husband that when he asked her how her head was she didn't recognise the sentiment immediately.

"My head is not the problem," she said setting the cup back on the table. She swiped at her mouth with the edge of her sleeve.

Nigel narrowed his eyes at her. "What is that supposed to mean? If this is about your medication--"

Joan cut him off with a shake of her head. "It's not

that. I saw something and I think I need to speak with the police."

"Joan," Nigel said gently. He moved around the table, his hands raised placatingly. "What could you possibly have seen that would make you think you needed to speak with the police?"

"It's Gwen." Joan drew in a shaky breath. "I know her husband killed her."

Nigel stared at her, incredulity crossing his features. "Excuse me?"

"I know he killed her, Nige. I saw it."

Joan waited for Nigel to speak. She'd played the conversation over in her mind for the hours she'd been sat at the table. He would sit next to her and take her hand in his. He would tell her how awful it must have been to witness something so terrible. He would tell her how sorry he was for not listening. It would heal the rift between them. He would finally understand that she wasn't crazy. He would--

Nigel's laughter took Joan by surprise. The sound of it short-circuited the thought process in her head. She stared blankly up at him as his laughter grew louder. When he held his side, and doubled over at the waist, one hand on the table to steady him, she felt shock settle over her. This wasn't how it was supposed to be.

"Nigel, I don't understand."

He laughed louder. Tears streamed down his ruddy cheeks. Humiliation burned in Joan's chest.

"This isn't funny, Nigel."

"I'm sorry," he said, swiping at his tears. "I know I shouldn't laugh, but I just..." He tried to straighten up and stifle his laughter, but immediately failed. "I know I'm not supposed to laugh, but I thought you were going to tell me something serious."

"This is serious," Joan insisted. "I saw Declan murder his wife. My friend, Gwen..."

Nigel shook his head, and choked off his laughter. "Joan, you can't be serious. Even you must see how insane this sounds." His laughter calmed and he wiped the tears from his cheeks.

"I'm very serious. I saw it, Nigel."

"No, you didn't," he said. The smile faded as his expression grew serious. "You can't just go around accusing people of things like that, Joan."

"You can if it's true."

Nigel shook his head. "Do you hear yourself?"

"You need to listen to me," she said. "I went over to Gwen's house that day. Do you remember? It was the day you confronted me about my tablets."

"Exactly," Nigel said triumphantly. "You weren't taking your medication."

"And I told you *why* I wasn't."

"Joan, without your medication you're prone to delusions."

She shook her head despite the mounting migraine. "No, that was different."

"Was it?" Nigel asked.

"That was entirely different," she said mutinously. "I wasn't well."

Nigel sighed and closed his eyes. "I know, Joan. And it's not something that just goes away." He turned and crossed to the kitchen sink. Grabbing a glass from the draining board he filled it with water before he knocked it back.

"Nigel. Please." Joan sucked in a breath. "You have to believe me. I wouldn't lie about something like this."

"And I wouldn't have thought you'd lie taking your medication," he said darkly. The smash of the glass in the sink made Joan jump. "This has to stop, Joan. Either you take your medication. You take it and we get back to some semblance of normality."

"I'm taking my medication." She cringed at the lie.

"Really?" Nigel swung around to face her. "Because I happen to know for a fact that you haven't been taking them."

"How could you know that?"

"Because I count the pills, Joan. Somebody has to keep you in line."

"Nigel..." Shock rooted her to the spot. "You've been checking up on me?"

"Of course I have. I can't trust you. You lie and you make up stories and unless I verify everything I don't know from one day to the next what's fact or fiction." The emotion in his voice took her by surprise.

"I'm sorry..."

"Either you take your meds, or..."

"Or what, Nigel?"

"Divorce."

Joan was on her feet and across the room in an instant. "You made a promise. You said in sickness and in health. You swore it."

Cupping her chin, he gazed down into her eyes. "I did," he said. "But I'm only human, Joan. Even I have my limits. You live under my roof, you do as I say. I've got my growing business to think of, Joan. I need to be able to trust you."

She tried to turn away from him, but his grip tightened on her face. "You're hurting me."

"Do you hear me, Joan? If you want this to work, then you need to do as I say."

"But they make me feel worse," she whispered. "I don't feel like myself when I take them. I can't think, I can't write..."

"This is not a choice. I'll be forced to report you to Dr Oswalt. You remember what happened the last time?."

She nodded. Her memories were a little hazy about the details, but she was perfectly clear about what it had been like to be locked up. "Fine."

"And there'll be no more accusations about innocent people?"

"He killed her, Nigel." The words were out of her mouth before she could even think to stop them.

Sadness registered on his face for a moment. "For God's sake, Joan, what did I just say?"

"But you don't understand--"

"You're right," he said. Anger radiated from every inch of his body. "I don't understand. God help me, but I've tried to help you. But you just don't want to be helped, do you? You're a malicious, twisted bitch determined to drag everyone down to your own toxic level."

Tears welled in Joan's eyes blurring her vision. Dashing them away with the heel of her hand, she tried to swallow past the lump that had formed in her throat. "Nigel, please, don't."

"Don't what?" he spat at her. Colour suffused his face, reddening his cheeks. The vein in his temple throbbed as he paced back and forth in front of her. "Don't tell the truth?" His laughter was bitter. "I know it's something you're not exactly familiar with, but the rest of us don't live on cloud-cuckoo." The mocking tone in his voice cut at what little remained of her self-confidence. Closing the space between them, Nigel pushed his face in hers. "You're a fucking lunatic. I don't know why I stay with you. You make me sick."

Joan cringed away from him, backing up until her spine hit the wall. She shrank in on herself as he dogged her every step. "Anything I felt for you, died a long time ago."

"Nigel, you don't mean that."

"Don't I?"

He laughed again and Joan squeezed her eyes shut. The sound was physically painful to hear. He could be cold, even callous sometimes, but he'd never been so cruel before. This wasn't the man she knew and loved. Nigel cared for her. Everything he did was for her own good. But everything he was saying now...

"How long has it been since I touched you?" There was an undercurrent to his voice now. "How long has it been since I fucked you?" He leaned in and whispered the last against her ear. At any other time it might have been an intimate action, but now it was threatening.

"Stop it," Joan whispered, tears falling freely down her face.

"I found someone else," he said softly. "Someone who gives me everything I could ever want."

"No..."

"Oh yes," Nigel said. "And do you know what else? When I found you on the floor that night I was happy."

"Nigel, don't say it."

"I was happy because I thought you were dead." He closed his eyes, a smile stealing over his face. "I thought I was free of you. I saw it all mapped out before my eyes. I'd have given you a good funeral. And then finally I would be free." When he looked at her again it was with pure hatred. "And then you moaned and all of my dreams were shattered."

"Nigel, I swear I'm not lying. Declan Campbell murdered his wife. I saw it."

"There you go again," Nigel said. He wasn't even listening to her anymore as he pulled away. "I've just told you I wished you were dead and you're still hung up on a delusion you had." He moved over to the medicine cabinet and pulled it open. Grabbing the packets of medication he took them down and set them out on the table. "You're going to take your pills, Joan."

"I don't want to," she said panic lacing her words. This wasn't the Nigel she knew and loved. He would never do this to her. There was something wrong, something she was missing.

Nigel crossed to her side and grabbed her by the shoulders. He jerked her forwards, pushing her towards the table. She went with him because to fight back was pointless. He was stronger than she was. When he forced her into the chair, he popped a pill out of its foil packet and held the tablet out to her. "Thou shalt not lie."

Joan lifted her eyes to his, pleading silently as she stared up at him. But there was nothing of the man she knew and loved there.

"Nige..."

"You heard me, Joan. Make your choice."

CHAPTER FORTY

SITTING on the side of the bed, Joan fumbled with buttons on her black blouse. It felt strange to be attending a memorial service for Gwen. Especially when they wouldn't be burying her. At least that was what Nigel had told her. There would be no burial. Not yet. The police had not released the body.

It felt wrong that they would hold onto her remains like that. Did they not realise that they were keeping her from her rest? Perhaps they didn't care. The police force were not exactly known for their respect for spiritual beliefs...

As she remained on the side of the bed, Joan became aware of Nigel's heavy tread on the stairs. Since that night when he'd returned to find her on the floor, things had changed between them. He was colder, harder. As much as she hated to admit it, the man she had married had somewhere along the line slipped away from her.

He paused in the doorway, his gaze slid over the clothes she wore, appraising her. He nodded and took another step into the bedroom.

"I brought this for you," he said. He held his hands out towards her, a glass of murky water in his right hand and in his left was a packet of medication. Joan's hands shook as she stood and crossed the floor. The carpet shushed softly beneath her stockinged feet as she took the offered packet of pills.

"What's wrong with the water?" She raised her gaze to Nigel's face. If she'd expected to find any kindness there, she was mistaken. Instead, he glared at her.

"Is that the thanks I get?"

"Nigel, I just--"

"How should I know what's wrong with the water? Do I look like I work for the water company, Joan? It's probably due to a burst pipe, or something."

"I'm sorry, I didn't mean..."

"No, you never mean to do anything, do you? But you keep on doing it just the same." He sighed and thrust the glass out towards her. Some of the grey brown water sloshed over the sides of the glass and landed on the simple black blouse she'd picked out for herself. The tremor in her hand increased as she took the packet of pills.

"Nige, I'm not supposed to take these ones no more. Dr Oswalt said--"

"And how would know what Dr Oswalt said, Joany-Pop?"

Her lower lip began to wobble, not that she would be able to cry. Her illness made it practically impossible for her to weep. And whatever chance she might have stood was quickly negated by the side-effects of her medications.

But Nigel saw the look on her face. His expression softened and he guided her back to the edge of the bed. "I'm sorry, love. It's just finding you on the floor like that the other night, well it really scared me. And then, to hear you haven't been taking your medication properly." He shook his head sadly as he sat her back down on the bed. "It's all really upset me. More than I can say."

"I said I was sorry," Joan said. "And I meant it. I really didn't mean to fall, but my legs." She dropped her gaze accusingly towards her skirt clad lap.

"I know." He patted her hand gently. "That's why I rang Dr Oswalt. We had a little chat this morning."

"Nigel, there was no need," Joan said. Embarrassment warmed her cheeks. What must Dr Oswalt think of her? Would he want her to return to the hospital? The thought of winding up back in there... It shook her to her core.

"There was every need, Joan, love. You know Dr Oswalt only wants what's best for you, same as me."

"But it was an accident."

Nigel shook his head. "Dr Oswalt isn't too convinced of that."

Joan's heart leapt into the back of her throat. "He wants me to go back in?"

There was a pause and Nigel continued to stare at the floor. Joan tightened her grip on the glass. "I'll do anything you say, Nigel. Just please, don't send me back in there. Please." Under normal circumstances, Joan knew better than to beg Nigel for anything. It never went in her favour. Sometimes, Joan wondered if begging him gave him the ammunition he needed, no wanted, to punish her. Not that she blamed him. She was a silly, wicked sinner who deserved all the punishment he doled out.

"We agreed it wasn't best to send you back in, yet." Nigel's voice was level. As soon as he said she would not be sent back in, Joan stopped listening.

Throwing her arms around his neck, she squealed with delight. The glass of murky water slipped out of her hand. Before she could stop it, the glass hit the carpet and bounced with a dull thud, spilling the contents across the rug.

"Now look at what you've done?" Nigel snapped. Exasperation was etched into every line of his body. But Joan did not care. All she could see, all she could hear was the man who had saved her from having to go back for another extended stay in the hospital.

"I'll fix it, Nigel. Don't you worry," she said,

bending down to snatch the glass from the floor. Getting to his feet, he bumped against her hip causing her to sprawl, face first, onto the damp carpet. The carpet burned roughly against her cheek.

"You're a mess," he growled. "How do you expect me to take you anywhere?"

Straightening up, she tried to smooth down her hair. "I'll fix it, Nigel. I can fix it."

"Just make sure you take your tablet," he said tossing the packet of tablets onto the floor next to her. With one last look of disgust, he walked away leaving her to sit on the damp floor as the water soaked into her skirt.

CHAPTER FORTY-ONE

ALONE IN THE PEW, Joan fought the urge to fidget. The memorial service had come to an end ten minutes ago and Nigel had told her to stay put while he fetched the car. She rubbed at the spot on her thigh where he'd been forced to pinch her during the service just to get her to stop biting her nails.

But now that he wasn't here to correct her, the urge to chew what was left of her nails down to the quick was overwhelming. Of course, if she'd taken the tablet he'd given to her then she wouldn't be struggling to sit still in the somnolent church.

This wasn't her church. It was too large for one thing. Cavernous was the word that came to mind. Sitting in the pew, was too much like being trapped inside the belly of a huge, monstrous creature. Maybe not its belly, Joan thought. Perhaps the pews were its ribs and if that were the case then she was trapped between two of its ribs. Closing her eyes, she imagined how the beast would writhe and wriggle as she sat there, like a bubble of indigestion that refused to give way. The whole thing made her want to laugh.

Opening her eyes, she tried to swallow the giggle that threatened to erupt out of her. Crossing and then uncrossing her legs again, she trained her eyes on the altar ahead. This was definitely not her church. In there there would be no quiet reflection.

It wasn't Gwen's church either, she thought. The idea of Gwen frequenting a soulless monstrosity like this wasn't one that sat easily with her. In fact, Joan knew for a fact that were Gwen here, they would both have had a wonderful laugh about it all. Perhaps she should tell Gwen's husband that he had picked the wrong church for Gwen's memorial service.

Movement off to the side of the seating area, pulled her attention back to the present moment. The young boy stood sullenly in front of the candles on the left side of the church. He was practically hidden from her view by the large pillar that separated both sections. But there was something deeply familiar about him that drew her in.

Glancing around, Joan was pleased to discover that most everyone else had left. Getting to her feet, she made her way over to the section where the boy stood.

"Are you all right?" Joan's voice was a little hoarse from disuse but the words still came out and so she was grateful for small mercies.

The boy, who was really more of a teenager, she decided, whirled to face her. His gaze raked over her, a sneer curling his lip as he took a step back. "What do you want?"

His question took Joan by surprise. And not just because she'd asked him a question first.

"I came for the service," she said, glancing over towards the altar where the large picture of Gwen had sat. They'd taken it away and Joan found that disappointing. She'd wanted to look at Gwen some more. To get close to the picture and examine it. She'd wanted to know if the photograph of Gwen had been the same as the memory she had in her mind.

"Did you know my mum?" The boy asked.

Joan whirled to face him. "She was your mum?" She shook her head. Gwen didn't have a teenage son...

"Si!" His voice was so familiar. It took Joan back to a time before. Glancing back over her shoulder, she watched Declan approach cautiously. "Hello." A tentative smile appeared on his face before he turned his attention back to the teenager. "Simon, it's time to go. Beth is waiting."

Bitter bile coated Joan's tongue. "Who's Beth?"

The question was blurted out before she could stop it.

Declan winced and cast a look back towards the altar. "I--"

"She's my step-mum," Simon said with a defiant jut to his chin.

Curling her hands into fists, Joan felt her anger build. How could they behave so callously? Gwen wasn't even gone that long and yet they had all moved on with their lives as though she'd never mattered at all. If Gwen were here now, what would she think of it all?

"What would Gwen think?" Joan turned her accusing stare towards Declan. "You can't just bring another woman in to replace her, you know? It's not right."

"Look, I don't know who you think you are, but--"

"She was my friend," Joan said hoarsely. "My best friend."

Declan stared at her uncomprehendingly. "What are you talking about? I've never seen you before in my life. You were never friends with my wife. I knew all of her mates and you're not one of them." There was an icy edge to Declan's voice that cut Joan to the bone. "Are you a reporter?"

Joan shook her head. Her mouth was dry, her tongue stuck to the roof making it difficult to form words correctly. "I was Gwen's best friend. She told me everything. Told me how unhappy she was..."

Declan took a step towards her and raised his finger, jabbing it towards her face. "If you ever come near me or my son ever again--!"

"Joan!" Nigel's voice echoed in the cavernous space of the church.

At the sound of his voice, Declan froze. Joan watched with detached interest as the colour drained from his face and a tremor started in his hand. She turned towards her husband as he hustled up the centre aisle.

"Joan, what have I said about wandering off!" There was an irritated snap to his voice. She stepped aside, allowing him a view of the others she was stood with. Nigel's expression shifted instantly. A smile stretching his lips into a false mask of cheer that Joan recognised only too well. That smile twisted as his gaze fell on Declan.

"Nige, this is Declan." The words were a whisper but they carried in the heavy silence of the church. "Gwen's husband."

"You..." The word came from Declan, a hoarse declaration of agony that caught Joan's attention. There was something important here. Something she was supposed to remember, but years of living in a fog made remembering far more difficult than it should have been. "What the fuck are you doing here?"

Joan glanced idly down at Declan's hands that

had again started to tremble. Rage rolled off his body in waves that threatened to drown her.

Nigel's hand locked around her elbow. He jerked her harshly and Joan stumbled against him.

"Nige, you're hurting me." He would not like her to question his actions but the pain of his fingers as they dug into the flesh of her arm superseded anything else. As though he'd never hurt her, Nigel tightened his grip. A low whimper of pain fell from Joan's lips and Declan's gaze raked over to her.

"Is there a problem?" The low rumbling voice came from the man who stood behind Nigel. Joan stared up at him. Nigel wasn't particularly tall, but she'd never considered him to be particularly short either. But the man who had apparently appeared out of thin air towered over them both.

The heavy khaki overcoat the stranger wore hung perfectly from his broad shoulders. Next to him, Nigel stiffened, his dark grey peacock coat gaping to reveal his pigeon chested torso. He released her arm and pulled his coat close across his body. It was, Joan thought with some amusement, an almost self-conscious move. She wasn't used to seeing Nigel flustered and yet, in the face of the man standing close-by, Nigel was practically floundering.

"No problem," Nigel mumbled.

"I was just giving my condolences," Joan said feeling somewhat braver than she had a moment ago. From the corner of her eye, she spotted a woman standing off to the side. Her shrewd gaze swept over the small group and paused on Joan. As she caught her eye, Joan felt herself smile in response to the warmth in the woman's eyes.

"This man--" Declan never got the chance to finish the sentence.

"Come on, Joan!" Nigel barked. "You've taken up enough of everyone's time."

"Nige, I was just..."

Something unreadable passed through the stranger's eyes as he took in manner in which Nigel manhandled her. The sudden urge to defend her husband swept through Joan but before she could form the words, Nigel had started to tow her away.

Leaning in towards him, she lowered her voice to a conspiratorial whisper. "Who do you think that was?"

Nigel marched her from the church, his pace never faltering as he led her towards the car. If he heard her, he never gave any indication of it.

As they reached the car, which Joan noticed had not moved from where he'd parked it when they'd moved. She contemplated asking him just what he'd been doing when he'd said he was going to bring the car up to the door, but seeing the look on his face, Joan thought better of it.

He pushed her towards the passenger door. "Get in."

"Nigel, who do you think that was?"

He paused on the opposite side of the car and glared at her. There was a glint in his eye that hadn't been there a moment before and it unnerved her. She shrank back against the side of the car, trying to make herself appear as small as possible. There was something about that look in his eye. Something so terribly familiar about it. The hairs on the back of her neck stood to attention. She'd seen it before. She tried to remember but her mind blocked the memories.

If archangel Michael wanted her to know, then he would reveal it all in time.

"Who do I think it is?" Nigel repeated the question back to her. He pursed his lips and glanced back towards the church. "That was the police, Joan."

Her stomach dropped. Gripping onto the door handle, Joan slid into the passenger seat of the car. Nigel climbed in opposite. He kept his gaze trained ahead on the road as he tightened his grip on the wheel.

"What do you think they were doing there?" Her voice was low but Nigel heard her.

"You know I've only ever tried to protect you."

She nodded.

"But sometimes you do terrible things, Joan. I try to keep you safe, but sometimes that's not always possible."

"Nige, you're scaring me."

He looked over at her then. "Do you remember what you did to Gwen?"

She shook her head but the fragmented images from her dreams washed through her mind. And then there were the things she'd written in the times she couldn't remember. Even though she didn't remember typing it out it sounded like her. It felt like something she would have written in one of her books before...

Joan bit her lip hard enough that the metallic taste of blood flooded her mouth.

"What did I do to Gwen?" Her voice was small.

Nigel sighed and started the engine. "It's all right, Joany-Pop, I'll protect you." He reached over and touched her cheek with his fingers. "I'll keep you safe, like I always do."

She leaned into his touch. Her heart had started to hammer in her chest, but feeling Nigel brush against her face settled her. He would look after her. He had in the past. She could trust him.

Opening her eyes, Joan pressed her forehead against the glass of the passenger window as Nigel drove away from the church. As they drove past the front of the building, Joan watched the police officer file out with the strange woman. Declan stood to one side and their gazes were locked on him as he spoke to his son.

Joan's stomach churned with guilt as she watched the scene unfold. Nigel would protect her.

He touched her arm, drawing her attention. "You do trust me, don't you, Joany-Pop?"

Joan nodded, a lump forming in the back of her throat.

"Good girl." He patted her hand affectionately before he returned his attention to the road ahead. "That's my good girl."

CHAPTER FORTY-TWO

THE SERVICE HAD PASSED in a blur. Harriet had barely heard a word that had been uttered. She was far more interested in the people who had turned up to pay their respects. Although, from what she'd seen it had been less about mourning the woman who had once been such a huge presence in the community and more about being seen by the reporters who had turned out for the event.

And then the altercation had occurred. Not that she could really call it an altercation as such. Nobody had raised so much as a finger in anger. Yet, there was no denying the tension that had passed between both men like a live wire.

"What do you think that was about?" Drew asked. They stood outside the church and Drew's attention was fixed on Declan Campbell and his family.

Harriet looked up at him. "Sorry, I was miles away,"

Drew gave her a tight lipped smile before he jerked his chin in the direction of Declan. "Back there with the odd couple. What do you make of it?"

"It certainly needs to be looked at," Harriet said quietly so as not to be overheard by the reporters gathered like vultures just outside the fence that surrounded the church. "You'll have to wait until you can get him alone."

"You don't think he'd be willing to discuss it in front of Beth?"

Harriet shook her head. "He won't talk about it in front of Simon. Things are already tense enough between them without adding to it."

Drew continued to stare over at the small group. "I suppose. We should follow them back to the house. See if Declan is willing to talk to us after everything that happened."

Harriet glanced down at the ground. "I should really head back to the university."

"You're going to miss me make a complete arse of myself," Drew said. The ghost of a grim smile hovered on his lips. There was something beneath his words, something he wasn't telling her. Harriet pushed the intrusive thought aside. If Drew wanted to tell her then he would. But it would happen in his own time.

"Dr Baig has asked me to come in and speak to

him about a matter I raised." The voicemail message she'd received had unnerved her. Something had undoubtedly happened, but Dennis hadn't told her anything useful in the message he'd left.

A frown line appeared between Drew's eyebrows. "Is it about what we discussed before?"

Harriet shrugged. "No idea. He gave me no clues."

"Well, if you're sure..." Drew pushed his hand back through his hair, causing it to stand on end as he looked back at the Campbell family who were at that moment loading into their family car.

"Drew, what is it?"

He glanced down at her and she could see the unspoken in his eyes. Was she doing this to him? Was Melissa right? Was she undermining his confidence in his ability as an detective? Harriet had never considered the possibility. As far as she was concerned, Drew wasn't someone who was so easily rattled. And yet...

If she abandoned him now, what would the implications be?

"It's nothing," he said as he straightened up. "You go and I'll fill you in when you swing by the office later."

"All right." Harriet kept her expression fixed as she watched Drew walk towards the Campbell's car.

With her hands in the pockets of her coat, Harriet curled her fingers into a fist allowing her nails to dig into the soft flesh of her palm. It hurt to think that she was abandoning him when he needed her help. But everything Melissa had said was still rattling around in her head. Harriet was no stranger to the dislike the other DI had for her. From what she could tell, she had never done, or said anything to upset Melissa. As much as Harriet felt like it was nothing more than playground politics, it didn't change the truth. Melissa had some kind of problem with her.

But Melissa, this was what had given Harriet pause, had known Drew a lot longer, so what if she were right?

CHAPTER FORTY-THREE

JODIE STARED at the lines of code as they flashed up onto the computer screen. Frustration wound its way through her body, tightening her muscles. With gritted teeth she added another line of characters to the code and waited for the program to respond. When it did, she groaned and pulling her glasses from the bridge of her nose, she buried her face in her hands.

Retrieving the remnants of the deleted video was proving far more difficult than she'd anticipated. When DS Arya had come to her with the phone and the task of digging out as much information as possible, she'd foolishly believed it would be easy. She'd also foolishly believed it would be a chance to spend a little time with the sergeant. Jodie had played it all out in her mind. She'd awe him with her unrivalled computer skills and he would, what exactly? Like her plan to wow him with her abilities, her plan to win him over was also half-baked.

She wouldn't be so naive the next time.

Replacing her blue-framed glasses, she squinted angrily at the screen. If willpower alone could have cracked the phone, she'd have long since retrieved the files they needed.

Snatching her coffee stained mug from the desk, she opened her drawer and took out the Tupperware box where she stored her ground coffee beans and spare filters and extra spoon. Getting to her feet, she stretched, her back popping as she rolled back her shoulders. How long had she sat in front of the screen?

Hustling out of her office and across the hall, Jodie made a beeline for the small staff kitchen. Stopping abruptly, she spotted DS Arya with his back to her. He stood, staring into the cutlery drawer as though mesmerised by something inside. Or more probably, Jodie thought, the lack of something inside. The urge to take a quick peek over his shoulder to prove herself right, was powerful.

Instead, she took a step back. Putting distance between them was definitely the safest option.

He muttered beneath his breath and Jodie guessed it was some kind of expletive judging by the set of his shoulders.

She contemplated returning to her desk and

waiting for him to leave. But her brain buzzed, a sure sign she was low on caffeine. She really did need to make some progress with the phone. That knowledge was enough for her to make the decision to stay. Clearing her throat softly, she moved into the room.

DS Arya glanced over his shoulder and his scowl disappeared. His brown eyes lit up and Jodie's stomach did a little flip.

"Jodie, I didn't know you were here."

"Where else would I be?" She self-consciously pushed her glasses further up her nose.

DS Arya frowned and glanced down at his feet. "I just meant..." He shrugged and lifted his gaze again. "Any luck with the phone?"

Jodie's smile faded. With a shake of her head, she crossed to the coffee machine. Ignoring the fancy pod machine that sat proudly in the centre of the counter, Jodie busied herself filling up the filter machine. The pods were, 'all fur coat and no knickers', her dad would have said. And Jodie agreed. "Nothing yet. It's harder than I expected."

"I'm sure you'll crack it," DS Arya said, returning his attention to the drawer.

"Are you looking for something in particular?" Jodie fed three tablespoons of coffee into the paper filter and closed the lid. Pressing the button, she waited for the beep. A moment later she was greeted by the welcoming scent of the coffee as it began to percolate.

"No spoons," he said, rifling through the cutlery.

Surprised, Jodie looked from him to the full sink. "I think you'll find them in there," she pointed a finger in the direction of the clutter.

"Why is it so hard to wash up and put the spoons back?"

Biting her tongue, Jodie decided answering the question would do more harm than good. Most of the officers and admin they shared the kitchen with had an aversion to washing up, DS Arya Jodie noted, was one of the office's biggest culprits. It was one of the main reasons she'd started bringing her own spoons, coffee, and filters with her to work. Well, that and the fact she did not enjoy sharing her things with others. Her teachers had always been quick to point out that she did not work well with others. As far as she was concerned it wasn't a problem.

Rolling up the sleeves of his pale blue silk shirt, he started to noisily rummage in the sink. "Where did you get your spoon?"

Jodie glanced down at the silver one gripped in her hands. "Home."

DS Arya paused his rifling and turned to face her. "Home? You mean you bring your own spoons from home?"

She nodded. Heat crept into her cheeks as he studied her a little more closely. There's was something about DS Arya that wound up making her feel a little stupid and ungainly. It was probably just in her head though. Martine, her flat-mate said she spent far too much time living in imagined situations, she was probably right.

"You're on to something there," DS Arya said. "I might start doing that myself." He turned back to the sink. "So what is it about the video that's proving so difficult?"

Jodie fiddled with the handle on her mug. "It's just not there. I've tried everything to retrieve it. But whoever deleted the video did a very thorough job."

"You think it was deleted on purpose?" There was a note in his voice that Jodie couldn't read.

"Well, yeah, obviously."

"Why obviously?" He stopped his searching and turned to face her. When he crossed his arms over his chest, Jodie shrank back against the counter. Had she done something wrong? Perhaps she had insulted him. It wasn't as though it would be the first time she'd insulted someone without fully comprehending it.

"Because there's a log of it."

When he continued to stare at her with a blank expression, Jodie sighed. "I've searched the phone for the video. Usually there's a way to track it. Most people's phones are automatically backed up to the cloud or whatever service they're using. And when they delete things they don't even think to check elsewhere for it."

"But in this case, they did?" DS Arya's eyebrows rose towards his hairline.

Jodie nodded. "Yeah. They scrubbed it. The only breadcrumb left for me to find is the date and time the video was deleted..." Jodie trailed off as another thought occurred to her.

Tossing her spoon on the counter, she fled from the room. Racing down the corridor, she ignored the voice of DS Arya that followed her.

Dropping back into her seat in front of the bank of computer screens, Jodie let her fingers fly over the keyboard. A couple of keystrokes later and she sat back against her chair feeling a little breathless.

"What is it?" DS Arya's voice cut through her silent contemplation. Jodie jumped and swung around to face him.

"What?"

"You raced out of the kitchen so fast, I figured you'd worked something out." He set her mug on the desk beside her, a lopsided grin on his face. "I thought you might want your coffee though. Milk and two sugars. Oh and..." From behind his back, DS Arya produced a packet of chocolate digestives. "You mentioned before your brain works best on sugar."

"Thanks..." A warm feeling settled in the pit of her stomach. He'd remembered. Pleased with the development, Jodie glanced back at the screen. "Our conversation got me thinking about back-ups."

DS Arya nodded encouragingly as he propped a hip against the desk. "Go on, I'll try to keep up."

"When I was downloading the contents of the phone earlier I noticed some oddities in how the phone was backed-up." She clicked open a new screen that displayed a list. Strings of numbers, dates and the corresponding time stamps appeared. Jodie scrolled quickly down to the entry that had caught her attention. "This one." She opened it, revealing a plethora of information that told a story.

DS Arya stared at it. A crease had appeared where his brows had drawn together. "I'm not sure what I'm looking at."

"Someone backed up the phone before the video was deleted."

"So you can retrieve it after all?" Excitement caused his eyes to light up.

"Don't get your hopes up. This is a long shot. So long as no back-ups have occurred since the files were deleted." Jodie chewed her lip. "The last back-up was a manual one. But we're going to need the original computer used for the back-up."

DS Arya stared at her. "But you think it could work?"

Jodie shrugged. "It's our best shot right now. But I need that computer, DS Arya. Without it we've got nothing."

"Do we know which computer?"

Jodie nodded. The sound of the printer whirring

to life took DS Arya by surprise. "I've printed out all the information you'll need. But the user name is Beth Smith so it seems pretty straightforward to me."

"Leave it with me," DS Arya said briskly, as he headed for the door. "Good work, Ms Meakin."

"Please, call me, Jodie," she whispered. But he was already gone and hadn't heard her.

CHAPTER FORTY-FOUR

LOCKING THE CAR DOOR, Harriet started up the path towards the university campus. There was something about the woman in the church which continued to bother her. But every time she tried to put her finger on the reason for her discomfort, it slipped out of reach. As she reached the coffee shop, Harriet caught sight of Misha as she exited the building.

The young woman kept her head down, her gaze focused on the ground beneath her feet. Despite the way she kept her face averted, Harriet had spotted the blotchy colouring on her face and the telltale sniffing that suggested she was upset. Had Dr Baig passed on the news?

Dennis could wait a few more minutes, Harriet thought as she hurried after the student. "Misha, wait up!"

Seeing the way in which the young woman stiffened as Harriet called after her, told Harriet to slow down. Misha glanced over her shoulder, her expression a mixture of fear and misery. As she laid eyes on Harriet she shook her head.

"Why can't you just leave me alone?"

"You're upset. I wanted to make sure you were all right?" Harriet halted a few feet from the unhappy young woman.

"And why do you think that might be?" Misha sniffed loudly, her voice rising in volume. "You keep following me around. I just want you to leave me alone."

"Misha, I can see I've upset you. I'm going to--" Before Harriet could finish the words, Misha's expression crumpled and she took a couple of steps back.

"Please, just leave me alone. I don't know what you want from me, Dr Quinn. You're really starting to freak me out."

Dumbfounded, Harriet stared at her. "I don't understand." Unease settled over her as she realised the way in which Misha had raised her voice was drawing a crowd of onlookers. From the corner of her eyes, Harriet could see the ripple of unease that spread through the group. They stared at her as though she were the problem.

"Misha?" A tall, athletic, young man broke through the crowd. His face was wreathed with concern as he pushed past Harriet. The way he bumped into her caused Harriet to take a stumbling step forwards.

Misha's watery eyes widened and she collapsed against his chest as he gathered her to him. "That's her, Xavi. She won't leave me alone."

"Just fuck off," the man she'd named as Xavi said. He glared at Harriet. Hostility darkening his eyes.

"I'm just going to leave," Harriet said, moving backwards into the crowd.

"You stay away from her, you hear?" He made to move after Harriet, but Misha clung to him, holding him in place.

Ice trickled down Harriet's spine as she pushed away through the group that had gathered to witness the argument, altercation? Harriet wasn't even certain herself what had happened. But there was something seriously wrong. Why would Misha have behaved like that? She'd certainly never given the student any reason to believe she was any sort of threat to her. But there was no denying Misha's fear.

Unsettled, Harriet hurried towards her own office building. Despite putting some distance between her and the group, she could still feel everyone's eyes on her as she kept her head down and crossed the campus.

Hurrying up the stairs to her office, Harriet thrust open and door and came to a halt as her eyes settled on Dr Baig. His lips were set in a grim line as he took in Harriet's shocked expression. Straightening up, he jerked his head in the direction of her office.

"Did you not get my message this morning?"

Swallowing hard, Harriet nodded. Her mouth was dry and she pressed her hand to the doorframe in an attempt to steady herself. "Yes, sorry, I--"

Dennis shook his head. "Never mind the excuses, Harriet. This is serious. We can discuss it in your office."

Harriet opened her mouth to argue but the look on Dennis' face stopped her. Her shoulders dropped as she pushed away from the door.

"I need to discuss an important matter with Dr Quinn," Martha interjected. Her tone was as it always was, brusque and professional.

Dennis shook his head. "It can wait. I--"

"It's all right, Martha."

Martha ignored Harriet as though she'd never spoken at all and glared at Dennis over the top of her glasses. "This cannot wait," she said primly. When Dr Baig seemed suitably surprised, she turned around. "Dr Quinn, I only need a minute or two."

Swallowing hard, Harriet with a shaky jolt of her head gave her assent. She caught Dr Baig's eye. "I'll only be a moment."

Disgruntled, he stormed into her office and slammed the door, leaving Harriet alone with Martha.

"What was it you needed me for?" Harriet pinched the bridge of her nose between her index and thumb. She was exhausted and a large piece of her wished she'd never left her bed that morning.

"Nothing," Martha said. She sounded grumpier than usual and Harriet cast a look of surprise in her direction.

"But you..."

"I know what I said," Martha snapped. "But it was him and his bossy attitude. You fall in the door white as a sheet and he pounces. It was uncalled for is what it was."

"You were trying to protect me?"

Martha huffed. "Someone had to." Leaning back in her chair, Martha looked Harriet up and down. "So, what did happen?"

Sighing, Harriet shrugged. "I'm not exactly sure. I've upset one of the students, but if I'm honest about it, I'm not certain what it is I've done."

"Let me guess," Martha said. "It's that same student who was in here the other day."

Harriet gave Martha a tired smile. "Got it in one." Gathering her bag close, Harriet straightened up. "I suppose I'll have to face the music at some point."

Martha swung her chair back around to the computer screen. "That one needs to mind his attitude."

"He's our superior."

Martha snorted derisively. "Don't let him hear

you calling him that. You'll only make his head bigger."

Laughing softly, Harriet crossed to the door. "Wish me luck," she said. Unease prickled along her scalp.

"You don't need it," Martha said. "You do good work, Dr Quinn. Don't let him make you think anything else."

"Thanks, Martha."

Her smile was sympathetic. "But good luck all the same."

"Actually, Martha, you didn't happen to see my appointment book, have you?"

The other woman screwed up her face. "Can't say that I have. Did you misplace it?"

Harriet nodded. "I think I must have. It's probably buried in the mountain of paper at home. Thanks again."

With a deep breath, she pushed the door open and stepped inside. Seeing Dr Baig's stern expression she immediately felt like a stranger in her own office. With a backwards glance at Martha, she closed the door behind her.

"We need to talk, Harriet."

Swallowing hard, Harriet nodded. She would need all the luck she could get.

CHAPTER FORTY-FIVE

WITH A NOD to the FLO who'd been assigned to the Campbell family, Drew stepped into the kitchen. Declan stood at the sink and stared vacantly over the garden outside the window.

Clearing his throat softly, Drew waited for the other man to turn around.

"Are you here to arrest me again?" Declan asked. His voice was oddly flat.

Drew shook his head. "Not at this moment in time," he said. "As I mentioned back at the church, I'd just like to have a chat with you about what happened."

"Nothing happened," Declan said a little too quickly. He grabbed a tea towel from the counter and roughly scrubbed it over his hands before tossing it back onto the draining board. "Just a misunderstanding."

"With all due respect," Drew said, hating the placating note in his voice. Not that he had much of a choice. They needed Declan's cooperation, without it, they were adrift. He sniffed loudly, wishing he'd had the time to take a Lemsip before calling around. "I saw that interaction back at the church. That wasn't nothing. The minute you saw that bloke, you--"

"Why can't you just leave it be?" The misery in Declan's voice was plain to hear. "They're all ready dead. Digging up the past won't bring them back." The man opposite buried his face in his hands.

Not that Drew could do anything about it. A woman and a child were dead and they deserved justice. Drew knew that Declan understood that on some level.

"But digging up the past is what will help us catch their killer."

"So you don't think I did it anymore?"

Drew bit his tongue and glanced down at the floor. "You're still a suspect, Declan." He glanced up at the other man and met his stony gaze.

"He didn't kill her," Declan said finally. He grabbed the tea towel and wrapped it around his fingers like it was some kind of noose.

"What, then?"

Declan's attention moved to the tile floor. "Before I tell you this I need you to promise Simon won't find out about it."

"I can promise you that I won't be the one to tell him anything you say here today."

Declan's lips twisted into a grimace. "I suppose that'll have to do." He heaved a sigh and gestured for Drew to follow him to the table. Declan dropped into one of the chairs surrounding the kitchen table as though all of his strength had suddenly abandoned him in one fell swop.

Drew took up a position across from him and he pulled a notepad from inside his coat. "Do you mind if I record the conversation?" He'd already set his phone on the table top, but he waited for Declan's permission before he clicked record. When the other man nodded, Drew hit the red button and watched for a moment as the seconds ticked up on the counter.

"You were going to tell me about the man at the church?"

Declan nodded. He still head the towel and he squeezed it hard, practically wringing it out. "His name is Nigel Harcombe. He's some kind of life coach, guru... it's all bullshit anyway. I tried to tell Gwen that it was crap but she wouldn't listen."

"Why was that do you think?"

A smile spread over Declan's face. "She was so stubborn. I suppose if I'd said I thought it was a great idea she'd have dropped it immediately. I fell in love with that stubborn streak of hers. When she got something in her head..." Declan sighed happily. "She was a sight to behold."

"So what changed?" Drew was hesitant to ask the question. This was the most he'd managed to get out of Declan since the investigation had started. One misstep now would cause him to clam up.

Declan looked up. "Hmm?" He seemed almost surprised to be in his kitchen and not deep in whatever memory he'd been concentrating on.

"Something must have changed between you for it to end the way it did?"

Declan nodded. "It was him."

"Mr Harcombe?"

Declan nodded. "He has this way of twisting everything around. I went and spoke to him when I found out about the affair. I called around to confront him and the things he said..." Declan physically shuddered. "The way he twisted our relationship around so that Gwen's cheating was somehow justified. That I'd driven her to it." Declan looked lost. "I loved her. The last thing I wanted to do was push her away. But he made her."

"You're telling me Gwen went to him for life coaching or something and she wound up having an affair with this man?"

A bark of laughter escaped Declan. Rough and caustic, it hurt Drew's ears. "You see how ridiculous it sounds? I tried to tell Gwen that she was being manipulated but she was having none of it." The animated look faded from his eyes and he slumped back in his chair.

Silence crowded around them in the kitchen. Drew waited for Declan to start speaking again. Finally, Drew cleared his throat, pulling the other man's attention back to the room. "What happened then?"

"Things soured between them. She never told me exactly what went down. But she came home one evening and told me it was over."

"You never contemplated leaving her?" Drew asked.

"Sure I did," Declan said. "But we had Si and Gwen had her online influencing business."

"And?" Drew prompted.

"My business wasn't exactly setting the world alight, DI Haskell." There was an unmistakable edge of bitterness to Declan's words. "Had I left Gwen, I would have been left with nothing."

Drew glanced at the recorder. He wasn't sure if the other man was aware or not that his admissions of the difficulties between him and his wife were the perfect motivations for her murder.

"So you what, you just forgave her?"

Declan shook his head. "No. I turned around and had an affair of my own."

"With Beth Smith?"

For the first time during the conversation Declan looked happy. "I don't regret it," he said. "That probably sounds weird but Beth was the best thing to happen to me. I mistreated her, jerking her along. There was a part of me that just wanted to punish Gwen. But God help me I fell for Beth..."

"You said in your statement that you and Beth had reconciled just before Gwen's disappearance?"

Declan nodded. "A couple of months after Gwen broke it off with Nigel she told me she was pregnant." He stared down at the towel in his hands as though he was surprised to see it.

Caught off guard, Drew leaned back in his chair. A rueful smile played around Declan's mouth as he met Drew's stare head on. "I know what you're thinking DI Haskell."

"And what's that?"

"You're wondering why I would stay when there was a possibility that she was pregnant with another man's child."

Drew shrugged. "It's really none of my business."

"But you are thinking it." Declan's face screwed up, making him appear harsh in the fading light of the kitchen. "I thought about leaving her. There was a chance the baby wasn't mine. And for a short while it looked like we might separate." A wistful note stole into Declan's voice. "And then we found out it was a girl."

"Why would that make a difference?"

Declan glanced down at the surface of the table. "A month after Gwen and I were married she found out she was pregnant. We were terrified. Neither of us had planned to have children so soon. But when we went for that first scan, it changed everything. And then time passed and we found out it was a girl..." He dragged in a ragged breath. "At seven months we lost the baby. Gwen was devastated. We both were..." His voice broke over the memory. He ran his hand down over his face as though that alone was enough to wipe the slate clean.

When he looked up at Drew, after what felt like an age, there was a haunted look in his eyes. "Do you have children, DI Haskell?"

Drew shook his head. For a moment he felt the pain of that admission but he quickly wiped it away and returned his attention to the man in front of him.

"It's like nothing else on earth." Declan wan smile was tinged with sadness. "But to lose a child..." He stared past Drew as though he wasn't present. "It's like someone tears out a piece of your soul and leaves you half formed and broken. There's no getting over it. Instead, you learn to move around this hole in your world. Sorry, maybe that doesn't make sense..." He cleared his throat and swiped at his damp eyes.

"We went on to have Simon and God, we were so happy. Terrified too. But when he arrived safe and sound and so perfect." Declan's laughter was like a ray of sunshine breaking through a cloud bank as he relived his memories. "You might not think it now, but he had a pair of lungs on him that could take the roof off. But we didn't care. Listening to him, it was proof, you know? Proof that he was here, with us. I could have listened to him all day, every day. I would sit for hours, just watching him breathe. This little miracle." He smiled at Drew. "It sounds mad, but I didn't care about the sleepless nights."

His expression darkened then. "And after we had, Si, we spoke about having another. But I think we still had that fear. So we just kept putting it off and time passed us by. We got busy and slowly the idea of having another it just went away. And that time, it put distance between us. We were so young when we married. Neither of us knew what we wanted." Declan splayed his hands in front of him. "I look back at it now and I think I should have broke it off. We weren't right for each other. Too much had come between us. But, when I found out she was pregnant with Evie, it was like I'd been given a second chance. I broke it off with Beth that same day. I was a fool."

"But it didn't last," Drew prompted when Declan fell silent again.

The other man shook his head. "After Evie, Gwen developed post-natal depression. For the first few weeks she wanted nothing to do with our little girl. And I can't say I helped matters. I was insensitive and I made her feel unwanted." He sighed. "I think I just expected her to snap back to being the Gwen I knew. And when she didn't..."

"You went back to Beth."

Declan nodded. "We reconnected at an event. She was so different, you know? She cared about the things I had to say."

"You were flattered," Drew said flatly.

"I was. And I was weak. But I didn't start sleeping with Beth until Gwen dropped the bombshell on me..."

Drew waited, but Declan no longer seemed to be forthcoming. "What bombshell?"

"My investments were failing and every time I tried to expand, something happened to block me. It happens sometimes. I really thought I would have to go back to my old job. And then Beth introduced me to Nate McCallister. He was looking for some investments and connections to a world only I had access to... I jumped at the chance to invest. It was the only way out, that I could see."

"You mean the mines."

Declan smiled. "Yeah. He offered shares in exchange for me setting up some meetings with some of my old clients." Declan looked down at the table. "I know it wasn't ethical, but I was trapped. Right before my eyes, I could see everything I'd built going down the drain. But this... This could save the business."

He met Drew's gaze. "I can still remember the day I came home and told Gwen about it. The look on her face..." He trailed off lost in his own memories. "She had planned to use her platform to help her run for council. It got her out of bed, so when she started talking about it, I was happy. And then, she started this new health kick, weight-loss and yoga. She'd gone back into therapy because of the post-natal depression. Real therapy this time, and not that other bullshit she tried before. The therapist suggested she try new things."

He traced the pattern of the wood grain with the tip of his finger. "I wasn't paying much attention to her at the time. I didn't see how much she'd changed." He paused and pushed the tip of his finger against the table top until it turned white. "God, she was disgusted by the new plan. Told me I was going to destroy our children's futures. That I was adding to the burden on the next generation." He laughed. "And then she told me she was going to seek a divorce. That Evie wasn't really mine anyway."

As he spoke, Declan's colour drained from his face. His anguish was palpable, as though the events he was relaying had only just happened.

"How did that make you feel?" The atmosphere in the kitchen shifted growing charged as Drew asked the question.

Declan looked up at Drew and there was a shrewd angry look lurking in the depths of his eyes. "How do you think it made me feel, DI Haskell?"

"Angry? It would have made me angry."

"But angry enough to kill, DI Haskell?" There was a challenge in Declan's voice that hadn't been there before. "I mean, that's what you really want to know, isn't it?"

"It would be remiss if I didn't ask the question," Drew replied. "Did it make you angry enough to kill your wife."

For a moment, Declan held his gaze. Finally, he glanced away. His shoulders slumped as he shook his head. "No. Not like that. It should have. But when she mentioned the 'D' word, all I could think was that there was nothing standing between me and Beth anymore..."

"What happened next?"

"I left. The night before she disappeared. I walked out and went straight to Beth. We spent the night together. I was with Beth the morning Simon said he recorded the argument between me and his mum."

"Did you return to the house at all?"

Declan looked sheepishly down at the table. "Not until Simon called me that evening and said Gwen hadn't come home..."

Drew couldn't believe what he was hearing. "Mr

Campbell... Declan, this doesn't fit with the story Beth told us about that morning."

"What story?"

"She claims to have seen the video."

Declan shook his head. "She can't have. The video is gone. Simon tried to show it to me months ago and it was corrupted. There was nothing to show."

CHAPTER FORTY-SIX

"SO WHAT ARE YOU SAYING, Dr Baig?" Harriet kept her hands clasped loosely in her lap. She wasn't going to give him the satisfaction of knowing his words were slowly ripping her heart out of her chest.

"I'm afraid, we'll have to suspend you without pay until we get this matter ironed out," Dennis said. He kept his gaze fixed on the desk in front of him. Her desk. It was the behaviour of a coward and it surprised Harriet. She'd never thought he was particularly brave, but she'd never thought of him as having no spine.

"I don't understand," Harriet said. "What has changed?"

"We've received a further complaint."

Harriet shook her head. "That's not possible. I haven't done anything wrong."

Dennis's expression said otherwise, and Harriet felt her stomach flip-flop. "I'm afraid there is evidence to the contrary." He sighed and buried his face in his hands. "How could you be so stupid, Harriet? I thought you were smarter than this. But to leave yourself so vulnerable..."

"Dennis, you need to tell me what is going on. How can I possibly defend myself, if I'm not even aware of the crime I've committed?"

He nodded thoughtfully. "Very well." He pulled his phone from his pocket and quickly tapped on the screen. "I'm only doing this because despite what you might think, I consider you a friend." He swallowed hard. "You were kind to me after the departure of Dr Perez."

Harriet wasn't sure she would agree with him on that point, but she wasn't exactly in a position to argue with him either. And right now keeping him as a friend didn't exactly seem like a bad idea, especially considering her job hung in the balance.

"The complainant is a Misha McDermid. She says your behaviour and actions towards her have been inappropriate." Harriet opened her mouth to argue, but before she could utter a word, Dennis held his hand up. "Initially, I was willing to overlook it because the complaint was anonymous. And mostly, because I knew there couldn't be any truth to it. I did my due diligence, but ultimately, there was nothing to support the claim, so I was willing to drop it."

"And now?"

His lips thinned. "Miss McDermid has come forward and claimed responsibility for the first complaint." Dr Baig paused. "And she has made a second complaint against you. In it, she states you suggested that you meet in the student bar under the pretence of discussing her research." Dr Baig turned the phone towards Harriet as a video began to play.

Harriet felt the colour leave her cheeks as she watched the footage from the bar play out.

"Why would you do that?"

"I said we could meet in my office," Harriet said quietly. "Misha wanted us to meet at her house."

"And that didn't seem odd to you?" Dr Baig asked, this time the note of incredulity in his voice was unmistakable.

"Of course it did," Harriet said. "But she said there was so much research..." She trailed off. Even she could hear how ridiculous it all sounded.

"And the bar, how did you wind up there?"

"She said it was closer to her house. She wouldn't have to carry her items as far." Harriet met his gaze. "I felt sorry for her, Dennis. And I came to you after and explained everything." Harriet could feel her shock giving way to anger.

"She says you've developed an unhealthy attachment to her due to your history with her mother. What does that mean?"

"I actually believe it's the other way around." The

look on Dr Baig's face said he wasn't particularly interested in her theories. "Her mother and I worked together when we both got our start as forensic psychologists." Harriet glanced down at her clasped hands. "I told you all of this when I came and asked for Misha-- Ms McDermid to be transferred. As you know, Louise McDermid died." She took a deep breath. "She was murdered. It was part of a case we were working on."

"And what, you blame yourself for her death, and you see Misha as a means to make amends?"

Harriet's head snapped up. "That's not it at all. I went to that bar thinking I was going to help her with her research. Once I knew her intentions were not as they had appeared, I left. And I came to you the next day and asked for her to be transferred."

Dr Baig shook his head. "Harriet, I really wish you hadn't gone to that bar. At least you came to me, but it's not exactly a lot of evidence in your favour. Ms McDermid has witnesses to your behaviour. And then there is the footage. This really leaves me with no choice but to suspend you."

"This is a mistake."

"And if that's true, then we'll get to the bottom of it," he said sympathetically.

"And by then my reputation will be in tatters," Harriet said, panic welled inside her. "Dennis, think of how this will play if the press get hold of it. My work with the police, everything will be in jeopardy."

He looked pained. "Don't you think I'm aware of that?"

She closed her eyes. "I can't believe this is happening."

"That makes two of us," he said. "But you need to understand, my hands are tied, Harriet."

Biting her lip and with her eyes still closed, Harriet nodded. "I do understand." And she did. He was right. There was no other option. If he didn't suspend her, the next time something like this arose at the university it could be used against him. These were the kinds of floodgates that simply could not be opened.

"I need you to clear out your office by the end of the day," he said. "I won't ask security to escort you from the premises..." It was a courtesy, Harriet knew he would not have extended to anyone else.

"Thank you."

"And I will try to keep a lid on this. But you should inform your colleagues at North Yorkshire Constabulary that a formal complaint has been lodged against you and that I have been left with no choice but to suspend you."

"Of course." Harriet got to her feet. She felt shaky, and as she turned to walk away her legs felt as though they were made from jelly rather than muscle and bone.

"Harriet, I'll get to the bottom of this as quickly as I can. You have my word."

"Thank you," she said quietly. Glancing back over her shoulder. "I appreciate it."

CHAPTER FORTY-SEVEN

"DECLAN, I need to have a chat with Beth," Drew said, trying to keep his voice level. "Where is she?"

"She went round to her sister's place," Declan said. "Si went to his friend's and Beth said she needed a break from the house here. You don't think she had anything to do with Gwen's murder, do you?"

"Right now, I just want to have a chat with her." Drew got to his feet. "Could you give me her address and..." Before he could finish, his phone buzzed in his pocket. "Just a moment."

Stepping out of the kitchen, Drew answered the call. "What is it?"

"Sir, we need to bring Beth Smith in for an interview. And Ms Meakin is going to need access to her computer so she can--"

"Wait, what?" Stunned, Drew reached up to

loosen his suddenly restrictive tie. "How do you know about Beth?"

"Jodie... I mean, Ms Meakin found something."

"She found the video?" Drew didn't bother to hide the excitement from his voice.

"Not exactly..."

"What then?" Impatient, Drew strode down the hall and paused in front of the small table by the front door. There were several framed pictures placed in small groups and Drew bent down to the examine them.

"She thinks she has a way to retrieve the video but she needs the Beth's computer."

"She's sure about this?" Drew cast a look back down the hall. He couldn't see Declan but that did not mean the man wasn't lurking nearby and listening in to the call.

"About as sure as she can be, guv," Maz said. "She's really good at her job. And I trust her."

Hearing Maz gush over their resident computer expert caused a smile to tug at the corner of Drew's mouth. "I'll get the laptop. I'm going to send you on an address and I want you--"

"DI Haskell." Declan's voice filtered out from the kitchen. He sounded off and the hair's on the back of Drew's neck rose slowly to attention.

"I've got to go." Before Maz could argue, Drew ended the call.

Drew paused in the kitchen door. Declan's face

was pale as he paced back and forth. "Come on, Beth, pick up."

"Mr Campbell, I would appreciate you not trying to contact Ms Smith right now..."

Declan shot him a withering look. "She didn't kill Gwen, DI Haskell. You've got the wrong end of the stick." He pulled the phone away from his ear and stared down at the screen incredulously. "She's not answering." He hit redial and waited, the call cut off abruptly as it went to voicemail.

"I just need you to give me her sister's address so I can go around there, and--"

"She's not there," Declan said, sounding utterly miserable. "When you left the room, I called her sister. "But she says she hasn't seen her all week. They haven't even spoken today."

"I'm still going to need her sister's name and address. Where else would Beth go?"

Declan moved to the table and dropped down into the chair. Burying his face in his hands, he moaned softly. "It's happening all over again..."

"Mr Campbell..." When the other man didn't respond, Drew crouched in front of him. "Declan, we're going to find her. But you have to listen to me and give me the information I need, all right?"

Declan's eyes were bloodshot but he nodded. "Fine. Whatever you need. You can have it."

"Good," Drew said. "We'll start with her sister

and I'm going to need access to Beth's laptop. Can you do that?"

Declan nodded mutely.

"Great," Drew said, straightening up. "We'll work from there... We'll find her, Declan. She's going to be fine because I'm going to find her." And Drew meant it. He wouldn't have a repeat of history on his hands. When Gwen had disappeared he'd been off his game, but not now.

This time he would find her.

This time he would get it right.

CHAPTER FORTY-EIGHT

BETH TURNED down a farmer's track and parked the car. At least the rain had eased a little. Of course, that wouldn't save them from the inevitable flooding. She'd already been forced to make several diversions on the drive over because the River Esk had started to rise and surface water was becoming problematic. If she was a superstitious person, she would have turned back by now.

Sitting behind the wheel, she peered at the large house that loomed over the hedgerows a few yards ahead of her. Was she making a huge mistake?

The question nagged at her. Self-consciously, she moved her hand to her bump as she continued to study the house. Seeing him at the church service had been the last straw. She'd come so far and the police did not appear to be any closer to figuring it all

375

out. Someone needed to do something. But did the someone have to be her?

The answer was blatantly obvious. She should take her information to the police and let them deal with it. But the idea of handing over months worth of hard work just didn't sit right with her. This was her chance at a big break. If she could just find the proof she needed then...

"Don't get ahead of yourself, Beth." The words dropped into the well of silence inside the car. There was still a slim chance that she was wrong in all of this. It was unlikely. She'd been thorough in her research. And none of it had been easy. Keeping secrets from Declan had been the worst of it. He wouldn't understand. And when she'd tried to broach the subject with him, he'd practically bitten her head off. No, this was down to her.

Gripping her phone in her hands, she opened the car door and climbed out. The moment her feet hit the ground, she sank into the soft mud, no doubt churned up by the machinery that traversed the track. Pulling a foot free, the sucking sound of the mud made her stomach flip uncomfortably. Careful to make as little noise as possible, Beth closed up the car and locked the door.

With one hand on the car's bonnet, she picked her way cautiously through the muck. When she was finally on level ground, she glanced back at the distance she'd travelled. In the fading afternoon light, the car's slick carapace gleamed as a shaft of light hit it. She could just go back. Return to her home. Declan would be waiting for her. Her hand touched against her bump. They could settle on the couch together and make plans for the nursery.

It would be so much easier than what lay ahead. She couldn't turn back.

Fixing her gaze on the house ahead of her, Beth straightened her shoulders. She could do this.

CHAPTER FORTY-NINE

THE RAIN HAD STARTED to pick up as Drew had left the Campbell house. It thundered against the windscreen, blurring the view beyond the glass. As Drew parked the car outside the small semi-detached house, he kept the engine running allowing the wipers to do their job. Two cars were already sitting on the small drive, neither of which belonged to Beth. Getting out, he glanced down at his phone half expecting to see a message from Harriet. Nothing waited for him. It was unlike her. She was always prompt in her responses to the updates he sent her about the case. But this time there was nothing. He contemplated calling her but changed his mind at the last minute.

Slipping his phone into his pocket, he pulled the collar of his coat up and braved the weather. Locking the car, he headed for the front door. It swung open before he even had a chance to knock. The young woman who stood in the hall peered up at him with large, expressive eyes. Her hair was pulled back from her heart-shaped face. He could see the familial resemblance instantly.

"Elizabeth Smith?"

She shook her head. "It's Elizabeth Evans. Smith was my maiden name."

"Sorry about that," Drew said, rainwater blurring his vision as it dripped into his eyes. "Could I come in?" As he moved, water seeped down inside the collar of his jacket, freezing him to the bone.

"This is about Beth isn't it?"

Drew nodded. "You spoke to Declan Campbell a short time ago?"

"Yes, of course come in..." She glanced nervously towards the kitchen.

"Is there someone else here?" Drew kept his tone neutral.

"Uh, yeah. Just a friend. He's in the kitchen with Toby, my son," she added quickly. "We can talk in the living room."

He followed her through the narrow hall into a small, heavily furnished space. The walls were painted in a gentle dove grey, and Libby directed him to a seat on a velvet grey armchair. Tentatively, Drew lowered himself into the seat. He sank into the cushions, and for a moment he worried he might sink all the way to the floor. He stopped before his knees struck his chest but he wasn't comfortable. Shifting, he tried to find a better position, but with nothing doing, he gave up and sank further.

Meeting Libby's eye, he smiled and pulled a notebook from his pocket. "Declan said you hadn't spoken to your sister recently."

Nodding, Libby lifted her hand to her mouth and began to worry at her fingernails. "It's just sister stuff, you know?" She stared down at the carpet. "We had a falling out last week."

"What about?"

Sighing, Libby glanced towards the living room door. "It's a little delicate." Getting to her feet, she crossed to the living room door and pushed it closed. "Beth doesn't approve of who I'm seeing."

Normally, Drew wouldn't push on domestic situations. And an argument between sisters regarding their love lives was definitely not something he wanted to get too involved with. But, there was something about the whole affair that didn't sit right with him.

"Your sister and your husband don't get along?" Drew glanced down at the notepad and pretended to scribble something as Libby made her way back to her seat.

"No, Hugh and Beth get on fine..." Libby took up her place on the couch opposite. "Hugh and I, well, we're separated."

"So when you said your sister doesn't approve of who you're seeing, you meant..."

"I'm seeing somebody else. It's the reason Hugh and I are separated." She glanced towards the closed door. "Look, I'm not sure what this has to do with Beth."

Drew's smile was patient. "I'm just trying to build up a picture of where your sister might have gone."

"Sure..." Libby resumed her assault on her nails. "There's not much Beth approves of when it comes to my life, DI Haskell," Libby said.

"Could you tell me about your argument? It must have been serious enough if you haven't spoken to one another in over a week?" Declan had been quick to tell him how close Beth and Libby were. "Mr Campbell seems to believe you're very close and are typically in contact with each other every day."

Libby smiled. "We are." She got back on her feet. "Could I make you a cup of tea, or..."

Drew started to shake his head but she was already halfway to the door. "Tea would be great."

"Good..." She nodded, but didn't appear to be listening to him. "I'll be back in a mo." She disappeared out into the hall, leaving Drew alone. Getting to his feet, he moved over to examine the framed pictures that took up a small section of an end table. Sudden raised voices from the kitchen quickly followed by the sound of a small child beginning to cry, saw Drew hurry from the room.

He made it to the kitchen door in time for it to be swung open. A whoosh of warm air rushed out to greet him, quickly followed by the loud wail of a child in a highchair. The man in front of him paused for a moment as though stunned to find himself face to face with Drew for the second time in so many hours.

"I'm sorry, I've got to go."

"And you are?" Drew raised an eyebrow. Not that he needed an answer to the question, Declan had told him about Nigel Harcombe. He just hadn't expected to see him quite so soon after.

"I'm a friend of Libby's," Nigel said, recovering quickly. He tried to edge around Drew in the doorway and failed. "She called to tell me about Beth, so I thought I'd come over and see if she needed anything." Nigel's smile was wide and disarming but it had the odd effect of making Drew's skin want to crawl off his body.

"That's very kind of you," Drew said, looking past Nigel into the kitchen. Libby was huddled near the end counter, with her son propped on one hip. Her eyes were wide and she looked like someone who'd been crying.

"I really should go," Nigel said. "Joan will be waiting for me..."

"And Joan is?"

"My wife," Nigel said. "She hasn't been well for

quite some time now. I don't like to leave her alone for long in case she does something silly..."

"Such as?" Drew prompted, noting the way Libby's expression crumpled as Nigel spoke about his wife.

Nigel sighed. "She has good days and bad... Today is a bad one. You see, she suffers from schizoaffective disorder, without me to manage her medications and such, well... let's just say I don't think she'd survive very long."

"She seemed fine earlier," Drew said mildly.

"Oh, that was you at the church, was it?" Nigel's pretence was not particularly convincing. "I thought I recognised you. Tell me, DI Haskell, do you plan to charge Declan Campbell with his wife's murder, or are you going to allow a murderer to walk free?"

"We're investigating all lines of enquiries," Drew said.

Nigel shook his head. "Such a shame about that other woman... Perhaps, if you'd done your job correctly to begin with she'd still be alive."

Drew narrowed his gaze at the man in front of him. "You seem to be very well informed regarding the investigation."

Nigel shrugged and glanced over at Libby. "I'm just a concerned citizen. I'll give you a call later, Libbs," Nigel said.

She nodded and Drew stepped aside allowing the other man to slink past him. "Perhaps, you and I could have a chat," Drew said. He watched the other man putting on his jacket in the hall.

Nigel froze, his shoulder's stiffening. For a moment Drew wondered if Nigel would turn him down. Instead, when Nigel swung around his face was wreathed in a smile. "I can stop by the station anytime you'd like, DI Haskell."

Drew shook his head. "Not at all, Mr Harcombe. I can come to your house. I wouldn't want to keep you from your wife. And that way, I could have a chat with her too."

Nigel's mouth twisted into a smile. "Of course. Anything to aid the police in their investigation."

Before Drew could say another word, Nigel stalked to the door. As he left, he made sure to slam the door behind him and Libby jumped.

"I'm sorry..." Her lip trembled as she held her son closer.

"Is he always so pleasant?" A wry smile tugged at Drew's lips.

"I've never seen him like that," she said quietly.

"Is that the man Beth doesn't approve of you seeing?"

For a moment, Libby looked surprised and Drew half wondered if she would deny being involved with him. But in the end, her shoulders dropped. "She says he's dangerous," Libby said softly. Her gaze rose to meet Drew's. "I never believed her before."

"But you believe her now?" Drew asked, trying to

keep his composure. He needed evidence and that was something he was sorely lacking in. He couldn't jump the gun again, not like he did with Declan Campbell. But that didn't mean he should ignore his gut either.

She stared down at the top of her son's head. "I don't know what to believe."

Drew could feel his frustration rising. What would Harriet do if she were here now? For starters she'd already have Libby talking. Slipping his phone from his pocket, he was disappointed to see she still hadn't responded to any of his messages. Where was she? Glancing over at the frightened woman, cradling her son, Drew cleared his throat.

"You take a seat Libby and I'll make us a brew."

With a watery smile, she did as she was told. Crossing to the kettle, filled it and then returned it to its stand. Pulling out his phone, he typed out a quick message to Maz asking him to send a car over to the Harcombe house. Something about the entire situation felt off to him and Drew was tired of feeling like he was always behind the curve.

Satisfied, he returned his attention to the matter at hand. Feeling like a contestant on Who Wants to Be A Millionaire, he stared at the row of cupboards in front of him. With Harriet AWOL, he would just have to figure it out himself. Determined, Drew began to open the cupboards.

. . .

TEN MINUTES, two mugs of tea, and a packet of Hobnobs later, he sat across from Libby.

"Tell me about Beth," Drew asked.

The ghost of a smile hovered on Libby's lips. "You've met my sister, DI Haskell. She's a force of nature."

The short time he'd spent in Beth Smith's company had not given him any indication of her character. "I've only spoken to your sister once."

Libby glanced down and then ruffled her son's hair. "Well, I suppose you'll have to take my word for it. She loves Declan and Simon. She loves her work... lives for it really." Libby trailed off.

"It's my understanding that Beth gave up her job a number of months ago."

Libby's head snapped up. "She took some leave but she hasn't quit her job. For a while she thought about working with Declan but when she found out she was pregnant..." Libby wrapped her hand around the handle of her mug. "It feels strange to talk about these kinds of things behind Beth's back."

"I'm just looking for some background informa-tion, Libby. Anything you can tell me so I can find your sister..."

She sighed. "Beth became interested in Gwen's disappearance about six months ago. She's been looking into it ever since then."

Drew sat back in his chair. "Mr Campbell never mentioned this."

Libby's face twisted into a grimace. "Well, he wouldn't now, would he? Beth didn't tell him. She wanted to do a little digging herself. She told me about six months ago that she'd found something on this website that we all go to..."

Scribbling a couple of notes, Drew raised his gaze to Libby. "What website is this?"

"It's sort of like a gossip site..." She shifted uneasily. "People go there to blow off steam, and..."

"Would it by any chance be called Rattle?"

Libby looked sharply up at him. "How do you know?"

"It's popped up on our radar too," Drew said, careful not to say anything that might put words in Libby's mouth. "What did Beth find on Rattle?"

Libby sighed. "She said Gwen used to post there years ago along with a few others from the area. She said they had it in for this writer. Olive Scott... Beth said they made all sorts of claims about her. That Gwen and the others were particularly cruel."

Drawing his eyebrows together, Drew struggled to understand what Beth could have seen in the poisonous conversations on Rattle. "Does Beth think this Olive Scott figured out who Gwen was?"

Libby shook her head. "Not exactly. Beth told me last week she'd worked out who this Olive Scott was. That she was some local woman writing under a pseudonym and that she could link Nigel to both this Scott woman and Gwen..."

"And that's why you two argued?"

Libby nodded looking miserable. "She said he was dangerous. That she knows he was involved with Gwen's death. But she didn't have any evidence. I told her it was ridiculous. That she couldn't just go around making accusations..."

"Why wouldn't she have come to us?" Drew asked.

"To the police?" Libby scoffed. "And would you have listened to her? She said you lot were so fixated on Declan, that you had tunnel vision. She reckoned you would dismissed what she was telling you as a desperate woman trying to get the heat off her boyfriend."

There wasn't exactly anything Drew could say in response. Beth had not been wrong. They had suffered from tunnel vision, him included. But he wasn't convinced that he would have ignored Beth had she come to them with her suspicions.

"She wanted to find some proof before she went to you lot," Libby said. "She said it was the only way you'd listen to her."

Drew couldn't shake the sinking feeling in his gut. "And where was she hoping to find this proof?"

Libby's lower lip trembled. "I don't know... But before you came into the kitchen Nigel got a phone call. I think it was from Joan, his wife. And afterwards, he was so angry..."

Pulling his phone from his pocket as he got to his

feet, Drew dialled Maz's number. "Any luck on getting a car 'round to Nigel Harcombe's place?"

"Guv, we're trying but so many of the roads have cut off due to flooding we're having to divert all over the place."

"Right, I'll see if I can get through on my side." Drew ended the call and met Libby's concerned gaze.

"She'll be all right, won't she DI Haskell?"

He knew he shouldn't make any promises but after everything that had happened on the Gwen Campbell case, Drew felt responsible. If he hadn't taken his eye off the ball when he did...

"I'll find her, Libby. I'll bring her home."

"Beth is good at her job, DI Haskell. And if she thinks she has evidence that points towards..." Libby swallowed hard as though the act of even mentioning his name out loud was somehow painful.

"Evidence pointing towards Nigel," Drew said for her.

"Yes. If she really has that and Nigel now knows..." There was no need for her to finish the sentence. They both knew what she was thinking.

"I won't let it come to that," Drew said, as he grabbed his car keys and made for the door.

CHAPTER FIFTY

AS JODIE WORKED her way through the forum posts, an alert caught her attention. Surprised, she let her fingers hover over the keyboard. The posts kept scrolling and it took her a moment to realise that what she'd been working on had disappeared off the screen.

Muttering under her breath, she got to her feet and hurried across the hall into the main office space. She scanned the area, her gaze snagging on the sight of DC Olivia Crandell with her head down as she worked at her desk. Ignoring the curious glances from the others in the workspace, Jodie made her way to Olivia's desk.

Moving from one foot to the other nervously, she waited for the officer to notice her.

"Oh, what's up?" Olivia started.

"Can you come and look at something?" Jodie kept her voice low.

"Do you have something?"

"Maybe--" Seeing the look on Olivia's face, Jodie hesitated. "Look, it'll be better if you come and have a look for yourself."

She didn't wait to see if Olivia was going to follow her. Instead, Jodie turned on her heel and strode back to her own office. Settling in behind her bank of computer screens, she pushed her glasses up the bridge of her nose. Olivia dragged a chair over to sit next to her.

"What have you got?"

"There's another murder."

Olivia stared blankly at her for a minute. "You mean the woman found in her flat?"

Jodie nodded. "Holly Thomas is her name. She was an influencer and Only Fans star."

"Right, I knew about the Only Fans account. It's the reason we got the call. An anonymous tip off actually. Like we can't trace a call from a landline. Uniforms went around today to have a word with the bloke who called it in." Olivia sighed. "But what does that have to do with the Gwen Campbell investigation?"

Jodie glanced back at the screen. "Well, technically nothing..." Seeing the look on Olivia's face she held up her hand to stop the officer from cutting her off. "But like I said, Holly wasn't just an Only Fans performer. She was an influencer too, like Gwen."

Olivia screwed up her face. "Even you must admit that's tenuous at best."

Jodie nodded. "True. But there's something else." A couple of clicks on her keyboard and Jodie pulled up the threads on Rattle."

"This again?" Olivia shuddered next to her. "Any luck on tracing the people posting?"

"Actually, yeah. I've got a small pool of people who've been posting across three different topics. I was missing something but Holly Thomas' murder has proved to be the key I needed."

Olivia perked up. Leaning forwards with her hand beneath her chin, Olivia's eyes scanned down the threads.

"Four names kept popping up through it all." Jodie drew up a short list of names. "The Greedy Truth, Sin Eater, Mard-Arse, and this last one, Gee Soup..." She waited for Olivia to read the forum entries.

"Wait, that Gee Soup person they only appear in the threads from years ago."

Jodie nodded. "It's Gwen Campbell."

"What, where did you get that from?" Olivia screwed her face up. "I mean, the name is pretty on the nose but anyone who wants to keep their identity hidden, they wouldn't be so obvious would they?"

Jodie shrugged. "It's the same as people who keep

their passwords as 1234, or use the names of their pets. Most people think they're being so clever when really they're quite transparent."

Olivia cringed. "Is it bad that I use the name of my dog from when I was a kid as my password?"

"You mean Hetty0486?" Jodie raised a brow at the woman next to her.

Olivia winced. "I guess that means I'll be changing it then."

Jodie grinned at her. "I think that's wise."

"How do you know it, anyway?"

"Best you don't know," Jodie said darkly. She returned her attention back to the computer screen. "Anyway, I tracked the IP address which is how I confirmed Gee Soup was Gwen. But get this. There was another influencer, well she wasn't really an influencer *per se*, she was an author." Jodie dragged up another page. "Olive Scott. She wrote romance novels. Sin Eater, Mard-Arse, and Gee Soup loved tearing her a new one."

Jodie waited for Olivia to read some of the entries. "Funnily, Sin Eater's IP tracks back to a home owned by a Joan and Nigel Harcombe. And this is where it gets really interesting."

"Well go on then, don't keep me hanging."

"Sin Eater and Olive Scott are the same person. At least they have the same IP."

"What?" Olivia's jaw dropped. "You're sure about this?"

"Olive Scott is the pseudonym of a woman by the name of Joan Harcombe. She has had some difficulties in recent years. Looks like she's been in and out of hospital over the last few years. She was sectioned by her husband in December 2016. Less than a week after Gwen disappeared."

"How do you know all of this?"

"It's public record," Jodie shot back. "That and her husband made a statement when she missed the deadline for a book. He told her fans that she'd been sectioned. Said it was nothing to be ashamed of and that he was going to stick by his ill wife."

"How kind of him," Olivia said drily. "I'm still failing to see how this is--"

"Because Nigel Harcombe is running some kind of life coaching business. He started it back in 2016 and one of his first clients was Gwen Campbell. And last year Holly Thomas attended a few sessions with him."

"We need to let the DI know what you've got here."

Jodie nodded. "I'll keep digging. I'm sure there's more to it. And maybe if I can get access to Holly Thomas' computers and accounts I'll be able to dig out more."

DS Arya poked his head around the door. Without thinking, Jodie straightened up and pushed her glasses up her nose. "Can I help you with something?"

"DI Haskell has goth the go ahead from Declan Campbell for you to look over Beth's computer. Got a uniform bringing it in for you now."

"If it's faster for me to go--"

DS Arya shook his head. "No need. They'll be here shortly. Beth was supposed to be at her sister's place but no one has seen her since the service this morning."

"Who's the sister?" Olivia asked.

"Elizabeth Evans."

"Do you mean Libby Evans?" Jodie's stomach clenched.

"That's the one. How do you know?" DS Arya took a step into the room.

"Jodie, what's wrong?" Olivia touched her arm.

She could feel the colour draining from her face as she scrambled through the pages of code. "Another one of the users, Libby-Lou89." Jodie clicked on the keyboard and pages of entries on the Rattle forum appeared. "She's another regular poster on the forum. But this person warned her away from Nigel Harcombe a week ago." Jodie brought it up so that it appeared on the main screen. "This is smaller defunct thread they're using."

TheGreedyTruthx0x0: For once Lib, trust me. He's bad news. NH is not the nice guy struggling with a mentally ill wife. He's a manipulator. He used Gwen and he'll use you up to.

Libby-Lou89: You don't know anything about the situation. If anyone is manipulating things it's you. What would Dec think if he knew you was snooping 'round and trying to dig up dirt on his dead wife? I should just tell him.

TheGreedyTruthx0x0: You can't do that. I don't have enough evidence yet. Messenger.

"The person posting as The Greedy Truth is using an IP blocker to mask her location. I think after this they took the conversation off the site to discuss things privately." She clicked her mouse. "I've been tracking The Greedy Truth and they're very interested in any and all mentions of Gwen, Olive, Holly, and Nigel. Just before Gee Soup went--"

"Wait, who's Gee Soup?" DS Arya asked, scratching the side of his head as he studied the screens.

"Gwen Campbell," Olivia and Jodie said in unison.

"Just before Gwen went offline for the last time she posted this." Jodie pulled up another thread.

> xoGeeSoupxo: I thought NH was a good guy but trust me he's anything but. When I blow the lid on what he's been up to with his 'clients', he's not going to have a business left.

They remained in silence for a moment. "You don't think Beth intended to go to his house, do you?" Jodie asked.

"Why would she?" Olivia leaned back in her chair.

"She said herself she didn't have enough evidence..." Jodie let her words drop into the well of silence.

"Shit..." DS Arya said under his breath. "Haskell asked me to send a car over to Nigel Harcombe's house but the flooding is getting really bad."

"We've got to get someone over there," Olivia said getting to her feet. "I can get us there."

"You're on desk duty," DS Arya said crossly.

"Maz, you can't expect me to sit here twiddling my thumbs with everything we know. Not to mention I know the area better than anyone..."

He screwed up his face. "It's not a good idea..."

"I'll stay in the car," Olivia said. "You won't even know I'm there."

"Gregson has to clear it," Maz said, turning on his heel.

"Maz, wait!" She called after him but he was already gone. "Shit."

"He's right. I know you want to get out there but not like this..."

Olivia let her head hang down. "I know, I just can't bear the idea that something awful will happen and I could have prevented it..."

Jodie touched her hand to Olivia's arm. "It'll be fine. DS Arya will make sure of it."

Olivia smiled. "I know you're right--"

"You better bloody stay in the car," DS Arya said appearing in the doorway again. He hastily dragged his jacket on as he tossed Olivia's in her direction. "I'll kill you myself if you don't."

"You're the boss."

"Good luck!" Jodie called after them, but they'd already left her behind. Dropping back into her swivel chair she stared at the screens in front of her. "I guess it's just you and me again."

CHAPTER FIFTY-ONE

WHEN DREW ARRIVED at the Harcombe residence, he was unsurprised to see Beth's car parked in a lane a short distance away.

He dialled DS Arya's number and waited for his sergeant to pick up. The moment he did, Drew didn't bother to wait for Maz to speak.

"Maz, where is everyone?"

"Sorry, Guv, they're on their way. We'll be there as soon as we find a detour around the floods."

Drew ended the call. He would have to do this alone. The rain had increased in intensity. As he got out of the car, it took all of his skill not to fall in the mud that lined the side of the road.

Hurrying to the door, he was somewhat surprised to find it ajar. Raised voices drifted through to him from somewhere near the back.

"Hello?" His voice echoed back to him. The argument continued. Drew stepped into the house, following the hall to a kitchen. The backdoor was open onto a small conservatory. Through the glass, he could see Nigel Harcombe standing beneath a canopy of trees that lined the edge of the garden.

A small, bird-like woman stood in the middle of the lawn, directly in front of a glass-fronted building. To Drew's mind it looked like some kind of home office set-up. Through the blurred glass of the conservatory, Drew struggled to recognise the woman. She stumbled, almost going down to one knee as Nigel shouted at her. As Drew moved out into the conservatory he spotted the weapon in the woman's hands. She waved it around in front of her. There was an almost imperceptible shift in Nigel's body and Drew wondered if he'd been spotted. But if the other man had seen him, Nigel made no move to acknowledge his presence.

At the door, Drew spotted another body slumped over, inside the glass-fronted office.

"You said you'd protect me!" The woman's voice was slurred. As the rain beat down on her and plastered her dark hair to her head, it took Drew a moment to recognise her. This was the same woman from the church.

Joan Harcombe waved the knife in front of her.

Nigel had tensed. "Why would do this, Joan? You had to know people would find out sooner or later?

Did you really think the police wouldn't figure out that you killed Gwen?"

For a moment Joan looked shocked. She staggered a couple of paces towards him, her face a blank mask of shock.

"I would never hurt Gwen. She was my friend!" The words were barely audible over the unrelenting downpour. "It was you. I know everything, Nigel, and when--"

Drew spoke. "Mr and Mrs Harcombe, I'd like everyone to calm down. If you put down the weapon we can all go back inside and--"

Before he could finish his sentence, Nigel started across the lawn. "She's already tried to kill Ms Smith. I can't let her finish the job."

As Nigel spoke, Joan turned and glanced back at the slumped body in the outbuilding. "I didn't..."

"Don't hurt her, Joan!" Nigel rammed into his wife, sending them both sprawling to the ground.

Drew was across the lawn in a flash. Nigel had pinned his wife on the wet grass beneath him. Drew grabbed his collar and attempted to haul Nigel up but the other man was harder to move than Drew had anticipated.

"She didn't mean it. This is all my fault. My wife is not a violent woman. She's just sick. She didn't mean it," Nigel continued to babble.

Conscious that there was still a knife in play, Drew fought to subdue Nigel Harcombe.

The sound of feet running across the ground told Drew his backup had finally arrived. He jerked Nigel onto his feet, away from the prone body of his wife. The colour had left Joan's face and from his position, Drew could see the blood that stained the knife in her hands.

"Knife!" Drew gave the shout as the uniformed officers piled into the space.

Joan didn't move.

"Is she all right?" Nigel's voice was pitched high. "I just didn't want her to kill Ms Smith. She was so angry. You saw her, DI Haskell. She was waving the knife around--"

Drew handed Nigel off to a uniformed officer. Crossing the lawn, he knelt in the wet grass next to Joan. Removing the knife from her grasp, he pressed his fingers to her throat and was relieved to find a weak pulse.

"We need an ambulance." He hastily handed out orders to the officers on the scene. Leaving Joan in the capable hands of another officer, he hurried to the home office.

"How is Ms Smith?"

The uniformed officer with Beth was checking her over. "She's got a wound on her head but she's conscious and she knows where she is."

"Beth, are you all right?"

She gazed up at Drew her eyes a little unfocused. "Where's Declan?"

"You can see Mr Campbell as soon as we get all of this straightened out."

"Joan!" Nigel's voice carried over the din. "Please be careful with her. She doesn't mean to lash out."

Maz appeared at Drew's elbow. "Looks like we missed all the fun here."

"This is a mess," Drew said. Sirens split the air. "Get him out of here. We need a statement from him. And Beth and Joan Harcombe will have to go to hospital."

Maz nodded and hurried away to do as Drew asked. Tugging his phone from his pocket, Drew dialled Harriet's number for what felt like the millionth time.

She answered finally.

"Drew, this isn't really a good time--"

"I need your help. Meet me at the hospital. I'll send you the address as soon as I have it."

Harriet hesitated and for a moment Drew thought she would turn him down.

"Okay." The line went dead.

Staring out over the chaos, Drew felt a knot of concern tighten in his gut.

CHAPTER FIFTY-TWO

DREW PACED the floor in the hospital corridor. As soon as Beth had arrived, they'd taken her in to be checked over. Joan had been whisked off in another direction. He had yet to hear how either of them were doing. And as more time passed, he grew more and more uneasy.

The sight of Harriet hurrying down the hall towards him lifted his spirits.

"How are they?" she asked.

He shrugged. "I've got no clue. No one is willing to tell me anything."

Harriet glanced down at the floor. "There's something I need to tell you..."

"Beth and the baby are both fine!" Declan's voice cut over Harriet's before she could finish speaking. "I've told her not to but she said it's important that she talk to you, DI Haskell."

"Go!" Harriet urged.

Hesitating, Drew studied her. "What's wrong?"

"Nothing that won't keep," she said. When she smiled at him, it was strained. "Honestly, go."

Without needing to be told twice, Drew did as she said. Following Declan down the hall, he was surprised when the other man paused in front of Beth's room.

"Look, I know you were just doing your job--"

"I am sorry," Drew said.

"I get that, but I just want you to hear Beth out and then leave us the heck alone."

"I'm investigating the murder of your wife, Declan. I can't just do that."

"I don't care how you do it, DI Haskell. But I never want to see you near me, or my family after this. If you had done your job correctly the first time, then Beth would never have had to..." Declan choked off.

Nodding, Drew stared down at his shoes. "I can't make promises but I'll try and keep this as brief as possible."

"Fine." Declan started to walk away down the hall.

"Are you not coming in to hear this?"

Declan shook his head. "Beth already told me everything I need to know. I don't need to hear it again."

Drew watched the other man walk away before

he pushed open the hospital door. Beth sat up in the bed, a small bandage sat over her left eye. She looked smaller than the last time he saw her. More vulnerable.

"Where's Declan?"

"Probably gone to get coffee. You gave him quite a scare."

She nodded and smoothed the sheets down over her lap. "I really messed everything up."

Drew pulled a notebook from his pocket. "When you're feeling better we'll need to get a formal statement down at the station but this will do for now."

"Are you going to arrest me for tampering with evidence?" There was real fear in her eyes as she met his gaze.

Drew paused. "Should I?"

"I didn't mean to damage the recording. It was an accident. The phone was old and when I tried to transfer it to my computer it wiped everything." A tear rolled down her cheek and she swiped it away quickly.

"Did you see the recording?"

She stared down at the bed covers and chewed her lip. "I did."

"And what was on it?"

"It's not Declan on the recording. You don't ever see the person Gwen is arguing with. She was on the phone having a proper barny with someone. You can hear her call the person on the other end of the line

Nigel. I only realised that was who she was talking to after Declan told me of her affair with Nigel Harcombe."

Drew jotted down a few notes. "Beth, how did you find out about the video in the first place? Declan told us that when Simon tried to show him the video it was already corrupted."

She nodded miserably. "That was after I'd tried to transfer it to my computer." She took in a deep breath. "Simon told me about the video. We had a fight. With the new baby coming, things have been tense." Her fingers played over the sheet. "I asked him to show it to me but of course he wouldn't. I knew Declan would never have hurt Gwen but Simon was saying he had proof of what his dad had done and..."

"And you wanted to protect your family?"

When she looked up, her eyes were swimming with tears. "I thought I could prove it wasn't Declan. I know what people think. I remember the looks and the whispers. Do you know what it's like to live with that accusation hanging over your head for so long? I just wanted to show everyone that Declan would never hurt anyone. I thought with the baby coming it would be the perfect chance to start over. But I needed to prove he was innocent first. So I started doing a little digging. You can check my computer but I'm telling the truth."

"And what did you find?"

"Nigel Harcombe is not the man everyone thinks he is. He's a poisonous manipulator."

"The fact he's in a relationship with your sister can't have made you feel too good."

She shook her head. "I tried to tell Libby. But he gets this hold on them." She looked up. "I don't know how he does it. One night, when they were in bed together, he choked her out. She didn't want to tell me, tried to hide the bruises. But I saw them. And when I confronted her about it, she said it was nothing. That it was just a game they'd been playing that went wrong. Can you imagine that? My sister, she's a smart capable woman, a brilliant mum to Toby and she let him get away with that!"

Drew continued to make notes.

"When I tried to tell her about Gwen, she told me I was exaggerating." Beth sucked in a deep shaky breath. "Said I had no proof. That Nigel had told her I was just lashing out to look for attention because everyone was so excited about the new baby coming. He told her to stay away from me. That I needed help..." Beth's shoulders began to heave as tears rolled down her cheeks. "And when you arrested Declan, I knew I needed to do more, so I went to his house."

"And what happened there?"

It took Beth a few minutes to compose herself. "I met Joan. She let me in. She was behaving so strangely."

"Strange in what way?"

"She was out of it and..." Beth took a moment. "She behaved like someone who was drunk but when I asked her she said she didn't drink. When I told her why I was there she didn't seem very surprised. She just took me back to Nigel's office, the one he has in the garden. And then she disappeared back into the house."

"How did you end up hurt and bleeding in the office?"

"I found pictures in the office," Beth said, her voice dropping to a whisper. "He keeps them in a lock box but when I got there the lock was bust and the box was already open and there were all these pictures of women in various states of undress. There were pictures of Libby and--" Beth looked away, squeezing her eyes shut. "She was naked and I could tell she wasn't conscious. And then there were pictures of Gwen in there too. Pictures from when she was already dead." She closed her eyes and swallowed hard. "There was something else in the box. He keeps a journal. I had a quick look through it and--" She cut herself off and swallowed hard. "Everything you need is in the journal."

Drew felt a jolt pass through him. He needed to get someone over there to do a thorough search of the house. If there was anything to find there, they would get it.

"Did you find my phone?" Beth asked.

"What?"

"My phone. I took photographs of the journal and the pictures that he had in his box."

"Where is it?"

Beth looked at him forlorn. "I don't know. I thought Joan had come back into the office. I heard footsteps and I started to show her what I'd found and then..." Beth touched her hand to her head. "Everything went black. I woke up with one of your officer's tending to me and I haven't seen my phone since."

"You should get some rest, Beth."

"Promise me you'll nail him."

"I'll do my best."

Beth slumped back against her pillows. Drew crept from the room.

MAKING his way down the hall, Drew was relieved to find Harriet still waiting for him.

"How is she?" she asked.

"She'll be fine. She had some interesting things to say about Nigel Harcombe though." As he spoke he quickly typed out a message to DS Arya telling him to send a team over to the Harcombe residence to go over it with a fine-toothed comb. At the end of the message, he asked how Nigel was holding up in the custody suite.

"Do you think she's telling the truth?" Harriet asked.

"She says there's evidence to be found at the house. I need to get someone over there to search it. And I'll have to go back to the office to interview Nigel Harcombe."

Harriet nodded. "That's great. It sounds like it's all coming together."

"It is. But I'd like to get in to have a chat with Joan first."

"They said she's awake," Harriet said. "A doctor came out a short while ago. She's in a bad state, Drew."

He looked at her surprised. "What do you mean?"

"They said they found some chemical compounds in her blood analysis. They think she tried to commit suicide."

"Shit." Drew shoved his hand back through his hair. "Beth said she was behaving oddly when she was at the house."

Harriet stared down at the ground. "The doctor's didn't sound too hopeful."

Drew's phone chose that moment to buzz in his pocket. Pulling it free, he was surprised to find Maz's name on the screen.

"Hang on," he said to Harriet. "Go for DI Haskell."

"Guv, I just got your message..." Something in the way Maz spoke set alarm bells off in Drew's head.

"Is there a problem with getting a team to go over the house?"

"Not exactly," Maz said. "I mean I can do that, but—"

"But what?"

"Well, you asked about Nigel Harcombe and we released him half hour ago. I took his statement myself."

"You did what?" Fury swept through Drew and it took all of his restraint to keep from shouting down the phone.

"He was a witness, guv. We couldn't hold him and he knew it. He spoke voluntarily to us and then he left. He had a lot to say about his wife. Reckons she's the one who murdered Gwen and Holly—"

"Who the fuck is Holly? And what do you mean you let him go?"

"Like I explained, guv, he was a witness. He wasn't under caution. You never said otherwise."

"Did he leave by himself?"

"We had a uniform drop him home."

"Great, get them to bring him back to the station and—"

"Sir, they already left his house." There was no mistaking the shake in Maz's voice.

Drew ended the call. "I have to go."

"What should I do?"

"See if they'll let you in to speak with Joan."

Harriet opened her mouth to argue and then

seeing the look on Drew's face, seemed to change her mind. "I'll try. Keep me posted."

Drew was already gone running down the corridor. Nigel had a headstart on him. But if he was lucky he would get there before the scumbag destroyed all of the evidence.

CHAPTER FIFTY-THREE

IT HADN'T TAKEN as much persuasion as Harriet had hoped to get in to see Joan. Apparently, the woman had been asking to speak to someone from the police from the moment she'd woken up.

Sitting in the hard plastic chair next to Joan's bed, Harriet studied the small frail-looking woman in the bed. Joan;s skin was paper thin, with an unhealthy yellow tinge. Black and blue bruising that suspiciously resembled finger marks had started to form around her chin and mouth. The chair creaked beneath Harriet and Joan's eyes slid open.

"Who are you?"

"My name is Dr Harriet Quinn."

"Another doctor..." Joan's eyes fluttered shut. "I asked to speak with the police. I don't need another of your lot to tell me I'm dying. I already know that."

"I'm not a medical doctor. I work with the police.

I'm a forensic psychologist." Harriet swallowed past the dry lump that had formed in the back of her throat. Considering she'd been suspended from the university, how long would it be before they took away her licence?

Joan's eyes opened again. "I'm not crazy."

"Who said you were?"

"Nigel wants everyone to think I am. He wants them to believe I killed those two women."

"Two women?"

Joan laughed softly, but the sound quickly turned into a heaving cough. "It hurts. They said my liver is failing. Everything is failing. I'd need a transplant to save me but I'm not going to get one in time."

It took several moments for Joan's features to smooth out as her pain subsided.

"You asked to talk to someone, Joan. What is it you wanted to say?" Harriet slipped her phone from her bag. "Do you mind if I record our conversation?"

Joan shook her head. "I don't mind. I just want someone to know it wasn't me. I need somebody to believe me."

"I'm listening, Joan. You can tell me anything I promise I won't judge. I believe you."

The woman in the bed reached out with a trembling hand. She wrapped her fingers around Harriet's and squeezed softly. "He said nobody would ever believe me."

"Who said that?"

"Nigel. I'm here because of him. He wanted to get rid of me. Bled me dry for every penny I was worth. I used to be a writer, you know. I was good at it, too. A Sunday Times Bestseller." Joan closed her eyes again, her lashes dark smudges against her jaundiced skin. "And then I got sick. Schizoaffective Disorder, Dr Oswalt called it. Manageable with medication. Nigel started his life-coaching business once I was settled on my meds.

"He took over the finances. He took over everything, really, while I was recovering. And I was doing well. I'd started going back to the slimming club up at the church hall. I was on track for my deadline. Things were looking up."

Joan drifted off and Harriet waited a moment before touching the other woman's hand. "What happened then?"

Joan sighed. "And then I found out he was having an affair with this woman he'd met while dropping me off at the slimming club. Oh, he pretended she was a client of his. She used to come around for 'sessions' in the outdoor office. And then they had a falling out. I confronted her about the affair and she confessed. We talked and she was actually really nice." Joan smiled. "I know that sounds nuts but it's true. She told me how manipulative he could be. And I talked to her about how he'd changed. We stayed friends. And then one day she saw him with another woman from the slimming club."

Harriet remained silent, simply absorbing the glut of information Joan wanted to share.

"She came around and told me. Said she was going to tell everyone about his predatory practices. Nigel didn't like it. They fought and..." Joan swallowed hard.

"It's all right, Joan. You're doing great. Take your time."

"She was in our house. Gwen followed Nigel upstairs. The next thing I knew she was at the bottom of the stairs. Evie, her little girl, was inconsolable." Joan fell silent again but Harriet could tell she was relieving the moment in her mind.

"What happened then?"

"Some things are still fragmented. I remember we were in the car out on the moors and Evie wouldn't stop crying. Nigel was so angry. He kept screaming at me that it was my fault. I can remember staring out the windscreen as he carried Gwen's body down the path. I was still holding Evie. And then he came back and took her away."

"Did you see Evie again after that?"

Joan nodded, her dark halo of hair *shushing* over the pillows. "I followed him. One minute she was crying and the next, silence. I remember sitting in the bracken as he buried them together."

"Why didn't you tell anyone, Joan?"

"He told me he would kill me if I said anything. I started getting ill after that. Hallucinations and delusions. I was hospitalised in early 2017. I was in and out several times and then Nigel took over my medication. Every time I thought I was getting better I would get sick again. But it was different this time. All I wanted to do was sleep."

"You think he was doing something to you?"

Joan nodded. "I know he was. After Gwen's memorial service I finally confronted him. He was saying all these things about what I had done to Gwen. But I've been remembering. I stopped taking my medications just over a week ago." Chagrined, Joan looked down. "I know that's wrong but I didn't know what else to do. I knew something was wrong. Things kept on appearing on my computer every time I would try and write. Things I know I hadn't written."

"What happened when you confronted Nigel?"

Joan swallowed hard. "At first he tried to laugh it off. Said I was slipping. He offered to make us both tea and I agreed. When he thought I was in the living room, I watched him pour something from a glass bottle into my cup. So I confronted him." Joan reached up and touched her hand to her chin. "He went ballistic. Said I was nothing but an ungrateful bitch. That I was just like the rest of them and that he wished he'd killed me back when he did Gwen in."

Joan released a shuddering breath. "I tried to run but he caught me. Held me down while he forced me to drink the liquid from his bottle. He was so happy when he'd finished. Stood over me and said he was going to see his bride-to-be. Told me that if I had any decency at all, I'd be dead when he returned."

Harriet sat dumbfounded as she listened to Joan's confession. "How did you survive?"

Joan laughed. "I didn't survive, Dr Quinn, I've only delayed the inevitable. I tried to vomit up as much of the poison as I could. And once I got back on my feet, I went to his office. I saw his pictures and his journal... So much cruelty from one man. He killed another one. He wrote about it in the journal. Said she'd gone to him for some life-coaching and when he made a pass at her, she turned him down." Joan squeezed her eyes shut. "But he still had photographs of her naked, Dr Quinn. I can only assume he did the same to her as he did to me."

"You think he drugged her?"

Joan shrugged. "I wouldn't put it past him. I didn't read any more of the journal. I couldn't. It made me sick. I do know that after she tried to black-mail him, he murdered her. I doubt it was a hardship for him. While I was going through his things, Beth Smith arrived. She'd worked it all out. She was just lacking the evidence to nail him. So I let her go into the office. I let her find his stash of evidence."

"And then Nigel came back and... He was going to kill her. I was frantic. I tried to keep him away from her with the knife. I wouldn't hurt her, Dr Quinn. I didn't touch her."

Harriet squeezed the other woman's hand. "It's all right, Joan. I believe you. And DI Haskell is going to find a way to get Nigel."

A wan smile broke out on Joan's face. "I'm not going to survive the month, Dr Quinn. Maybe I won't make it to the end of the week. Nigel will get his wish in the end. And he'll tell anyone who'll listen that it was me." Joan's hand trembled against the covers. "What time is it, Dr Quinn?"

Surprised, Harriet glanced down at her phone. "It's eight thirty. Why?"

Joan's smile grew wider. "When I found his little lockbox of treasures, I found another glass bottle. It smelled just like the one he'd forced down my throat before he left."

A cold sweat broke out on Harriet's skin. "What did you do, Joan?"

Joan turned her head towards Harriet. "Retribution, for Gwen, and Evie, and Holly. But mostly, retribution for me."

CHAPTER FIFTY-FOUR

DREW PARKED HAPHAZARDLY outside Nigel Harcombe's house. His phone started to ring and he snatched it up. "What is it?"

"Drew, Joan just told me she put poison in Nigel's wine."

"What?"

"Just hurry. She said he always has a glass of wine in the evening and she poisoned the bottle."

"Right, I'm there!"

Drew ended the call and raced towards the front door. Pounding against the wood, he prayed for Nigel to answer. This was not the way to nail a slippery bastard like him. He needed to be brought to justice. He couldn't be allowed off the hook so easily.

With no answer, Drew hurried around the side of the house. Peering through the glass walls of the conservatory he could see a light on in the kitchen.

He banged against the glass door but there was nothing stirring in the house. Grabbing a rock from the flowerbed next to the side of the house, Drew used it to smash the glass. Letting himself inside, he was greeted by the soft sounds of classical music that drifted from the general direction of the centre of the house.

"Nigel Harcombe! It's DI Haskell. I need to speak with you in regards to..." Drew trailed off as he rounded the corner and entered the kitchen.

Nigel's body was splayed out on the floor. Foamy vomit coated his mouth and chest. A smashed glass lay on the floor next to him and a half drunk bottle of wine stood open on the kitchen counter.

Drew stared at the body. Crossing to the fallen man, Drew crouched beside him and pressed his fingers to Nigel's throat. Nothing. He checked his wrist but was unsurprised to still find nothing.

How had it come to this? The sound of sirens ripped the air. Drew's gaze snagged on the open lock box on the counter next to a paper shredder and his heart sank. He was too late. Much too late.

CHAPTER FIFTY-FIVE

DREW SPOTTED Harriet across the office. She sat in one of the swivel chairs at his desk, her gaze fixed on the floor beneath her feet.

"You look about as happy as I feel," Drew said as he reached her.

"It's not exactly the outcome we'd hoped for," Harriet said. Her face was pale as she knotted her fingers around the strap of her bag.

"No, but I'm certain Jodie will salvage something from Beth's phone. He shredded a lot of the items before I arrived but we still have some pictures and pages from the journal."

"So it was definitely Nigel then?" Harriet stared up at him.

Drew shook his head. "Honestly, I don't think we'll ever know the truth. I read the statement Nigel gave to Maz. He puts the blame squarely on Joan.

And in her chat with you, she put the blame solely on him. The evidence seems to point in his direction but we found a sample of his handwriting in his office and it doesn't match what we found in the journal." Drew sighed. "It's a complete shit-show."

"Neither of them will ever hurt anyone again," Harriet said softly.

"Well, Joan might recover--"

Harriet was already shaking her head. "Her organs are failing. It's a matter of days, maybe hours. Joan doesn't really realise that yet. She still thinks she has more time." Harriet squeezed her eyes shut. "How did it all go so wrong?"

"Look, at the end of the day we'll have enough to close the Gwen Campbell case and clear Declan Campbell of any wrongdoing."

"I don't mean that," Harriet said. "But I'm glad of it all the same."

"What do you mean then?"

"We can't work together anymore, Drew." Swallowing hard, she met his gaze head on.

"What? What do you mean? Of course we can."

She shook her head as tears welled in her eyes. "I've been suspended from the university for inappropriate conduct with a student."

Shock rendered Drew momentarily speechless.

"Dr Baig suggested I tell you that effect of immediate I will no longer be able to work with you."

"But that's... That's bullshit!"

Harriet smiled at him and tilted her head to the side as a tear streaked down over her cheek. "It's just the way it is. If I'm cleared--"

"Who made the complaint?"

"Misha McDermid."

"Well, she'll come to her senses and--"

"No, Drew. It's done. She has a witness. Even if I'm cleared, I won't ever be able to go back to the university. And my professional reputation will be tarnished."

"This isn't right. There has to be something I can do. You wouldn't behave inappropriately. She must be lying."

Harriet got to her feet. "I just wanted you to hear it from me." She held a hand out to him. "It's been a pleasure working with you all."

He pushed her hand away and got to his feet. "No. I don't believe this. We can do something. I'll contact Dr Beige and--"

Placing her hand on his arm, she shook her head. "Drew, no. There's nothing to be done. He will conduct his investigation. By morning I expect the media will have caught wind of it and it's better if you and everyone here are as far away from me and the situation as you can be." She started to walk away and Drew went after her.

"'Tell me how I can fix this?"

She paused and smiled up at him. "Keep fighting

the good fight, Drew. And remember you're brilliant at the work you do here."

"No."

She pulled free of his grip. "Don't make this harder than it needs to be."

"Harriet, I--"

She cut him off before he could say anything. "I've got to go. Look after yourself, Drew."

And with that she was gone. She moved swiftly through the desks and was out the door before Drew could fully comprehend everything that had happened. He started to follow her, but stopped as he reached the door. She would come around in time, he was sure of it.

For now, he would let her go.

The story continues in Lake of Tears

GET THE NEXT BOOK!

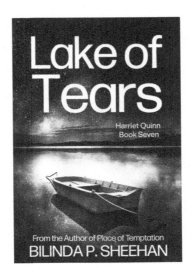

Harriet and DI Haskell return in the next book in the
series.
Lake of Tears

GET THE NEXT BOOK!

Join my mailing list

ALSO BY BILINDA P. SHEEHAN

Watch out for the next book coming soon from Bilinda P. Sheehan by joining her mailing list.

WANT A FREE BOOK?

Sign-up to the mailing list to receive a copy of my psychological thriller - Wednesday's Child

https://dl.bookfunnel.com/ch0039wgz7

Or Join me on Facebook
https://www.facebook.com/BilindaPSheehan/
Facebook: The Armchair Whodunnit's Book Club

Alternatively send me an email.
bilindasheehan@gmail.com

My website is bilindasheehan.com

Made in the USA
Las Vegas, NV
21 August 2023